Love Finds You
in

VALENTINE
NEBRASKA

Love Finds You
in
valentine
nebraska

BY IRENE BRAND

summerside
PRESS

Love Finds You in Valentine, Nebraska
© 2008 by Irene Brand

ISBN 978-1-934770-38-2

All rights reserved. No part of this publication may be reproduced in any form, except for brief quotations in printed reviews, without written permission of the publisher.

All scripture quotations, unless otherwise indicated, are taken from the HOLY BIBLE, NEW INTERNATIONAL VERSION®. NIV®. Copyright © 1973, 1978, 1984 by International Bible Society. Used by permission of Zondervan. All rights reserved.

Scripture quotations are also taken from the King James Version of the Bible.

The town depicted in this book is a real place, but all characters are fictional. Any resemblances to actual people or events are purely coincidental.

Cover and Interior Design by Müllerhaus Publishing Group | **www.mullerhaus.net**

Published by Summerside Press, Inc., 11024 Quebec Circle, Bloomington, Minnesota 55438 | **www.summersidepress.com**

Fall in love with Summerside.

Printed in the USA.

Acknowledgments
....

During the writing of this book, I worked with a very supportive editorial team at Summerside Press. I especially value the encouragement and help of Rachel Meisel and Jason Rovenstine.

I also owe a debt of gratitude to my agent, Chip MacGregor, who believed in my work and forwarded the beginning of this manuscript to Summerside Press…and to a group of fellow authors who have encouraged me and prayed for me when all was going well and commiserated with me when I was discouraged.

Thanks are also due to the kind people of Valentine, Nebraska, including:

Lisbeth Sherman and Pauline O'Dell at the ARK

The staff at *Midland News*

Marsha Bauer and Carleen Buechle at the Holiday Inn

Shelly Frank at Cedar Canyon Steakhouse

Members of the First Baptist Church

Vickie Cumbow, Flower Land florist

And I wouldn't forget to acknowledge the support of my readers, some of whom have been reading my books for twenty-four years.

Lastly, but not least, I couldn't have started or continued my writing career without the love, encouragement, and help of my husband, Rod, who proofreads my manuscripts, accompanies me to book fairs and writing conferences, and who carries a large load of our household/ business responsibilities to give me the opportunity to fulfill my Christian writing ministry.

Chapter One

....

Uncertainty had plagued Kennedy Blaine since she'd boarded an early-morning flight at the Los Angeles International Airport and landed in Omaha, Nebraska. Her doubts escalated while she drove to her destination through the abundant grasslands of the Sandhills region of the state. Apprehension washed through Kennedy's heart with the power of an ocean wave when she eased the rental car to a stop before the driveway framed by a metal arch bearing the words CIRCLE CROSS RANCH.

A warning voice whispered in her head, *It's still not too late to turn back.*

Tormented by conflicting emotions, Kennedy forced herself to settle down. What had happened to the confidence, courage, and hardheadedness that her father had often told her was the only inheritance she'd received from her maternal relatives, the Morgans? Considering Kenneth Blaine's resentment of his wife's family, it hadn't been a compliment. Kennedy's personal annoyance increased when she noticed that her hands were shaking like leaves buffeted by a strong prairie wind.

"Hey, get hold of yourself," she said aloud, in an attempt to bolster her self-confidence. "The Circle Cross Ranch belongs to you, so why shouldn't you visit the place you've wanted to see all your life?"

This personal scolding calmed Kennedy to the extent that she released the brake and turned left onto the graveled driveway. Most of the trees still weren't in full leaf, but Valentine was apparently too far north to expect summer foliage by the first of May. She immediately crossed a cattle guard of folded parallel ridges and troughs, with the car shaking as if she'd driven across a corrugated roof. Hereford cattle grazed in wide, luxuriant pastures, and many of them turned to watch her as she drove slowly up the lane, eagerly looking for her birthplace, Riverside, which had been built by a Blaine ancestor more than a century ago. After a few miles she entered a large open area surrounded by barns, machinery sheds, several other metal and wooden buildings, and a one-story frame residence. The whole area was bordered on the north and west by thickets of evergreens.

With a sweeping glance, she noted the absence of the large white house she'd expected to see. Still, the ranch had a homey atmosphere. Several horses grazed in a corral. A few cows stopped chewing their cuds to look her way. Chickens industriously scratched the ground behind a woven wire fence.

Wondering if she was at the wrong place, Kennedy stopped the car not far from the dwelling. A man and a black-and-white dog came around the side of the house, and Kennedy stared in disbelief. Fleetingly, her misgivings changed to amazement.

Marshal Matt Dillon in the flesh, she thought humorously. During her teens, Kennedy had watched Western reruns by the dozens, having a big crush on the handsome hero as he engaged in gunfights, righted wrongs, and rescued women in distress. And here he was strolling toward her, tall and straight as a sequoia tree.

The cowboy walked gracefully with an air of self-confidence, exactly like her television heartthrob, James Arness, who had fascinated Kennedy each time he appeared on the screen. Scanning him from head to toe, she took in every aspect of his appearance. A wide-brimmed hat was pushed back on his forehead, revealing brown hair that curled around his ears. A leather vest and plaid shirt covered his massive shoulders. His slender thighs and long, sturdy legs were encased in denim. And his well-worn brown leather boots had pointed toes and high heels, just like the ones her favorite TV cowboy had worn.

Kennedy stepped out of the car and waited for him. She considered herself to be above average in height for a woman, but this pseudo–movie star towered over her by at least a foot.

The dog barked, and a low growl rumbled in its throat.

"Quiet, Wilson," the man demanded in a deep voice. The dog stilled, but he took a rigid stance and bared his teeth at Kennedy.

The man's dark eyes appraised Kennedy skeptically. "What can we do for you, ma'am? Are you lost?"

Up to this point, Kennedy hadn't decided whether or not to reveal her true identity, but she spoke impulsively, "I'm Kennedy Blaine. I own this ranch."

The man's expression changed from disbelief to amusement to cynicism to anger. His eyes narrowed suspiciously.

"Yeah? Well, I own Rockefeller Center in New York City."

Kennedy's temper flared. She longed to slap him, and it took all of her willpower not to stamp her foot. "I tell you, I'm Kennedy Blaine. I inherited this ranch two months ago when my father died."

"Now, lady," he said. His condescending tone angered Kennedy even more than his words. "If you are who you say you are, why didn't Smith Blaine tell me you were coming? I can't allow every woman who stops by here to take ownership."

Anger sharpened her normally gentle voice. "Let me ask *you* a few questions. Who are you?"

"Derek Sterling."

The name was unfamiliar to her. Smith Blaine, her father's cousin and the Circle Cross's accountant, handled all the ranch affairs. Kennedy searched her memory for some mention of Derek Sterling from her father. But she was certain she hadn't heard anything about this man who moved menacingly closer to her. Hands on his hips, his dark eyes blazed down into hers.

Too late, Kennedy wondered if her impulsive decision to visit the ranch unannounced had been wise. Should she have heeded the mental warning that had nagged her all day? She was among strangers, and she hadn't told anyone, not even her lawyer or her housekeeper, about this surprise visit to the ranch. Though they knew she was going out of town, she'd never given her destination.

Her anger quickly changed to concern, and Kennedy turned toward her car. Although retreating from the battle, she still wanted to have the last word. Over her shoulder she said, "I hadn't expected a cordial welcome in Valentine, but I certainly didn't think I'd be chased off my own property by a cowhand and his mongrel dog!"

* * * * *

Derek Sterling had had a bad day. A herd of cattle had broken through the fence and eaten an acre of alfalfa before they'd been discovered. He and the other ranch hands had spent the morning rounding up the cattle and fixing the fence. And the worst blow was when one of his own horses had broken a leg, causing the animal to have to be put down. No matter how hard he worked, he just couldn't get ahead. Was he destined to always work for someone else rather than to buy a ranch of his own?

It was the last straw when this young woman barged in unannounced. He rather admired her fighting spirit, and he smothered a smile when she called his registered Australian Cattle Dog a mongrel. But it cut pretty deep when she labeled him a cowhand. He was glad she was leaving. If she *was* Kennedy Blaine, he could deal with her tomorrow.

Derek's annoyance turned to concern when he saw her lips tremble and tears fill her eyes as she opened the car door. A shaft of sunlight struck her face, and the moisture in her emerald eyes reminded him of early morning sunlight mirrored in a Sandhills lake. His heart hammered against his ribs, a shock ran through his body, and he was totally and compellingly attracted to her. In all of his twenty-eight years he'd never experienced anything like this! So unexpected and unusual was the emotion that Derek was momentarily too stunned to know what to do about it.

But when she slid into the seat of the car and lowered her head on the steering wheel, he galvanized into action. With one long step, he reached her.

"Ma'am, I'm sorry. I've had a rough day, but that didn't give me any reason to take my rotten mood out on you. Let's start over."

Swiping at her eyes with a delicate long-fingered hand, the woman reached into a leather bag beside her and took out her billfold. When she lifted her tearstained face to him, Derek experienced a ripple of anticipation unlike any feeling he'd ever known.

"I really *am* Kennedy Blaine," she said. She opened the billfold, which displayed her driver's license, and handed the billfold to Derek. "See, that proves who I am."

Derek no longer doubted that she was who she claimed to be, but to get his emotions in check before he dared to speak, he glanced at her license and noted that her age was twenty-six. She was five feet seven inches tall and weighed 130 pounds. She had green eyes and blond hair and, as usual, the license photo didn't do justice to her beauty.

Handing the billfold back to her, he said, "I'm sorry for giving you such a poor welcome to the Circle Cross." He held the car door open. Motioning to the house, he said, "I live here with my mother, and she has supper about ready. Come on inside and eat with us."

Kennedy stepped out of the car, and the wind ruffled through her blond hair that spread gracefully over her shoulders.

"By the way, I'm the ranch manager."

Seemingly embarrassed, Kennedy exclaimed, "And I called you a cowhand!"

"That, too," he said. "My father managed the ranch for a long time, and when he died a few years ago, Mr. Blaine asked me to take over." They climbed the steps to the porch of the house. Derek opened the screen door into a combination living/dining/kitchen area. "This has been my home since I was a teenager."

"But where's Riverside, the Blaine home?"

"About a mile from here. I'll take you there as soon as we eat." He hung his hat on a hall tree. "Hey, Mom," he called. "We've got company."

A tiny woman, about five feet tall, turned from the kitchen stove and moved toward them. Momentarily, Kennedy was amazed that such a small woman had given birth to a hunk like Derek.

"Mom, this is Kennedy Blaine, the owner of the Circle Cross. I invited her to supper. Miss Blaine, this is my mother, June Sterling."

Kennedy hardly knew how to take Derek—he had completely changed from the skeptical man who'd practically ordered her off the ranch to a friendly, congenial host.

"Oh, my!" June said, and she swiped at the gray hair that framed her oval face. She quickly surveyed the large room with a critical gaze. "I'm afraid we're not fixed for company. I'd have prepared a big meal if I'd have known you were coming."

Chagrined, Kennedy said, "Don't let me be a bother to you. I'm going to spend the night at a motel in Valentine. I can eat there and come back tomorrow to look around. I wanted to check out the ranch, but I should have let you know that I was coming."

"Now, Mom, you know you always have twice as much food as we can eat. Miss Blaine can have supper with us, and I'll take her to Riverside before she goes into town."

"You're right, son," Mrs. Sterling said. "It flustered me a little to have a visit from the owner of the ranch. Come into the kitchen. I was ready to dish up the food." She reached toward Kennedy to shake her hand.

Kennedy felt a tinge of remorse that she'd barged in like she had and grasped the woman's hand warmly. "I tried to contact Cousin Smith to tell him I was coming, but his secretary said that he and his wife are vacationing in Europe for two weeks. I've dealt with all of my father's estate except the ranch, and I didn't want to wait until Smith came back to see what has to be done here."

June nodded and quickly put another plate and silverware on the table. "The bathroom is down the hallway on the left if you want to freshen up," she said.

Kennedy excused herself and left the room. When she returned, June invited Kennedy to be seated before placing the food on the table, which consisted of a bowl of red beans, a platter of baked pork chops, a salad, and a pan of corn bread.

"Not much of a meal for a Blaine," she said apologetically. "My husband would turn over in his grave if he knew I'd set you down to a meal like this."

Trying to put Mrs. Sterling at ease, Kennedy said, "Dad never lost his fondness for Nebraska cooking. We often ate corn bread and beans."

After a brief prayer of thanks, June passed the food and Kennedy served herself. When their plates were filled, June said, "Mr. Blaine told us he's had an offer to sell the ranch."

"Yes, he called and talked to me about it," Kennedy said. "That's the main reason I made this trip to Valentine."

"We didn't know the ranch was for sale until a week or so ago," Derek commented.

"I didn't know, either," Kennedy answered with a slight laugh. "Dad had apparently given Smith free rein on ranch matters, and he seemed to think I'd okay the sale without question. I might have if I hadn't had an overwhelming urge to see Riverside while it was still in the family. I was born in the house and lived there until I was almost two. Besides, this ranch has been in the Blaine family for years and years. I couldn't let it go without seeing it."

Kennedy noted the quick glance that Derek's mother slanted toward him, before she quickly said, "I think you did the right thing. This is a fine ranch, and not one you'd want to sell without knowing something about it."

After the main course, Mrs. Sterling served them apple pie à la mode. After her first bite, Kennedy said, "This is the best pie I've ever eaten! I've loved your food—thanks for sharing it with me."

"It's just plain ranch grub, but I'm mighty pleased that you enjoyed it," June responded genuinely.

By the time they finished the meal—and after Kennedy had been told to call them June and Derek—she felt that she really *was* welcome in their home. June poured cups of coffee for all of them, and Derek pushed back from the table and crossed one leg over his knee. "So tell us about yourself, Miss Blaine."

With a grin, she said, "I will if you'll call me Kennedy."

He nodded, and Kennedy wished she could interpret the mystery of his gaze, which awakened a strange surge of excitement in her heart. She lowered her eyes to hide her thoughts from him.

"That's a pretty name," June said. "I don't believe I've heard it before."

Smiling, Kennedy said, "Probably not. My mother was convinced that I would be a boy, and she planned to name her firstborn Kenneth, Jr., after Dad. When I arrived instead of a boy, she didn't have a girl's name in mind, so she called me Kennedy."

"I like to learn different names, and I believe your mother made a good choice," June said.

"I suppose you know about the age-old feud between the Blaines and the Morgans," Kennedy began.

"We don't hear much about it anymore," June said. "Sometimes during elections the old hatreds flare up, but most folks don't pay any attention to it nowadays."

"You see," Derek explained, "many out-of-state people have moved into the county over the past few years, and the Blaines and the Morgans are outnumbered now." He chuckled and added, "But some of the old-timers still remember what a fracas it caused when Kenneth Blaine and Grace Morgan got married."

With a wry grin, Kennedy said, "My parents! They stayed here until Dad finished college, but they didn't want to raise me in a hostile atmosphere, so they left Nebraska. They both liked California and felt at home there. Mother never came back, although Dad did when his parents died. A few Blaines came to visit us, but I've never met any of the Morgan family."

"Several of your relatives still live in the county, including your grandfather, Gabriel Morgan, who must be around ninety," Derek said. He added with a grin, "But he's still as ornery as he always was."

"Derek!" June scolded.

A smile curved the corners of his mouth. "I'm sure I didn't say anything that Kennedy hasn't heard before," he said.

Hearing her name spoken with warmth and gentleness in his deep, rich voice caused Kennedy's pulse to leap. A wave of heat spread upward from her body, and she was glad that June misunderstood the reason for her red face.

"Now look what you've done! You've offended her."

Mastering her emotions, Kennedy said as calmly as she could, "No, not at all. Mother seldom mentioned her father, but Dad had plenty to say about him. He never forgave him for disinheriting Mother, and it wasn't because of the money involved. To be separated from her family was a wound she carried all of her life."

"Mom's right, though. I shouldn't put down your grandfather. I'm sorry," Derek apologized. "He's never done anything to me, so I shouldn't judge him." Standing, he asked, "Do you want to look at Riverside now?"

"I'd like to, but I think I'd better reserve a room at a motel first."

"We have only two bedrooms, Kennedy, but you can have Derek's room," June invited. "He won't mind sleeping in the bunkhouse with the other men."

"That's okay by me," Derek readily agreed.

Kennedy rejected the offer with a wave of her hand. She was too much aware of Derek Sterling now—she didn't want to sleep in his room, either. "I won't put you to that trouble. I don't know how long I'll stay, and it's only a short distance to town."

When she started to stand, Derek quickly moved to pull back her chair.

"Then we'll see you tomorrow," June said, "and I'll fix a *real* dinner for you."

Impulsively, Kennedy hugged June. "I consider this a wonderful meal. Thanks so much."

"There are several good motels in Valentine," Derek said. "Let's go to my office, and you can call from there."

They left the house through the back door and walked toward a small building, with the dog frolicking around them, apparently accepting Kennedy as Derek and June had done. Kennedy looked upward to the cloudless blue May sky and heard the soft gentle whir of the windmill behind the barn.

Derek unlocked the door and stepped aside to let Kennedy enter. He flipped a switch, and several strips of florescent lights revealed a neat, modern office. A workstation with a computer, a large flat-screen monitor, a copier, a fax machine, and several metal filing cabinets were located behind an old wooden desk, a vivid contrast to the modern office equipment.

"I'm impressed," Kennedy remarked.

"You should be," Derek said, mirth shimmering from his large brown eyes. "Your money paid for most of it. The desk belonged to Dad."

He looked up the number of the Holiday Inn in Valentine, and when the line rang busy, he said, "While we wait, I'll explain a bit about the way the ranch business is handled. Dad wouldn't consider using a computer, and he did everything the hard way. After I became the manager I talked to Smith about it, and he readily agreed that the ranch records should be computerized. I set up a program to make my reports to him online. It saves both of us a lot of time."

"That's neat *and* interesting," Kennedy said, taking another look at Derek. Behind the cowboy facade he affected so well, the ranch manager obviously possessed tons of wisdom and knew when to use it.

Kennedy tried the motel number again and shook her head when the line was still busy.

"Let's go on to the family home," Derek said, "and we can use my cell to call from there. A storm two days ago messed up the phone lines, so we may not be able to get through."

"Then maybe I should go into town before it gets dark. I don't know these roads at all, and I could easily get lost. Besides, there may not be any vacancies if I wait much longer."

Derek shrugged his shoulders, and Kennedy breathlessly watched the way his muscles moved beneath his shirt. She looked away quickly.

"You make the decision. But if you don't get a motel room, you can have my room and I'll sleep in the bunkhouse with the other *cowhands*." He sliced a grin toward her as he put emphasis on the last word.

Kennedy covered her face with her hands and peered at him from one eye. "Don't remind me of that. It's not my habit to be so nasty. I'm really sorry."

"I was just joshin' you," he drawled. "I take all the blame for us getting off on the wrong foot. I thought you were a spoiled city girl at first, but I'm changing my mind mighty quick."

She turned away when the warmth of his smile reached her. With a deep intake of breath, she said, "I won't take time to look inside the house tonight since I want to reach town before dark, but I would like to see where it's located. I'll go into Valentine and come back tomorrow to check out the house by myself so I won't be bothering you."

He took a ring of keys from a hook beside the door, saying, "There's a gate across the road, which we keep locked." He closed the door behind them. "Let's go in my truck."

"Okay. Wait until I lock my car."

"You don't have to do that. Nobody around here bothers anything."

She activated the locks from the keypad. "I've lived in the city too long—I never leave my car without securing it. Besides, this is a rental car and I feel even more responsible for it."

He opened the truck's passenger door and held her arm as she stretched to reach the running board and get into the truck. He whistled to the dog. "Let's go, Wilson." With a flying leap, the dog landed in the truck bed.

Derek motioned to a graveled road to the left of the one that Kennedy had followed to the ranch. "This is a private road," he said. As he accessed the road, Derek lifted his hand to greet two men who were lounging on the porch of a long, wooden building. "We only have two men, Al and Sam, who live on the ranch, but one other full-time man, Joel, is married and lives in town. That's the bunkhouse, but we don't have any housing for families. We hire others to help during roundup time and the haying season."

"I'm ashamed to show how ignorant I am about the ranch, but Dad didn't discuss his business affairs with Mother and me. He probably would have, but I've been busy with college and taking care of the household management after Mother died, and I didn't have time to take on anything else. As it is, the last two months have been terrible. Not only have I missed my father, but I didn't have a clue as to how to settle the estate. I had to depend on his lawyer, who's thankfully an old family friend. So you'll understand why I ask so many questions."

"Did your mother die recently?" Derek asked softly.

"No, she died five years ago," Kennedy answered. Because the loss of her mother still hurt, she changed the subject. "How big is the ranch?"

"Roughly twenty thousand acres. I'll tell you everything I can, but Smith will have more answers than I do."

They followed the narrow road until they came to a steel gate. From there, the road veered to the right along a river. Derek jumped down from the truck and unlocked the gate, and when he sat in the cab again, he pointed to a nearby tree-lined river.

"That's the Niobrara River," Derek explained. "It's a long stream and winds through the Circle Cross's range. It's spring-fed, and even in the driest season, there's enough water for irrigation and watering livestock. That's what makes the ranch so profitable."

Kennedy didn't want to cause any waves, but she was sure that her dad had commented on the decrease in income from the ranch, and she hadn't been interested enough to pay attention. Still, she'd come to Valentine to gain information, so she said slowly, "I seem to remember Dad complaining the past year or so that the ranch was losing money."

Derek glanced sharply at her. "What? We've had several good seasons. We haven't lost any money since I've been the manager, and I have the records to prove it."

"I must have been mistaken then," Kennedy replied quickly. "Dad had several investments, and I didn't pay much attention to what they were. After his sudden death, I wish I had listened to him. As far as I knew, he was in perfect health until he had that massive heart attack."

"As the owner, you *should* know what's going on here at the ranch," Derek agreed. "And I hope you'll take the time to let me show you the records I've kept since I've been manager."

"I suppose it won't make much difference if I sell the place."

"No, I guess not," Derek said slowly, "but you're welcome to check out anything you want to."

They rounded a sharp curve, and directly in front of them stood Kennedy's ancestral home. A knot formed in her throat, for it looked just like the picture hanging in her father's office.

Derek shifted into a lower gear, and the truck crept toward the house. Built by Kennedy's great-grandfather in the latter part of the nineteenth century, the white-framed, two-story dwelling was one of Queen Anne architecture. A veranda with banisters spread across the first floor from the gazebo on the left to a driveway on the right. A similar veranda wrapped around the second floor, and a round corner tower with a conical roof was located behind the gazebo. Six stone steps led to the front door that included an ornate window in the upper half and a transom of stained glass above that. Staring silently at the house, Kennedy wondered how her life would have differed if she'd grown up in this environment. Tears filled her eyes, and she swiped them away.

When Derek stopped the truck and exited the cab, Wilson jumped to the ground and tagged at Derek's heels as he rounded the truck to open the door for Kennedy.

Once she stood beside Derek, sniffling, she said, "You must think I'm a crybaby, but today is the first time I've cried since Dad's funeral." Slanting a timid smile toward Derek, she continued, "I know I'm assuming a lot on such short acquaintance, but this is a difficult experience for me. Do you mind if I hang on to you for support?"

He didn't answer, but when he reached out quickly and wrapped his large warm fingers around her hand, she knew he didn't mind. They walked slowly around the house, and occasionally Kennedy touched places in the old siding where the paint had peeled. When they returned to the front of the house, she sat on the edge of the porch facing the river a mile away. Derek dropped down on the first step and turned to face her.

They enjoyed a comfortable silence for several minutes before Kennedy said, "Growing up as I did in Los Angeles without any of my extended family around me, I've always felt rootless, looking for something out of my reach. Today I feel as if I've finally come home."

"This *is* your home, Kennedy, and I hope you'll stay around long enough to get to know the country. The roots of the Blaines and the Morgans dip deep into Nebraska history. This *is* your home," he repeated.

Chapter Two

· ·

Leaning against a porch post, Kennedy observed her surroundings with a rapt expression on her face. Derek hesitated to break into her reverie, but dusk was settling over the valley. If she intended to spend the night in Valentine, she should be heading that way.

When the dusk-to-dawn light came on, Derek said, "Kennedy." She jumped slightly, and he apologized for startling her. "Do you want to call the motel now?"

"Will you do it for me?"

He took a phone from his shirt pocket and punched in the number.

"I'm still getting a busy signal, so the line is probably out of order. Let me call Mom and tell her to fix my room for you."

Looking appealingly at him, she said, "Why can't I stay here? I've understood that the house is still like it was before my grandparents died."

"Yes, I suppose it is. Mom comes every two or three months to clean and dust everything."

Derek didn't like the idea of her staying alone in the house. Anyone coming by car had to drive past ranch headquarters and the locked gate. But there was nothing to keep people from coming across the river in the few shallow places. There wasn't much crime in Cherry County, but remembering his childhood, Derek was always alert to any possibility of trouble.

"Have you ever been totally in the dark, Kennedy?"

"At Carlsbad Caverns once. It was crazy!"

Pointing to the pole lamp, he said, "That lights the area close to the house but nothing else. And if the power should go off, you'd be completely in the dark. I don't even have a flashlight in the truck to leave with you. I can't tell you what to do, but I wish you'd spend the night with Mom. I'll bring you here first thing in the morning."

"I'd rather not impose on your mother, but I suppose you're right. This is a nostalgic place for me, and to be honest about it, I'd rather not be alone."

"It won't be any trouble." He dialed his phone again and explained to his mother that Kennedy would be staying overnight. "She said to tell you that she changed the bed linens today, so the room is ready for you."

As they drove away, Kennedy kept looking back at the house. Derek didn't like the tormented look on her face. She was too quiet to suit him, and he said, "I've always wondered why your parents moved away."

"As I understand it, Grandfather Blaine wasn't as antagonistic toward the Morgans as they were against him. He welcomed Mother into the family, but she was very unhappy living at Riverside. Not only had she been cut off from her family, but her friends didn't stick by her, either. Back then, Gabriel Morgan was so influential that everybody was afraid to cross him. He made it plain that Mother was no longer his daughter. As soon as Dad finished college, they moved to California."

Kennedy twisted a few strands of her hair with trembling fingers. Derek figured that was a nervous gesture she did unconsciously when she was stressed.

In a monotone, Kennedy continued, "When I was born, not even my grandmother came to see me, and that hurt Mother more than anything her father had done. She told me once that she couldn't have lived with his rejection without her deep faith in God."

Sympathetically, Derek said, "And you've suffered for it, too."

"Yeah, big time! My grandfather's unforgiving spirit ruined the complete happiness my parents could have had. And I paid for it, too, when I grew up without an extended family. As a child, I felt left out when my friends had big family gatherings."

They passed through a copse of trees and, except for the headlights of the truck, darkness surrounded them as they traveled.

"Whoa! Now I know what you mean by darkness."

Derek stopped the truck and turned off the headlights, and Kennedy scooted across the seat until their shoulders touched. "I feel as if I'm in a cave."

"I kind of like total darkness," Derek said thoughtfully. "It's great to be out on the range during roundup when it's dark. I lie on my back and watch the stars spread across the sky—and when a full moon rises over the plains, it's awesome." He rolled down the window, and a myriad of insect sounds filtered into the truck. "People think it's quiet at night, too, but it rarely is."

A hoarse howl sounded in the distance, and Wilson, behind them in the cab, belted out a long response. His clamorous barking pierced the quietness of the night.

"What's that?" Kennedy asked, clutching Derek's arm.

"It's a coyote. Wilson, shut up!" The barking stopped immediately, but when Derek started the engine again, Wilson gave one low growl.

"Derek."

"Yeah."

"Thanks for talking me out of staying at the house. I think I'd have been scared out of my wits before morning," Kennedy admitted.

"Probably so. And you'd have been lonesome as well as scared."

* * * * *

June rustled to the door when they arrived, and her pleasure in having Kennedy in their home was so apparent that Kennedy was glad she had agreed to stay at the ranch. Derek put Kennedy's bag in his bedroom, and

June invited her to sit with them. Kennedy glanced quickly around the living room. A massive fireplace dominated one wall. An elk head with a wide rack of antlers was mounted above the mantel.

"Where should I sit?" she asked. "I don't want to take someone's favorite chair."

With a humorous look toward her son, June pointed to a large, leather lounge chair that had seen better days. "Sit anyplace except in *that* chair. My husband had it for years, and Derek took it over after his daddy died. The chair's a disgrace, but I'm not allowed to get rid of it."

Kennedy sat on the couch, and Derek grinned sheepishly as he sat down, lifted his feet, and relaxed in his favorite chair. June chatted with Kennedy about her impressions of Riverside until Kennedy yawned widely.

Embarrassed, Kennedy said, "I'm sorry, but I've had a long day. Do you mind if I go to bed shortly?"

"Not at all," June assured her. "But if you aren't too sleepy, you can share my evening devotions. My husband always read a chapter in the Bible and had prayer before bedtime, and I've continued it since his death."

"I'm not too sleepy for that. I read the Bible before I go to sleep, too." She settled into the couch and waited while June took a well-worn Bible from the coffee table. She opened the Bible, saying, "I'm reading in the book of Hebrews now, beginning with chapter 13." Glancing at the text, a kind smile spread over her face. "Looks like that's a good place for me to read tonight."

" '*Keep on loving each other as brothers,*' " June read. " '*Do not forget to entertain strangers, for by so doing some people have entertained angels without knowing it.*' "

Kennedy understood why June had thought the words were appropriate, but she shook her head, indicating to June that she wasn't an angel. She peered sideways at Derek, wondering if he, too, considered her an angel. He was reading a magazine.

In her slow voice, June continued to read reverently, and the words that spoke most clearly to Kennedy's needs were, " '*Never will I leave you; never will I forsake you,*' " found in verse 5. She needed this biblical assurance that she was never *really* alone when the Spirit of God lived within her heart. After watching the warm comradeship between Derek and June, Kennedy had realized afresh how much she missed her parents.

When June finished the chapter, she laid the Bible aside. "Join me in prayer if you want to. I always kneel when I pray."

Without hesitation, Kennedy slid to her knees on the floor, lifted her elbows to the couch, and cradled her head in her hands, but she felt a wall between her and God. Jesus had been specific in His admonition that if people didn't forgive those who mistreated them, God wouldn't forgive their sins. The intense dislike she'd harbored all her life against her grandfather Morgan had surfaced today, and it stood between Kennedy and the spiritual growth she wanted. Here in the area where the Morgans lived, the loathing for her grandfather seemed to be intensified. Why couldn't she forgive the man for the way he had treated her mother?

After June's short but sincere prayer, which included her thanks for Kennedy's visit, she paused, and although she wasn't in the habit of praying aloud, Kennedy said quietly, "God, bless the Sterlings for the way they've welcomed me into their home and lives. This morning we were strangers, but now we're friends. Father, I have so many decisions to make. Please give me the wisdom to make the right choices and the grace to forgive the sins of others. Amen."

Kennedy heard June standing, and she scrambled up from her knees. Wondering why Derek hadn't taken part in the family devotions, she turned toward his chair. It was empty! She had heard Derek stirring as his mother prayed, and she thought he might be kneeling in prayer, too, but apparently he didn't share his mother's faith.

* * * * *

Temporarily bewildered by the unfamiliar surroundings, Kennedy awakened suddenly and sat up in bed. Outside her window, a rooster announced the dawning of the day.

She peered at the illuminated face of her travel alarm. Five o'clock? She yawned and looked again, but her eyes hadn't deceived her. It *was* five o'clock in Nebraska but only three o'clock at home. She slipped out of bed and went to the window. Daylight was filtering through the haze that hung over the river valley, and birds sang lustily to herald the beginning of a sunny morning in early May. She must be facing east, for a narrow layer of pink indicated the rising sun.

How strange it was to wake up in Derek's room. She got back into bed and snuggled beneath the handmade quilt, feeling lost in the king-sized bed. Considering Derek's height and his brawny shoulders, he needed a large bed, but it was too sizable for her. The room reminded Kennedy of her father's bedroom.

Derek was a puzzle to Kennedy. Would his room help her see beyond his attractive male physique and learn what he was like as a person? She'd been too tired last night to pay much attention to the room, but she glanced around now with interest. Knowing she wouldn't go to sleep again, she stuffed two pillows behind her back and surveyed the large room that seemed to fit Derek's character. As her eyes adjusted to the dim light, she saw five wide-brimmed hats hanging on the wall. A wooden rack on the back of the door held several bolo ties and a display of ornamental belt buckles.

When Kennedy had hung up her garments the night before, she had noticed shirts, jeans, vests, coats, and several pairs of boots in the closet. One garment bag evidently held a dress suit, but every other garment was casual wear. Derek obviously didn't go in for the elaborate outfits of some

Westerners she'd noted on television. Kennedy had a feeling that she had seen Derek as he would always be. Nothing fancy about him, but she had a feeling that he would be a good man to have around when things got rough.

Kennedy stretched out in the bed with a sense of well-being as the new day broke around her. Through the open window, she heard horses stamping their feet in the corral, cattle bawling, and the clear, lilting call of a bird—an exuberant, bubbling medley of rich flutelike calls. Could it be a meadowlark? That was one of Nebraska's birds that her mother had missed hearing in California.

Kennedy couldn't believe that this time yesterday she had been in Los Angeles and had never heard of Derek Sterling or his mother. Their way of life differed so much from hers that it was inconceivable that she felt so comfortable, safe, with them. But she couldn't impose on the Sterlings any longer. She had come to Nebraska without any long-range plans, so what was she going to do now?

Kennedy dozed a little until she heard water running in the bathroom beside her. June soon knocked on her door.

"You awake, Kennedy?"

"Yes."

"Breakfast is in thirty minutes. You'll have the bathroom to yourself until then. Derek will wash up in the bunkhouse."

Kennedy hurried out of bed and opened the suitcase she'd brought from the car last night and chose her personal items for the day. She had hung up a pair of green cotton slacks and a short-sleeved blouse before she'd gone to bed, which might not be warm enough, for she had already noticed that it was colder here than in Los Angeles. But she had a sweater in the car if she needed it. When she took her clothes from the closet, she noticed that they had picked up a musky, masculine scent, one she'd always associated with her father's closet. Would the fragrance of her perfume and makeup be left behind for Derek? Amused, she figured a he-man like him wouldn't appreciate having his clothes smell like women's cosmetics.

She took a cosmetic bag from the suitcase and went to the bathroom. She showered but didn't take time to wash her hair, for although she wasn't hungry, she didn't want to be late for breakfast. She'd already caused the Sterlings enough trouble.

When she entered the kitchen, the delicious aroma of ham and perking coffee tempted her taste buds. "Good morning," Kennedy said.

June, busy at the stove, turned her head and greeted Kennedy with a smile. "Same to you. You still look sleepy—I should have let you sleep in."

"Oh, I was already awake. The rooster took care of that."

While June placed food on the table, Kennedy looked through the screen door that opened out onto a porch and saw Derek sauntering toward the house. She opened the door for him, and he looked surprised to see her.

"I thought our city girl would still be in bed," he drawled.

"I didn't want to miss one of your mother's meals," Kennedy answered pertly.

As they ate and chatted about life on the ranch, Kennedy compared her life to theirs. It all seemed a novelty to her now, but she was sure she could never adapt to their lifestyle on a permanent basis.

"What can I do for you today?" Derek said when he finished his breakfast.

"I want to look over Riverside. Now that I know where it's located, I can go alone. I don't want to take you away from your work."

He shook his head. "There's always work to do on the ranch, but there's nothing pressing today to keep me from showing you around. Your only interest seems to be in the house, but I'd like for you to see the ranch itself—the rangeland, the cattle, the vastness of it all—and let you experience the kind of work we do. It's important for you to know what your birthright includes before you sell it."

She gave him a curious gaze. "Let me ask you a question. If you owned this land, would you sell it?"

"Never in a million years."

"Why don't you buy it, then?" Kennedy asked.

Derek took a quick, sharp breath and stared at her. "Do you have any idea what a spread like this would sell for?"

Kennedy shook her head.

"Depending on who buys it and what they aim to do with it, it would probably sell for a million dollars or even higher. That's more money than I could ever hope to have," he added bitterly.

He stood and walked to the screen door. Kennedy was stunned at Derek's quick change of temperament, and she glanced guiltily at his mother.

With his hand on the doorknob, Derek turned halfway toward her. His eyes were as sharp as summer lightning. "I know it isn't any of my business, so I shouldn't even say it, but I can't imagine why anyone who had the Circle Cross given to her would ever consider selling it!" He took a hat from a nail by the door and jammed it onto his head. "I'll be waiting to take you to the house when you're ready," he said over his shoulder, as he stalked out the door.

Chagrined, Kennedy stared helplessly at June. "What's that all about?"

June reached across the table and patted her hand. "You touched a raw nerve, but his anger wasn't aimed at you. Derek would like to have his own ranch. He knows it isn't possible, and he's touchy about it. We did the best we could for him, but we've never accumulated any money. It's too bad he's from a poor family with no one to back him."

After their first stormy meeting she and Derek had been on amiable terms, and Kennedy was heartsick that she'd unintentionally wounded him. She thought of how supportive he'd been and how he had held her hand last night when coming home to Riverside was so difficult for her.

Her distress must have shown in her expression, for June said, "Derek isn't one to hold a grudge—he knows you didn't mean to hurt him."

"I hope so. Will you let me help with the dishes before we leave?" Kennedy asked.

"No need of that," June insisted. "You go on and enjoy the day."

"I really appreciate how kind you've been to me," Kennedy said.

"You're not leaving today, are you?" June asked.

"I don't know how long I'll stay in the area, but I won't impose on you any longer. I'll get a motel in Valentine. Frankly, June, I don't know what I expected to achieve by coming here. Dad let his cousin handle the ranch affairs, and maybe I should have left it that way. Smith thinks I should sell. Derek thinks I shouldn't. What's your opinion?"

As she started clearing dishes from the table, June said, "I don't mean to pry into your affairs, but from what I've gathered through the years, you don't need the money from the ranch to live on, do you?"

Kennedy shook her head slowly. "No. Dad used to say that the Circle Cross income was peanuts compared to his other investments. I often wondered why he kept the ranch, unless it was to annoy Grandfather Morgan." A thought popped into Kennedy's head. "Do you think *he's* the one who wants to buy the ranch?"

"I wouldn't be surprised. And since you asked for my opinion, here it is. If you don't need the money, I can't see any hurry to get rid of this property, *and* I'd find out who wants to buy it and not sell to the first person who comes along. I'd also want to know *what* the purchaser intends to do with the ranch."

Kennedy drew the older woman into a close embrace. "Thank you. I needed some motherly advice, and I'll do what you say. Dad wouldn't want the Morgans to get ahold of his home place. I figure you're going to see a lot of me while I check out what's going on."

"God bless you, Kennedy. I pray that He'll give you the wisdom to make the right decision."

"I'll be praying, too," Kennedy said, "as well as reading the Bible for guidance."

* * * * *

Derek sat on the corral gate watching for Kennedy. Why had he taken his frustrations out on her? There was no excuse for his outburst. But rich people had no idea how it felt to be poor. If they wanted something, they bought it. It was as simple as that! If he could only admit that he would never make enough money to buy property and be content to work for someone else all of his life, as his father had done, he would save himself a lot of grief.

When Kennedy stepped out on the porch, he slid off the fence, noting as she approached how her beauty enhanced an otherwise ordinary house. He took the bag she carried. "Leaving us?"

Smiling, she said, "Not right away, but I'm going to check into a motel today. I'll admit that it was comforting to spend the night in your home, but I won't stay here any longer and make extra work for your mother. And I know you can't be comfortable sleeping on a bunk when you're used to a king-size bed. But I won't go back to California yet, at least not until Cousin Smith comes home. When you have free time, I'd appreciate having you show me around the ranch."

"I'll make the time."

Derek wondered if he should apologize for his eruption at the breakfast table, but she didn't seem offended, so he said nothing. "Let's go."

As they headed toward the blue pickup, Wilson came running and looked up at Derek. "Yes, you can go," Derek said. Wilson jumped into the truck.

Kennedy's mouth quirked with suppressed laughter. "Can that dog understand English?"

"Better'n some people."

A smile hovered on Kennedy's lips as she eagerly looked at the landscape where cattle grazed in the pastures and cottonwood trees formed an arch over the road. Derek hadn't had much interest in women and seldom sought their company. It was a novelty to be entertaining the lady owner of the ranch.

Derek carried her suitcase to the car before he opened the truck door and gave Kennedy a boost into the seat. "We'll look over the house at Riverside first, and then if there's time we can see some of the ranchland. It's a wonderful ranch, Kennedy. My dad was a good caretaker, and I've tried to be." Derek loved the ranch and hoped that Kennedy would see why.

"Does Cousin Smith take much of an interest?"

Derek shrugged his muscular shoulders. "Not much. I report to him if there's a problem, and he receives the quarterly reports. I pretty much operate the ranch as I want to."

As he stopped the truck and unlocked the gate, he marveled at how comfortable he felt with Kennedy. She was rich and he was poor, but it didn't seem to matter. And the fact that she was his boss didn't bother him at all—but he figured he was still in shock from her sudden appearance into his life. After a few days, he would come down to earth and realize that Kennedy Blaine was as far out of his reach as the moon and stars. But for a woman who'd been born with the proverbial silver spoon in her mouth, he had to admit that she wasn't a bit stuck-up, except for yesterday when she'd called him a cowhand and labeled Wilson a mongrel. Of course, he'd provoked her to anger, so he didn't hold it against her. And if he came right down to it, he *was* a cowhand.

Chapter Three

....

When they came in sight of the house, Derek stopped the truck and Kennedy studied the scene before her. Sunlight filtered through the leaves of the cottonwood trees behind the house, and it looked like a different building from the one Kennedy had seen the night before. The evening shadows had caused it to look like a fairyland, but in the morning sun, the house looked old and neglected. The white paint was peeling. A few of the shutters were askew, some palings on the porch rail were missing, and the shrubbery around the foundation needed to be trimmed.

Derek must have noticed her disappointment in the appearance of the place, for he put the truck in gear and moved forward. "The upkeep of this house isn't my responsibility. As I told you, Mr. Blaine asks Mom to clean once in a while, and we mow the grass a few times every year."

When Derek stopped the truck again, Kennedy said, "I suppose I expected it to look like the picture I've known since I was a child. It hangs on the wall of Dad's office, and I often wondered why he kept it when he didn't want to come back here. Although I suppose it was Mother who couldn't return, and he wouldn't come without her."

"But you kept in touch with some of your family," Derek said.

"None of the Morgans. Cousin Smith and his wife came to see us a few times. And Dad's parents visited us every year until Grandmother died. You probably know that after her death, Grandpa spent winters with us in California."

Derek nodded. "There hasn't been a caretaker on the place since he died—so it would naturally be run-down," he said, as if he was sorry she had to see the house in this condition.

As they got out of the truck and walked toward the house, Derek asked, "What caused the ruckus between the Blaines and the Morgans? I've often wondered."

"Oh, it was one of those crazy feuds that started years ago, and the next generations wouldn't let go of it. Jonathan Morgan and Alexander Blaine were best friends. They came west in the 1870s and made their fortunes in the Black Hills Gold Rush. They started back East with their gold, saw the lush grasslands of this area, and decided to settle here. Then they both fell in love with the same woman, and when she chose Alexander Blaine, my Morgan ancestor declared war on all Blaines. His hatred affected succeeding generations, but according to Dad, the animosity has about died out."

"Except for Gabriel Morgan."

"Yes. Dad said the bickering will never die as long as he lives." Grimacing, Kennedy added, "I don't have a very good legacy, Derek."

"That's true about a lot of us," he said quietly.

He inserted the large metal key into the lock of the front door, and the lock snapped back with a squeak. He held the door open for her, and she walked into semidarkness.

"It's dark in here because we keep the shutters closed. Stay put until I open the ones in the living room, and then I'll go to the back porch and turn on the power. We keep the electricity on all the time to have some heat during the winter."

She halted in the foyer. To the left was a living room, and a bedroom was on the right. They walked into the living room, and the windows squeaked when Derek opened them to unhook the shutters. "Mom keeps dustcovers on most of the furniture. You can take some of them off if you want to, while I get some more light." But she was still standing in the middle of the floor when he came back, so without speaking, he started uncovering the furniture.

The house had been vacant for a long time. *What else could I have expected?* Kennedy thought. She stirred out of her reverie and helped Derek fold the cloth he'd taken from a Windsor reed organ.

"You probably think I'm foolish for expecting the house to look like a mansion, but I've always thought about it the way Mother described it having come here as a bride. When my grandmother died, I didn't come with Dad because Mother was still living and I wouldn't leave her. When Grandpa died, I was in finals and didn't come back for his funeral, either."

From the living room they moved into an octagonal sunroom then into a large parlor and the dining room. The kitchen was the most modern room in the house, with fairly new appliances, but the rest of the furniture had probably been bought forty or fifty years ago. Only a few antique pieces remained.

"It seems rather futile for me to be here now," Kennedy said. She was disappointed that she didn't have any sense of *belonging* in the house.

Almost in silence they walked upstairs, where there were four bedrooms and a bathroom. The furniture was similar in each room—an oak bed, a dresser, an armoire, a rocking chair, and a nightstand. Most of the furnishings could have been there since the house was built. In the first room, Kennedy checked out the dresser drawers. Each drawer had papers or items of clothing, piles of mutilated paper, and a stale odor indicating that the house at one time or another had been infested with mice.

"I've seen enough for today," Kennedy said wearily. She'd looked forward to seeing her ancestral home, but all she felt now was a horrible feeling of emptiness. She had hoped to find contentment here, but she had experienced nothing but disappointment.

Derek locked the door and pocketed the large key. Pointing northward, he said softly, "The family cemetery is in that direction. It's only a short walk, if you'd like to go."

She shook her head. "Oh no, I can't deal with that today. But if you've got time, I'd really like to see some of the rangeland."

"On horseback or by truck?" he queried with a slight lift of his heavy brown brows as he and Kennedy got into the cab of the vehicle.

"I've never ridden a horse in my life," Kennedy admitted.

"Well, City Girl, that's the best way to see your ranch," he said with a mischievous arching of his left brow.

"Well, Cowhand, you'll have to teach me how to ride," she countered.

His brow arched again in a way that she found most fascinating. With a hint of humor in his intense brown eyes, he waved his hand in a gesture of defeat. "I sure can't do that in one afternoon. We'll go in the truck."

Kennedy didn't answer. She figured his good-natured ribbing was designed to ease the unhappiness that visiting the house had caused her, but she wasn't in a talkative mood. Besides, she was wrestling with a preposterous idea that had popped into her head out of the blue. She couldn't erase hang-ups from the past if she kept running from reality. Was it time to face the hurdles head-on?

Derek's impersonal gaze swept over her. "I'm not sure you'll be comfortable in that getup. We may do some walking, and your arms could get burned from the wind and sun."

She grinned, remembering how much "that getup" had cost her.

"Do you have jeans and a long-sleeved shirt?" Derek continued.

"Yes, but the shirt is silk, probably no more suitable than this 'getup.' I bought the jeans especially for my trip to the country," she answered, although now she realized that they were too stylish for the ranch. She needed plain Levis like her father had often worn.

"When we get back to the house, you can change into jeans, and Mom can loan you a shirt." He surveyed her body again, but not quite as impersonally as before. "No, I think you'd better wear one of my shirts—hers won't fit you."

Laughing, she said, "And I suppose yours will!"

"You can roll up the sleeves. It's better to have a shirt too big than too small. While you change, Mom can fix us a lunch."

Kennedy retrieved her jeans from a garment bag in her car and went to the bathroom and changed. June brought her one of Derek's shirts that was too small for him. The sleeves were several inches too long, but June shortened them with safety pins, agreeing with Derek that Kennedy needed a long-sleeved shirt. "When you're not used to our sun and wind, you can sunburn mighty quick."

When Kennedy rejoined Derek, she detected laughter in his eyes as he said, "Where did the city girl go?"

"I'm still the same, Cowhand. Clothes won't change me into a cowgirl."

He didn't respond as she expected him to. Instead he said, "I still think you'd better stay with Mom at night, but if you won't, do you want to try to reserve a motel room before we leave?"

"How long will we be gone?"

"As long as you want to be. This is a big ranch, and even in a truck it takes awhile to cover all of it. We'll only see a small portion of it today. Some places are too rugged to take the truck and we'll *have* to ride horses to get there."

Pleased to know that she would have a good reason to extend her stay, Kennedy said, "I'll probably have seen enough in a few hours, and we can be back by mid-afternoon. I'll call about reservations then."

A half hour later Derek was explaining about the crops grown on the ranch—alfalfa, wheat, and oats—and how they were needed to feed the stock during the winter months. Kennedy had never been surrounded by so much open country in her life. Next they came to the grasslands—large pasture fields where Black Angus cows and white-faced Herefords grazed.

She counted more than a hundred horses in another field. "These are mostly used at roundup time," Derek explained. "We ride the ones in the corral at headquarters just about every day."

After an hour had passed, Kennedy realized that they were steadily ascending. When they came to a rocky embankment, Derek put the truck into four-wheel drive, and the vehicle laboriously climbed a rough trail that took them to the top—giving Kennedy a bird's-eye view of the terrain they'd been driving. The grasslands extended for miles. As the strong wind stirred the green blades, the grass moved sinuously like ocean waves toward the pine-crested buttes of the Niobrara in the far distance.

Awestruck by the beauty before her, Kennedy gasped. "Oh, it's beautiful! Derek, what do you think a new owner would do with the ranch?"

"I don't know. It depends on the buyer. You hear all kinds of rumors when a piece of property is up for sale. If the buyer is someone who loves the land, it would probably continue as a ranch. But I've heard it might be turned into a housing development, providing large building lots for rich people. There's also talk of a country club or a shopping mall." He paused. "Do you want to get out? This is a pretty view, and you can get a good look at the rangeland from here. We can eat before we start back home."

"Oh, yes," Kennedy said, her eyes glowing. "I could look at that scene for hours."

Derek circled the truck and opened her door. Still looking at the scenery while exiting the truck, Kennedy missed the step and tumbled forward.

"Oh!" she squealed. Derek stepped forward and caught her in a close embrace. Still frightened, she clutched his arms and looked up to thank him. His protective arms wrapped around her like a warm blanket. Time stood still, and Kennedy could feel his heart thudding against her own. Was it fear or something else that caused her to gasp for breath?

His nearness kindled emotions she had never experienced, and she felt wrapped in an invisible warmth. His eyes swept over her face, and she lowered her eyelids a little to avoid his searching gaze. She sensed that he was leaning toward her, and she stared at his lips, which were coming closer and closer.

Suddenly she felt his body stiffen. He released her quickly and stepped back. In a husky voice he asked, "Did you hurt yourself?"

Not physically, she thought. Although she was breathless, she made an effort to speak calmly. "No, thanks to you. I shouldn't have been so clumsy."

Derek seemed to have gained control of himself, for he said, "That's a high step."

She had to get away from him. She walked to the promontory, where stunted pine trees provided some shade. The promontory was covered with grass and clumps of yucca. "This *is* a good place to picnic, and the view is spectacular."

"Yeah, I think so." Derek dusted off a rock with his bandanna, and she sat down, still looking out over the river valley. She couldn't meet his gaze. Whatever had happened to her must have affected Derek, too, for when she slanted a discreet glance in his direction, his face seemed a shade lighter than usual.

* * * * *

As they ate, Derek pointed out the ranch headquarters, the general direction of Valentine, the Niobrara River, and the approximate western boundaries of the ranch, saying that they couldn't see the eastern sections from this point. Kennedy had a lot of questions, and he fielded them as well as he could.

After a while she said, "I've seen enough new things for one day, but let's just sit here for a few minutes before we go back. That is, if you have the time."

Thinking he might as well put their relationship in perspective, Derek said coolly, "You're my boss. We'll stay here as long as you want to."

She frowned at him. "I *am not* your boss."

"With Smith out of the country, you're the nearest thing I have to one." The reproachful look in her eyes hurt his conscience, but he had to do something to counteract that fiasco between them a short time ago. "But we needn't argue the point right now. Let's talk about something else. You've lived in Los Angeles all of your life, but that doesn't tell me much about you. What do you do there?"

"Oh, it's the same as the life of any city girl." She gave him a sassy look, so he figured he was forgiven for hugging her. That is, if she'd been offended in the first place. "I graduated from high school and went to college all within the same city."

"What'd you study to be?"

"An attorney," she told him. "I specifically prepared to represent underprivileged people who need legal counsel. I've finished my college work, but I haven't taken the bar exams yet. With the pressure of finals and dealing with Dad's death, I needed some time off before I start reviewing for the exams. In California they're given in October and February. I hope I can be ready by October, but I'll have to review tons of information we covered in law school."

"I suppose you were at the top of your class," he said with a slight smile.

"Hardly that, but I did graduate from the university with honors."

"Have you traveled much—outside of California, I mean?"

"I've been in Europe a few times, and to Hawaii," Kennedy replied. "For my high school graduation present, my parents took me on a Mediterranean cruise. But that's enough about me. What about yourself? I'd never heard of you until yesterday, so now it's my turn. For starters, did you and your parents live anywhere else before moving to the Circle Cross? Do you have any brothers or sisters?"

Derek wasn't too keen on revealing his family background, but perhaps it was best that she knew now. He knew that there wasn't any place in his life for a girl like Kennedy. Although he would like to be her friend, he wasn't sure he could handle that without being hurt. Grief over her father's death had made her vulnerable, and Derek knew that nothing must happen between them that they would both regret when she left Valentine.

He'd almost kissed her when she fell into his arms an hour ago, and he doubted that she would have objected. But what was probably a summer fling to her could mean a lot more to him. He wasn't one to flirt with a woman. She had a right to know the worst about him, if for no other reason than because he worked for her.

"I grew up in the slums of Chicago. I have no idea who my parents were or if I have any siblings. As a matter of fact, I don't even know my birthday. When I was about two years old, the police picked me up. I was wandering the streets. They took me to a children's shelter and the staff tried for a year to find some clue as to my parentage, but they never did."

Kennedy's eyes widened. "And you still don't know?"

Determined not to sugarcoat the facts, Derek said laconically, "Nope! The director listed my birthday as August 15, the day I was taken to them. They recorded my age as two. After I was shifted from one foster home to another, Dad and Mom adopted me when I was eight."

A wide range of emotions flitted across Kennedy's face—shock, concern, disbelief, and another emotion he couldn't define—perhaps it was disgust. He couldn't tell for sure, so he added harshly, "So you see, while you were traveling overseas and living in luxury, I was living from hand-to-mouth. There's a big difference in our backgrounds, Kennedy."

Tears misted her majestic green eyes. "But how could you have turned out so well when you had such a poor start?"

"All the credit goes to Mom and Dad. He was originally from Nebraska, and after a few years, they decided that Chicago was no place to raise a boy. He got a job on the Circle Cross, and we moved. I was fifteen and way behind in my studies, but I wanted to better myself, so I studied hard. I graduated from high school and got a football scholarship to the university, but I didn't graduate with honors."

"But don't you see," she said earnestly, placing her well-groomed fingers on his hand, "that you've accomplished more than I have? I had *every* advantage, so it wasn't any big deal for me to make good grades. You're the one who deserves a pat on the back."

"I haven't gotten many of those," he said without rancor.

Playfully, she reached over and patted his broad shoulders, and the uncomfortable moment passed.

"But what about guys?" Derek asked, figuring she would tell him to tend to his own business. "I can't believe that someone like you hasn't had a lot of romance, but I don't notice an engagement ring."

"I had my share of teenage romances, but they were short-lived," Kennedy admitted. With a smile, she recalled, "Dad accused me of being too picky. The last two years I've been seeing another law student, Steve Martin. But what I considered friendship must have meant more to him. He asked me to marry him a few months ago. I didn't want to hurt him, so I told him I'd think about it. He's traveling in Europe this summer, and I told him I'd give him an answer when he comes home in September."

"What kind of a man is he?" Derek demanded, as if he had the right to question her.

"Oh, he's a good guy and would make a fine husband, but"—she regarded him with a steady gaze—"I don't think I'll marry him. There's no spark between us, if you know what I mean."

Derek knew exactly what she meant, and he wondered if she, too, had experienced the electric-like bolt that had shattered his composure when she fell into his arms. He cleared his throat. "Well, I sure can't give you any advice," he said. He forced himself to add, "I've avoided women, for the most part. I have nothing to give a wife and children. Besides being poor, I don't have a name, and I have no idea what kind of background I'd bring into a marriage. So I'm better off to leave women alone when I don't intend to marry."

"Oh," she said and turned from him to look out over the plains. He watched her profile, hoping she didn't turn quickly, for he figured his face revealed the perplexing emotions he'd been experiencing since she'd suddenly come into his life.

After the silence continued for ten or fifteen minutes, he said, "It will take an hour to drive back to the ranch. The tourist season is starting now, so if you want to be sure of getting a motel room, we'd better hit the road."

She shook her head. "I'm not ready to leave yet. I'm thinking."

He smiled, knowing that whether or not she admitted it, she *would* make a good boss. He lay back on the rock and covered his face with his hat. He was dozing when she said, "Derek?"

He sat up and put on his hat. "Ready?"

"Not quite. What would you think if I told you that I'm thinking of moving into Riverside for the summer?"

"I think it's insane if you're figuring on living there alone," he answered bluntly.

She glanced at him crossly. "I thought you'd agree with me."

"Why would you want to live there?"

"In the first place, I don't want to go home yet. I need to wait until Cousin Smith gets back so I can find out who wants to buy the ranch and why. If he doesn't want to tell me, I definitely won't sell. Also, I want to meet some of my cousins while I'm here. I can't see any reason to pay motel rent when I own a perfectly good house."

"A perfectly good, isolated, mice-infested house! Don't forget that. The place is almost a mile from ranch headquarters. You'll be afraid, and I've judged that you've never really taken care of yourself. Can you even cook?"

Ignoring his question, she looked directly at him. "I thought you might *want* me to stay."

He avoided her gaze. "As far as that's concerned, I'd enjoy having you around. I believe we could become friends if we had a chance. And I hate to see this ranch go out of the family. But I feel responsible for you until Smith gets home, and I can't watch you and do the ranch work, too. We're going to start the spring roundup soon and be branding the calves, which will take at least two weeks. It's a dawn-till-dusk job."

"I'll cause you as little extra work as possible, but I've made up my mind. I'd like to do this. I'll go into Valentine and get a few groceries, and tonight I'll set up light housekeeping in my ancestral home."

Derek stood and brushed the dust off his clothes. "You're living in a make-believe world, but I know there's nothing I can do to stop you." He wondered at his audacity in talking to Kennedy like that. After all, he'd only known her for a couple of days, and she owned the Circle Cross, where he'd spent the happiest years of his life. She had every right to fire him for meddling. But somehow he didn't think that was going to happen, for already they were on a first-name basis and sharing confidences and opinions as if they'd known one another for years.

The return trip was largely made in silence. When he reached the road that would have taken them to the ranch, Derek said, "I'll drive you into Valentine to get the things you need. It would take time for you to find a store, and if you're determined to stay at Riverside, I need to turn on the water before dark. There's a deep well that provides water, and we keep the pump turned off, but it's available in case of a fire. I'll need to make sure that the appliances are all working, too."

"Thanks."

Kennedy wondered if she was being stubborn to stay at Riverside when Derek was so set against it. She wished she could make him understand that with her father no longer living, the Circle Cross was her only tie to the past that hadn't changed.

Chapter Four

....

Realizing that it was impossible for him to be irritated at her for long, when they drove into Valentine, Derek said, "Now that we're here, you might as well take a quick look around town. Valentine is a progressive, friendly town. Its 2,800 residents won't measure up to where you live in California, but we're proud of it."

He turned left onto Main Street, and Kennedy was obviously interested in the wide streets, craft shops, and old brick buildings. Derek pointed to Young's Western Wear on the left of the street. "If you're going to stay around for a while, you may want to go into that store and buy some Western clothes. For a small town, you can find anything you need here."

Kennedy's luminous eyes widened in approval as they turned from Highway 20 onto the main street of town. A small smile of enchantment touched her lips as she reminisced. "When I was a child, Dad and Mother talked a lot about Valentine, and I'll probably remember some of the places that were dear to them. Derek, I owe it to them to stay here for a while."

"It's sometimes called the Heart City, and you'll eventually learn why."

"Oh," Kennedy exclaimed, "look at the beautiful facade of that building."

"That's the First National Bank of Valentine, where the Circle Cross accounts are. Those brick relief murals were created by Lincoln artist Jack Curran in the early 1990s. The top mural has running longhorn cattle to symbolize the movement of the cattle industry into the Sandhills. That smaller mural at the bottom tells about the first century of progress in Valentine. The inside of the building is cool, too. Be sure to go in and introduce yourself."

Derek turned onto a side street and parked in front of Scotty's Ranchland Foods, where his mother shopped. He waited until she came out with a small bag of groceries.

"This is enough for overnight. I'll have a better idea of what I need tomorrow," she said.

"I'm glad you didn't buy much. One night alone will be enough for you. You'll either move into town or stay with Mom."

A look of unyielding determination crossed her face, and her green eyes flashed impatiently. "Wanna bet?"

"Nope. I never bet on a sure thing."

A hint of anger flitted across Kennedy's pale, beautiful face, but she bit her lip and remained silent as she climbed into the cab.

They stopped at ranch headquarters to pick up her car, and he asked his mother for a set of bed linens and some towels. He whistled for Wilson, and the dog jumped onto the front seat with Derek.

Kennedy waved to June and followed him as he drove toward Riverside. He carried in her luggage and put it in the downstairs bedroom. He puttered around for an hour or more, working on the water system, checking the plumbing in the bathroom, making sure the windows were locked, and helping her remove the slipcovers from all the furniture on the first floor. He helped her spread the sheets on the bed. He tested the big flashlight he'd picked up at the Circle Cross bunkhouse and laid it on the bedside stand.

Finally, with a resigned shrug of his shoulders, he said, "I've done all I can do." He scribbled his cell phone and house phone numbers on a sheet of paper and gave it to her. "You've got your phone, so call if there's the least hint of trouble. I don't suppose I'll sleep anyway."

After she gave Derek her cell phone number, Kennedy followed him to the door. "You worry too much. I'll be all right."

Derek saw Wilson nosing around in the underbrush near the house. He whistled. The dog came running, and he directed Wilson to the porch.

"Stay!" he commanded, and although he whined, the dog dropped to the floor at Kennedy's feet.

"I don't need a watchdog," she protested. "Besides, Wilson doesn't like me."

Ignoring her comment, Derek stepped off the porch and turned to look up at her standing in the doorway. "You're stubborn, aren't you?"

"I suppose so," she admitted. "Dad told me more than once when I disagreed with him that, although I had been born a Blaine, I was Gabriel Morgan through and through."

Smiling in spite of his concern, Derek noticed how much she did resemble her maternal grandfather. "I reckon there are worse things than being stubborn," he said. He took a quick glance around the clearing, wondering if there was anything else he could do to protect her. He might as well leave, for he knew he couldn't keep her from doing what she wanted to do. "I had a good time today."

"So did I. Don't worry, Derek. Everything will turn out all right."

* * * * *

She watched him drive away. Derek stuck his hand out the window and waved just before he disappeared from view. When Kennedy knew he could no longer see her, she threw a kiss in his direction and walked into the empty house with Wilson at her heels.

* * * * *

Startled out of an uneasy sleep, Kennedy screamed and bolted out of bed with a shiver of panic. In the darkness of the room, she stubbed her toe on the bedpost and almost fell. Her body stiffened in shock when she realized what had caused her to wake up so abruptly.

Someone was in the bed with her! Her pulse beat erratically, and panic like she'd never known swept through her. With shaking hands she groped in the darkness for the large flashlight Derek had left. After she saw who had invaded her bedroom without waking her, she could use it as a weapon. How could she have slept so soundly that she hadn't heard someone enter the bedroom? She doubted it was Derek, but who else had a key to the house?

Splaying the beam of light on the bed, her eyes widened in astonishment. She took a glance of utter disbelief before she gasped, "Wilson!"

Lying on his side with his head on a pillow and his forepaws on the pillow slip, the dog snored softly. It would have been an amusing sight if she wasn't so frightened. Kennedy picked up her pillow and threw it at the dog.

"Get off my bed, you mongrel!"

With a terrified howl, in one leap Wilson scampered off the bed and crawled under it. Kennedy swung the light in that direction and saw his reproachful eyes staring at her. Her legs were shaking so much that she couldn't stand. She collapsed on the side of the bed. It had been a miserable night, for it seemed that every joint and beam in the old house creaked. As she lay awake, Kennedy thought of the past when her mother had come here as a bride. She had wondered in which of the upstairs rooms she'd been born. She had many questions about the past, but her restless night didn't provide any answers. Her sleep had been troubled, and to wake up in terror was the last straw!

During her wakeful hours, she had conceded that Derek had been right. Her impulse to spend the night in the house *was* a mistake. More than once she'd considered calling him, but her obstinate Morgan pride kept her from admitting that she'd been wrong.

Daylight was creeping into the room, and knowing that she wouldn't go to sleep again, Kennedy shrugged into her long robe and slippers. As she started out of the room, Wilson, still under the bed, whined piteously.

"Well, come on," she said. "But if you're going to be my houseguest, we're going to find some other place for you to spend the night."

Wilson crawled from under the bed and, with his belly almost scraping the floor, came toward her. She bent over and patted his head. He wagged his tail and barked joyfully. "Don't get carried away," she said with a grimace. "I'm still mad at you. Let's eat breakfast."

Wilson sniffed disdainfully at the cold bread she gave him to eat. He took one bite of the bread, chewed it languidly, settled down on his haunches, and peered up at her with liquid, begging brown eyes.

The dog's actions amused her, and she leaned over and scratched behind his ears. "Sorry! When I bought groceries, I didn't know you were going to be foisted on me. And I've never had a dog, so I don't know what they eat."

She boiled water, made a cup of tea, and, not seeing a toaster, put butter on a slice of cold bread. She'd finished eating when the phone rang.

"Just checking to see if you were up," Derek said cheerfully when she answered.

Smiling and wondering if her pleasure was obvious in her voice, she said, "Of course. Aren't all ranchers supposed to get up bright and early?"

"Mom fixed your breakfast—I'll bring it over right away."

"I've just finished eating, so don't bother."

"You're mighty independent all of a sudden," he said, and Kennedy sensed that he was smiling. "At least I'll bring something for Wilson."

Laughing, she said, "He'll appreciate that. He turned up his nose at what I served him."

"See you in a few."

Kennedy hurried to the bedroom and changed quickly into the jeans and shirt she'd worn yesterday. She brushed her teeth and had just run a brush through her hair when she heard Derek's truck approaching the house. With a yelp, Wilson hurried toward the door, his toenails clacking on the hardwood floor like hailstones on a tin roof. When Kennedy opened the door, he bounded out on the porch and down the steps to circle Derek. The dog barked excitedly, sniffing at the bag of dog food and a small basket, which Derek carried toward the house. Kennedy stepped out on the porch to greet him.

* * * * *

Derek's eyes swept her face speculatively. She watched him through dark, lowered lashes, but her eyes were unfathomable. He had no idea whether she resented his visit.

"Good morning," she said, holding the door open for him. Wilson tagged at their heels as they walked toward the kitchen. Derek glanced at the table with its meager food.

"I see you're living high on the hog, all right."

Without comment Kennedy found a bowl in the cabinet, watching while Derek filled it with dry food and put it on the back porch for Wilson.

He opened the basket and removed a foil cover from a plate that held a bowl of fresh fruit, a cinnamon roll, and a small bowl of oatmeal lavishly covered with brown sugar. Placing it on the table, he said, "Mom had an idea you wouldn't want a rancher's breakfast."

"She's right," Kennedy said, as she got a fork and spoon from the cabinet and sat down to eat the food. "I haven't found a coffeemaker yet, but you can make yourself a cup of tea."

He shook his head and sat down opposite her.

"So, how was your night?" he asked, watching her closely. "Were you afraid?"

Smiling slightly, she said, "If you want the honest truth, I was terrified at the quietness, the darkness, and the strange surroundings."

Relieved, he said, "So you'll stay with Mom or in a motel while you're in Nebraska."

Her voice was firm and full of determination when she answered. "No. I'm going to stay right here and overcome my fears. If I'd gotten used to the area during daylight, I'd have been all right. I can study for the bar exams in Nebraska as well as at home, so I've decided to spend the summer here."

His heartbeat accelerated to know that she wouldn't be leaving his life right away, but Derek shook his head. "But you said you were scared."

"I was and probably will be again, but I intend to get over it." She looked at him, as if pleading for understanding. "You see, it's lonely at home, too. With Dad gone, our house seems so empty. Last night, as I looked through photo albums and saw pictures of him I'd never seen— from a few days old until he was a young man—I felt closer to him than I did in California. I know you think it's just stubbornness, but, really, it isn't. I believe I can deal better with his death here than at home. Can you understand?"

Her eyes seemed to ask for confirmation of what she wanted to do. "I think so," he said slowly, "and I'll help you any way I can. If staying here is that important to you, we'll manage to keep you protected."

"I don't suppose I slept more than an hour all night, and I did a lot of thinking. While I'm here, I want to meet my cousins, *Morgan* cousins as well as the Blaines. And I think I have some aunts and uncles on the Blaine side. Now that I have no close family, I want to get acquainted with my extended family."

With a grin, he said, "But not Grandpa Gabriel?"

She shook her head. "No, not even if he wanted to see *me*, which he won't. I'm not proud of it, Derek, but I can't forgive him for being so mean to my mother." She stood up and looked out the window for a few minutes before she turned toward him with a small tentative smile. "You asked what you could do for me. I suppose more than anything, I need someone to understand why staying here is so important to me."

Somehow Derek had never expected to hear such a pleading note in her voice—he had judged Kennedy Blaine as a woman who had it all together. As he studied her face thoughtfully, he detected uncertainty and a need for belonging. He couldn't think of anything more to his liking than to see Kennedy every day throughout the summer. But could he handle it? His sleep had been fitful the night before, and Kennedy's soft but clear, velvety voice had provided a melodious background for his wakeful and slumbering thoughts.

Was he building up heartache for himself? He was halfway in love with her already, and that feeling was bound to increase every time he saw her. After avoiding women for years, why did he have to take an interest in Kennedy Blaine, a woman as far out of his reach as the sun and the moon? In order to get his emotions under control, Derek went to the back porch and turned Wilson outside, wondering how he could be Kennedy's friend without ruining his own life.

"For what it's worth," he said when he reentered the room, "I completely understand why you want to connect with the past. It worries me considerably that I don't know anything about my roots. I'll do everything I can to help you. We don't start the roundup for a few days, when I'll be busy from daylight until after dark, so how can I help you until then?"

Still standing by the window, she said, "Just advise me. The first thing is to get the house fit to live in and put the grounds in some kind of order."

"Mom can clean the house."

She shook her head. "No, I was thinking more on the order of a cleaning service—several people who would come in and clean

everything over several days. Is there anything like that in Valentine?"

"I don't know about a cleaning service, but there are several women and men in Valentine who do domestic work. Mom will know more about it than I do. You can ask her. What else?"

"How do I go about finding my cousins?" Kennedy asked.

"Smith Blaine will be the best one to tell you who your relatives are, although some of them attend church where Mom goes. You can go with her on Sunday, and she can introduce you."

"Don't you go to church?" Kennedy asked, remembering that he had taken no part in June's family devotions.

"No, I outgrew church when I was a boy."

She frowned at him, and from the smile she saw lurking in his eyes, she knew he was trying to ruffle her feathers. She ignored his remark.

"I need to take my rental car back to Omaha and rent a car locally to drive this summer," Kennedy said. "If you don't have time to take me, I'll understand and can wait until Cousin Smith returns. He's supposed to be back in a week or ten days, and I can ask him to help out with the car. I don't think he'll mind."

Derek walked into the hallway. "I'll take you to turn in the car on Sunday afternoon, and I'll mention the housecleaners to Mom. You can check with her later to see when they can come." He hesitated at the door. "It depends on how fancy a car you want," he said, "but I might have the answer to your transportation problem."

"I drive a small two-door car at home. Dad made his money by being frugal—and he passed the habit on to me. I'm not hard to please." When he threw a skeptical glance toward her, she smiled and added, "Not about cars, at least."

He motioned for her to follow him, and when she stood by his side on the back porch, he pointed to a garage behind the house.

"Your grandfather's car is still in there. I imagine it's about twenty years old, but I don't think it has much mileage on it. If you have a mechanic put it in shape, I imagine it would take you anywhere you want to go this summer."

"Let's look at it," she said.

He took a ring of keys from his pocket, and when they got to the building, he held up the key marked GARAGE, which she recognized as her grandfather's writing. A knot formed in her throat when Derek opened the door. He removed a dusty tarp from the car to reveal a maroon four-door sedan. They walked around the car, and Kennedy noticed that two of the tires were flat. But the body of the car appeared to be in good condition.

He raised the hood and looked over the engine for several minutes. "I figure an oil change, some new tires, and a battery—just a general overhaul—would get the car in super shape. I can ask a mechanic in town to come out and look it over. He might be able to tow it into his garage for repairs."

"I really want to do that," Kennedy decided. "It would be neat to drive Grandpa's car. I'll use it while I'm here, and I can use it other times when I come to Valentine."

"Then you don't intend to sell the ranch?" Derek said, with an inquiring lift of his heavy brows.

"Not until I learn more about the Circle Cross."

The beginning of a smile curved Derek's lips.

"Does that make you happy?" she asked.

"Of course! And if you stay around here a few weeks, the beauty and mystery of this country will get a hold of you and you'll never want to leave."

The conversation was progressing into matters that Kennedy wasn't ready to consider, and she looked away. "I'm just taking a day at a time, Derek—not looking too far into the future."

She couldn't determine his thoughts when he said in a resigned voice, "That's all any of us can do."

They walked around the house toward his truck in silence, with Wilson tagging at their heels. The dog jumped into the truck bed, and in a firm tone, Derek said, "No!" Pointing toward the house, he added, "Stay here!"

Whining, Wilson jumped to the ground.

"Take him with you," Kennedy said. "I'm mad at him."

"What happened?" Derek asked, staring at her in astonishment, as if he thought Wilson could do no wrong.

"I don't think I'll tell you," Kennedy said—but she couldn't keep her lips from twitching. "You'll think it's funny."

"Try me."

She quickly related how she'd awakened to find Wilson in bed with her, and before she finished, Derek threw back his head and burst out laughing. His amusement was infectious, and she couldn't suppress her own bubble of merriment.

"It's funny now, but I've never been so scared in my life."

"I told you he was a smart dog," Derek said, and Kennedy decided she wouldn't even dwell on the meaning of his words. "But I'll take care of that. I have a short leash for him where you can anchor him to a chair before you go to bed. If you're determined to stay here, you must have some kind of protection."

Knowing that she *would* be more comfortable with Wilson's company, Kennedy didn't argue.

Chapter Five

After Derek left, Kennedy showered and put on fresh clothes and then dialed her home phone in California. When her housekeeper answered, she said, "Rosita, this is Kennedy, checking in."

"About time," Rosita retorted with the freedom of a longtime employee. "Where are you?"

When Kennedy told her, Rosita was speechless for a moment, and then she shouted, "In Nebraska!"

Kennedy smiled at the housekeeper's surprise. To Rosita, who had never been outside of California, Nebraska must seem a long way off.

"Yes, and I've decided to stay for several weeks. I'd like for you to pack some clothes for me and ship them by UPS. I'll get together a list of things I want and telephone you in the next day or two. As soon as you send the box to me, you can take time off until I get back—with pay, of course."

"All right, Miss Kennedy, just let me know. But you take care, now," Rosita added. "That Nebraska must be a wild place."

Kennedy laughed away her concerns. "Don't worry about me. I have a handsome cowboy and his dog for protection," and she hung up after hearing Rosita's indignant snort.

When she called her father's lawyer and financial advisor, Elliott Talbot, to explain her absence and location to him, he assured her that he would contact her if anything needed her immediate attention.

"In the meantime, have a nice vacation," Talbot said. "You've been through a lot in the last few months. Enjoy yourself."

The rest of the day passed quickly for Kennedy. June contacted a family of three who were free to help at Riverside. They promised to come next week to clean the house. She left Wilson at the ranch while she went into Valentine to make preparations for her extended stay at the Circle Cross.

Kennedy parked diagonally in front of the First National Bank and entered the lobby, pausing to look at the murals Derek had mentioned the day before. The lavish interior of the bank and mementoes of Nebraska's past surprised her. She was received graciously by the head teller, especially when Kennedy wrote a sizable check, out of her checking account in California, to open a local account. After she left the bank, she walked several blocks along Main Street in both directions, thrilled to see hundreds of large red hearts painted on the sidewalks.

"No wonder they call Valentine the Heart City," she murmured aloud.

To finally visit the town she'd heard about all of her life was a bittersweet moment for Kennedy, as she remembered that her mother and father had walked these very same streets. If it hadn't been for Gabriel Morgan, she might have grown up here among her family rather than living in California all of her life. But the time had come to put the past behind her and look to the future. Nothing could change the past. She had to move on with her life.

She sensed the curious glances of people she met, and she appreciated their casual greetings, realizing that Derek was correct in his assessment of Valentine as a friendly town. She returned to her car and drove to the large IGA grocery store on the outskirts of town to buy groceries and other items she'd need to set up light housekeeping before she returned to Riverside.

* * * * *

Derek had called an auto repair shop, and he came to Riverside when a mechanic drove out with a wrecker to look at her grandfather's Buick.

After the mechanic kicked the tires, peered at the motor, and surveyed the paint, he said, "I can give this car a complete overhaul, put on new tires, and give it a good cleaning inside and out, and you'll have a better automobile than if you bought a new one."

"That's what I'll do then. What will it cost?" Kennedy asked.

"If you'll let me do it the way I'd repair the car if it belonged to me, it could cost two or three thousand dollars. That's just an estimate; I don't know what parts will need to be replaced until I start working on it."

Kennedy turned to Derek. "What do you think?"

He looked pleased and a little surprised that she'd asked for his opinion. "It's a fair price," he told her. "And you'll have a car to be proud of."

"And also one that belonged to my grandfather." Turning to the mechanic, Kennedy said, "Go ahead and take the car to your garage. How long will it take you to do the repairs?"

"It might take a week or more. I'll start on it on Monday."

After he loaded the car onto the tow truck, Kennedy said, "If you have any questions about it, please call Derek. I've always taken care of my own cars, but I don't know anything about this one." Wondering if she was taking too much for granted, she turned to Derek. "You don't mind, do you?"

"No, I'm glad to help."

Derek and Kennedy watched until the wrecker was out of sight, and then she said, "I'll keep the rental car until the mechanic finishes with Grandfather's. I don't have to return the rental yet…so we'll postpone our trip to Omaha until you're finished with the roundup."

"Sounds good. Mom told me to invite you to supper, by the way. And I want to discuss my bookkeeping for the ranch so you can look at everything when you have the time—like when I'm too busy branding your calves to take you horseback riding." He tugged playfully on her long hair and said with a teasing smile, "That should keep you out of trouble."

In spite of the teasing, Kennedy read a different message in his eyes.

Derek took Kennedy to the ranch for supper and afterward into his office to explain the records he kept on the Circle Cross. He gave her his password and insisted that she use the computer for her own personal use as well as to look over the ranch's operation.

"No matter what decision you make," he said, "you should know everything about the operation of this ranch. I never work on the computer during the day, so use it whenever you want to."

"Super. I was considering whether to ask my housekeeper to send my laptop, but that won't be necessary now. I always carry a zip drive with all of my files. So when I want to study, I can come here to work."

Before she went back to Riverside, Kennedy went inside the ranch house and made arrangements with June to go to church with her the next morning. Derek walked her to the car, whereupon she asked, "Where's my bodyguard?"

"He's in the back of the truck. I'm going to follow you to the house to make sure you're settled in."

She didn't argue with him, and when they arrived at Riverside, a cool breeze was wafting in from the Niobrara River. Kennedy stepped out of the car and looked around. The tall grass blown by a stiff wind looked like waves in the waning light. The sun hovered on the western horizon, and the setting was serene and peaceful.

She sat on the top step of the porch. "It's too nice to go inside. I'll stay here for a while."

"Want company?" Derek asked, a hint of uncertainty in his quiet voice.

She nodded and patted the step beside her. When he joined her, Wilson jumped out of the truck and took his place between them. They sat mostly in silence as night settled around them. The quietness that had seemed so intimidating the previous night now brought peace to Kennedy's heart.

When they could no longer see the western horizon, Derek got up and unlocked the door. Kennedy followed him inside. He checked the windows and the doors on the first floor to confirm that they were locked and then took a quick tour of the upstairs. He also put the leash on Wilson's collar and hooked it to a chair in the bedroom.

Looking around, he seemed uneasy as he said, "I don't know what else to do."

Not since her mother's death had Kennedy known anyone who was so concerned about her comfort, and her heart sang with gladness.

"You've done enough," she said softly. "Go on home and don't worry about me. I'll call you if I have trouble."

He wouldn't leave until she locked the door behind him, and, feeling protected, Kennedy entered the house and prepared for bed.

The night passed without incident, and Kennedy felt rested when she woke up. She had pulled the heavy draperies the night before, so the room was in semidarkness but daylight was shining through the transom over the front door and into the hallway. Stretching, she turned onto her side. Wilson lay with his head on his front paws, watching her, just as he had been when she'd turned out the light last night. She wondered if he had kept guard all night long.

She looked at the clock and saw that it was eight. The worship service at June's church started at ten thirty, so Kennedy got up, put Wilson on the back porch, and filled his bowl from the bag of food Derek had brought. Then she returned to the bedroom to decide what to wear. She preferred casual clothing, and although she owned a few dressy outfits, she hadn't brought them with her.

Because she hadn't intended to stay in Nebraska more than a few days, Kennedy had only five outfits, but they were pieces she could mix and match. She could manage until Rosita sent more clothes. She chose a fuchsia shantung silk blouse with three-quarter sleeves and turned-back cuffs, an open collar, and small pearl buttons down the front. Her white-and–black-gingham-check pants were made of linen, so she chose a black jacket to wear with them. She put on silver loop earrings and a silver-plated stretch bracelet featuring embossed Victorian hearts interspersed with beads of sterling-plated metal. She eased her feet into a pair of black sandals.

Before she left the house, she called June to ask if she would be her guest at lunch in Valentine. After protesting that it wasn't necessary, June agreed.

Derek stepped out of his office when she drove into the yard and came toward the car to open the door for her. Wilson barked a greeting, and after Kennedy exited the car, the dog scrambled across the driver's seat before running circles around Derek.

"Any trouble last night?" Derek asked.

"Not at all," she assured him. "I got a good night's sleep."

"Which is more than I did," he said grumpily. "I don't like for you to be alone."

"Hardly anyone knows I'm there. What trouble could I possibly have?"

Before he answered, June came out of the house and called to Kennedy. "Let's go in my car. It's easier for me to drive than to give you directions."

Noting that June was wearing a dress, Kennedy said, "I don't have a dress with me. Do all the women wear dresses to church?"

June laughed. "Oh no! You'll see jeans, slacks, shorts, knee pants—most anything during the summer. You look fine—doesn't she, Derek?"

Grinning, he said, "I hadn't noticed."

Kennedy ignored his remark. "I've already asked June to be my guest at lunch. Will you meet us after the service and eat with us?"

"Yeah, I will," he said. "Mom has my lunch ready to pop in the microwave, but I won't pass up a free meal."

"Derek!" June scolded, although Kennedy was aware by now that almost anything Derek said or did was okay with his mother.

"Where are you going to eat?" he asked.

"I thought Kennedy might like the Cedar Canyon Steak House," June suggested.

Derek nodded his approval, saying, "I'll be there at twelve o'clock."

Kennedy waved to Derek as they got in the car and drove away. "Why won't he go to church?"

June laughed lightly. "Stubbornness, more than anything else!"

"And he had the nerve to accuse me of being stubborn!" Kennedy commented.

"Derek is a Christian, and he went to church with us until he went away to college. He sets a strict standard of conduct for himself, and it bothers him that so many church members don't live Christlike lives. It irritates him when he goes to worship and sees people who've tried to cheat him on a business deal taking an active part in worship. I've tried to tell him that he's not their judge, but I can't change his mind."

"I wondered why he didn't stay when I shared your family devotions."

"He never participates, but he stays most of the time. I don't remember what happened that night. He might have heard a disturbance among the animals in the corral and thought a coyote was lurking around. But he's a good man, Kennedy. He's never given me any trouble."

Kennedy nodded. "I know. Although I go to church every Sunday," Kennedy said, "I'll admit that I'm a little uneasy about going today. What if people shun me like they did my mother? Or do many people know that I'm here?"

"Well, I haven't been spreading the news," June said. "I thought that was up to you, so your appearance is going to surprise most of the congregation. But don't let that bother you. Your cousin Tony Morgan is the pastor, but he's out of favor with your grandfather, too, so he'll welcome you. Besides, some of your Blaine relatives and their friends will be in the congregation. You won't be ignored. I'll see to that!" she added with determination.

"I should have stayed in California, I guess," Kennedy said slowly.

"You should not have!" June said, and her eyes blazed with indignation. "You're a landowner in this county and have as much right here as anyone else. I want you to walk into that church with your head high, your shoulders straight, and a smile on your face!"

"Yes, Mother," Kennedy said with a mischievous smile.

June's face flushed, and she looked slightly abashed. "Sorry," she said. "I don't have the right to order you around. But for the life of me, I can't imagine how Gabriel Morgan could hold a grudge for more than twenty years and not want to see his granddaughter. I'd like to give him a piece of my mind!"

"I don't want to see him, either," Kennedy said, "but I would like to be introduced to some of my father's family, if any of them attend your church."

The organ was playing when they climbed the steps and walked into the building. June tugged on Kennedy's hand and found seats for them about halfway down the aisle on the left hand side of the sanctuary.

Kennedy judged that the building wouldn't hold more than two hundred people, but it was a peaceful room. The organ prelude continued after June and Kennedy were seated, and Kennedy bowed her head and prayed silently. *God, thanks for giving me this opportunity. I'm so confused now. Sometimes I feel that I belong to Nebraska, but the pull of California is strong, too. I'm like a displaced person regardless of where I am. But I'm thankful that no matter what state I'm in, You are there. Take control of my life and lead me.*

The service was less formal than the ones Kennedy was accustomed to, but when she stood for the final song and benediction, she felt that she had truly worshiped.

After the benediction, June introduced her to many of the people seated around them, and as they moved toward the door, they were approached by a tall, regal, dark-eyed, brown-haired woman. Kennedy judged her age to be in the midforties.

"Did I understand you to say that your name is Blaine?" the woman inquired.

Before Kennedy answered, June said, "Kennedy, this is Robin Donovan. Her maiden name was Blaine."

"Oh," Kennedy said, pleased. "Then we must be cousins."

"Yes, I believe so, if it was your father who owned the Circle Cross."

"He did," Kennedy said, "and the ranch passed to me after his recent death."

Robin held out her hand, and Kennedy grasped it. "I'm so glad to meet you," Robin said sincerely. "You and I share the same Blaine grandfather. My father is John Blaine, but he and my stepmother live in Texas now. I'd like to talk with you while you're here. How long will you be in the area? My husband and I would enjoy having you visit us for dinner."

"As of now, I intend to stay for several weeks—probably most of the summer," Kennedy answered. "It will take me a few days to settle into Riverside, but when I do, I'll call and invite you to visit me."

"I would like that very much," Robin said. "I haven't been in the house for a long time." She reached in her bag and handed Kennedy a business card. "My residence and business phone numbers are on this card."

Several other people spoke to Kennedy and welcomed her to Valentine before they reached the door where the pastor, Tony Morgan, greeted guests. He was of medium height, with dark brown hair and eyes and a captivating smile that reminded Kennedy of her mother.

"So I have the pleasure of meeting you at last," he said to Kennedy as he shook hands with her. "My father has often talked about your mother.

They played together at family reunions when they were children and became good friends as they grew older."

But not good enough friends to stand by her when she was ostracized, Kennedy thought. She had hoped to mend fences, however, not make more enemies, so she smiled and greeted Tony.

"I'm glad to be back in Valentine," she said. "Although I dreaded to come, not knowing how welcome I would be."

With a grimace Tony said, "We have a lot in common. It might help you to know that I'm not in the good graces of our grandfather, either."

"Then come visit me at Riverside. I'd like to talk with you. I know very little about my Nebraska relatives." She wrote her cell phone number on a slip of paper and handed it to Tony. "I don't know what I'll be doing, so call before you come."

As they walked to June's car, Kennedy said, "I was a little nervous about showing my face in Valentine, but it has been a wonderful morning. I suppose I was expecting some Morgan to take a potshot at me," she added with a grimace. "And Mrs. Donovan seemed *very* nice."

"She is," June agreed, as they pulled out of the parking lot and drove toward Main Street. "Her husband has a state job, and Robin is somewhat of a social leader in town. As a member of the county historical society, she's doing a lot to preserve frontier sites in the county."

The Cedar Canyon Steak House fronted on Main Street, and when June slowed down, Kennedy pointed and said, "I see Derek. There's an empty parking place beside his truck."

Derek stepped out of his truck when June pulled in beside him. He had changed his jeans and flannel shirt for a pair of navy blue slacks and a white knit shirt. Instead of his well-worn work boots, he had on boots with higher heels that looked as if they were new. One of the white hats Kennedy had noticed in his room was tilted back on his head. As usual, her heart responded to his presence with a series of flip-flops. His vibrant strength drew her like a magnet, and she wanted to throw herself into his arms. She hoped her face didn't betray her.

Derek opened the door and took his mother's hand as she stepped out. He came toward the passenger side, but Kennedy jumped out before he reached her—she couldn't bear for him to touch her at this moment. Forcing casualness she didn't feel, Kennedy said, "Well, I see the cowhand is on time for his lunch."

"I wouldn't have missed it, City Girl. And I warn you, I've got a powerful appetite."

* * * * *

Derek noticed Kennedy's heightened color. His first thought was that she'd been mistreated at church. "Everything go okay this morning?" he asked sharply.

She smiled happily. "Yes, it did. The sermon was good, and I met several people who were friendly. I've invited Tony Morgan to visit. And Robin Donovan made it a point to speak to me, too. We're going to get together in a few days."

"Good! She's quite a historian, and she can tell you anything you want to know about your father's family. And probably about the Morgans, too."

A hostess greeted them when they stepped inside the restaurant, which was located in what had once been a hotel.

"This is our guest's first visit to the Steak House," Derek said. "Find a good table for us, please."

"You bet!" She led them to a table by the window. Derek suggested that Kennedy sit facing the windows to have a good view of Main Street.

The restaurant was crowded, and his mother told Kennedy that this was normal for any Sunday once the worship services were over.

After their beverage orders were taken, the waitress explained the daily specials on the buffet. Derek ordered the twelve-ounce steak dinner with the salad bar, but June and Kennedy opted for soup and salad bar only.

"But I want to order dessert," Kennedy said, as she scanned the menu. "The lemon pie sounds good."

The waitress soon brought their iced teas and a carafe of ice water with a large wedge of lemon. Sunbeams filtered through a few wispy clouds to illuminate the century-old brick buildings, and one beam spotlighted Kennedy's hair, making it seem as if a golden halo encircled her head. Derek groaned inwardly. Why did she have to be so beautiful?

"The wainscoting was made from local cedar," June said. "And I especially like the brick-front fireplace with gas logs. It makes the room cozy during the winter months."

Kennedy made herself at home, as she had since she'd arrived at the Circle Cross. Derek kept watching to see when she would show distaste of their down-home customs, but she took every new experience in stride. He marveled at how well she got along with his mother, and he listened to their comments on the people she'd met in church. His conscience hurt that he hadn't gone with them.

Derek didn't have any desire to attend corporate worship service, but that didn't mean he didn't pray. He prayed often when he was alone on the prairie at night. He felt nearer to God there than any other place, but he wasn't much of a witness to others when he did all of his praying in private. Still, he recognized that his spiritual life was far from perfect.

As he studied Kennedy's face through half-closed eyes, he wondered how much she'd influenced his change of heart. He was pleased with her reaction to the restaurant, and she had taken to the ranch activities right away. But he warned himself that this lifestyle was a novelty to her now. Soon she would get tired of the glamour of the Midwest and go back to California. Not once but dozens of times in the past few days, he'd told himself that he needed to accept Kennedy's friendship and not expect anything more. She was city; he was country—and the two wouldn't mix.

Derek felt his face flush when he realized that Kennedy watched him with clear, observant eyes.

"A penny for your thoughts," she said.

"You'll have to pay more than that, City Girl."

When the waitress brought their check, she paid it with a credit card, and while they waited for her receipt, Derek said, "I think it's about time for the city girl to learn how to ride a horse."

She looked at him uncertainly. "I don't know about that."

"Anyone who owns a big ranch ought to know how to ride a horse."

"Says who?" she retorted.

"It's Article III, page 15, in *A Cowhand's Guide to Ranching*." He couldn't keep his lips from twitching, and she was quick to realize that he was teasing her again.

"Who's the author?" she retorted.

He laughed loudly but sobered when he realized people were staring at him.

"With my experience, I could have written it, but I didn't. Seriously, it's a nice day; we should take a short ride. I'll be too busy next week to spend much time with you."

Skeptically, she stated, "I've watched enough Western movies to know that cowboys like to play tricks on 'tenderfeet.' Are you going to be nice?"

"Of course," he said, but she must not have trusted the amusement that flickered in his eyes, for she said, "Make him promise, June, or I won't go with him."

"Derek, stop pestering her. What's come over you?" June said. She turned to assure Kennedy. "He'll be patient with you. And I agree that it's a good idea for you to learn to ride. I altered his shirt to fit you, but you'll need a hat."

"She can put a scarf around her head today and buy a hat later." To Kennedy he said, "I promise you won't get hurt *if* you do exactly what I tell you to do."

"I'm good at taking orders," Kennedy said, adding with a grin, "most of the time."

"I want to take the trail along the river, so when you get back to the ranch, go to Riverside and get ready. I'll bring the horses to your home, and we can set out from there," he said.

Derek could tell by her skeptical expression that she still didn't trust him. He followed his mother's car to the ranc,h and try as he might, he couldn't stifle his excitement at the prospect of spending the afternoon with her.

Chapter Six

. . . .

At the Circle Cross, Kennedy collected the altered shirt from June and then got into her car and hurried to Riverside to dress before Derek arrived. She put on the shirt and the jeans she'd worn when Derek had taken her on the tour of the ranch. The wind was brisk, so she tied a red scarf over her head.

Derek had kept Wilson at ranch headquarters, so when Kennedy was ready, she locked the front door and sat on the porch steps to wait. The view of the river valley from this spot was fast becoming a favorite of hers. She glanced toward the gazebo, realizing what a pleasant place it would be to relax. She decided to buy some porch furniture for it. In some ways it distressed Kennedy that she was becoming so satisfied at the Circle Cross.

She heard the *clink-clink-clink* of shod hooves on the graveled road and knew that Derek was approaching, although it was several minutes before he came into view. As the horses came closer, she noticed the faint murmuring *swish* of saddle leather, the clinking of spur chains, and the snort of the horses as they tossed their heads and fought the bits between their lower jaws. She remembered similar sounds from Western movies and was thrilled to be experiencing these sensations firsthand.

Derek rode a rangy brown horse and led a mare with a golden coat and a silvery mane. She had a streak of white from her forehead to her nostrils. Kennedy waited for Derek at the foot of the steps. He stepped out of the saddle with one fluid motion and dropped the reins of his horse.

"Do you want to mount from the steps or have me give you a boost into the saddle?"

73

She shrugged her shoulders as she walked down the steps to join him. "You're the teacher. What's the simplest way?"

"I'll boost you into the saddle, but first I need to explain a few things." Eyeing her skeptically, he said, "You're serious about not knowing how to ride?"

She nodded. "This is the closest I've been to a horse in my life. You would have thought that because Mother and Dad were raised in ranch country, they would have taken me to a riding stable when I was a kid, but they didn't. Perhaps they wanted to put their Nebraska days behind them."

Derek motioned for Kennedy to come closer and told her to pet the mare. "She's a palomino, and her name is Santee."

Kennedy sliced an inquiring glance toward him, and he explained, "It's a Sioux name. She's about middle age for a horse, and she's very gentle. I bought her two years ago."

"You have your own horses?"

He nodded. "When you look over the ranch records, you'll see that part of my salary includes the privilege of accumulating a limited number of cattle and horses for myself and grazing them with Circle Cross stock." He pointed to the rear flank of the palomino. "That's my brand."

"Oh, a DS. That's cool."

"I'm limited to ten horses and forty head of cattle," he said. "I only have nine horses now. I told you the day you came to the ranch that I'd had a bad day. I'd had to put down one of my best horses that morning. But let's get on with your lesson."

His teasing manner was gone, and he patiently and slowly pointed out the bridle, saddle, and other parts of the riding equipment, explaining the purpose of each.

"The first thing is to learn how to mount a horse. You mount from the horse's left side. Take hold of the reins in your right hand and then the horse's mane with your left hand. Put your left foot in the stirrup and grab the cantle on the saddle with your right hand. Take a little springy step like you're pushing off the ground, lift your right leg over the horse's body, and move your right hand from the saddle to the pommel. Then sit down and put your right foot in the stirrup."

Perhaps he sensed how confused she was, for he said, "I know it sounds like a lot to remember now, but with practice you'll mount automatically, not even thinking about what you're doing. Stand back a little and let me show you."

He slowly mounted and dismounted several times, and in spite of her nervousness, Kennedy was physically aware of his powerful physique and his skill as a rider. After he explained how to start walking a horse, how to control its movements, and how to stop the animal, he said, "You try it now. I guessed at how to adjust the stirrups, but once you're in the saddle, I'll fix them to fit you."

"I'm not sure I can do this," Kennedy protested.

"Sure you can! A woman smart enough to be a lawyer can learn how to ride a horse. Try it," he urged.

Derek was standing close beside her, so Kennedy knew he wouldn't let her fall. After several tries, she finally got her foot in the stirrup.

"That's great. Now push off and I'll boost you into the saddle." She did and he did, but once in the saddle, she lost her balance and tipped toward the right side of the animal. Derek's arm quickly encircled her waist and steadied her, but the near accident unnerved Kennedy. Santee had stood patiently during the mounting, and Kennedy leaned forward to pat the mare on the neck, trying to hide her discomfiture from Derek.

With his hand supporting her back, Derek said, "How do you feel?"

"Like I ought to fasten my seat belt," she answered.

Derek laughed lightly. "I guess I could tie you into the saddle, but you won't need that." He swung into his own saddle. "Stay close beside me and don't grip the reins so tight. Try to relax. You're doing fine."

They rode slowly, with Derek giving instructions on how to use the reins to guide her mount and sway with the movement of the animal rather than to sit ramrod-straight in the saddle. But not once did he give her the feeling that she was a slow learner. He rode so close to her that she knew, if she started to fall, he would catch her immediately. This gave her a sense of security, and Kennedy relaxed slightly and began to enjoy the ride and look at the landscape.

They followed a wide trail lined by willow and cottonwood trees, with occasional clearings where they could see the Niobrara. The sun shone brightly, but a steady breeze kept the temperature pleasant. Vast rangeland on their right was populated with grazing cattle, and Derek pointed out the Circle Cross brand on the animals. After a few miles, Kennedy realized that her legs were getting numb, her back ached, and she was tired. Derek must have been watching her closely, for he soon halted the animals and dismounted.

He secured the horses to a fence beneath a tree with spreading branches. Coming to Kennedy's side, he explained the proper way to dismount, adding, "But you've learned enough new things today. Just take your right foot out of the stirrup and lean toward me, and I'll lift you down."

After she dismounted, he held tightly to her arm. When she took a step, her legs felt like cooked spaghetti, and her knees buckled. Derek put his arm around her waist. "Just walk a little more and the feeling will come back."

"I guess I really am a tenderfoot," she said.

When she could walk on her own, Kennedy said, "I'm all right now. I can ride if you want to go on."

"I wanted to stop here anyway. Let's walk down to the river—it's only a short distance."

A few minutes' walk brought them to the river, which was bordered by high banks. At Riverside, the river was wider and the banks lower. Derek called her attention to a long, two-story concrete building on the opposite bank.

"All of the Circle Cross land is on the northeastern side of the river except that eighty-acre plot. We don't do much with that property; there's no bridge across the river at this point. It's called the West Eighty, and we use it for grazing in the summer. It's shallow enough that the cattle have no problem crossing. Some outfit bought it with the idea of building a conference center and motel, but they ran out of money before they finished. It's not part of the original ranch, and you might want to sell this piece of land."

Puzzled, Kennedy asked, "But how did the Blaines get it?"

"That's something else you'll have to ask Smith. I've heard that when it was put up for sale, both of your grandfathers put in a bid for it, but Mr. Blaine was the successful bidder."

"So that's another thing causing bad feelings between the Blaines and Morgans?"

"Probably, but I don't know."

"I suppose I'm just like they were. If I do sell any property, I wouldn't want my mother's father to get it." She smiled grimly. "I don't feel very Christlike when I have such an attitude."

"Maybe you're the one to bring peace between the two factions," Derek said. "Have you ever considered that?"

She shook her head. "I doubt it."

"Let's go back to the horses," he said. "Whatever you do with the ranch, you should find out about those eighty acres."

"Thanks. I appreciate how good you've been to me. You could have kept your first opinion of me and not been a bit helpful, but you've gone out of your way to make me feel at home and introduce me to my parents' homeland. That's exactly why I came to Nebraska. Since you're not a relative, I feel that you'll give me a less biased opinion than Cousin Smith will."

"I'll tell you what I think," Derek said, "but that might not always be right."

"Where are we going now?" she asked when they reached the horses.

"Back to Riverside but by a longer trail, so I think we'd better sit awhile before we start."

They sat on the ground and leaned back against the trunk of a large cottonwood tree. While they rested, Derek plied her with questions about her college years and the city of Los Angeles.

"Southern California is a terrific place," she said. "When I go back home, you'll have to come visit me. I would make a good tourist guide."

"When, or *if*?" he asked, with a piercing glance in her direction.

She quickly glanced toward him. "*When*, of course! I have my life in California. Even if I keep the ranch, I'll have to go home."

She thought his face blanched, but he said evenly, "Yes, I can understand that."

Kennedy was tired, and she closed her eyes. She dozed a bit until Derek said, "We'd better go if you've rested enough."

The sun was setting when they reached the house. Derek helped her dismount and held her arm until her legs were steady. "Tomorrow morning you'll have sore places where you've never had them before, but that will soon wear off. It would be better if you rode a little every day, but I'm going to be herding cattle until late evening most of the week. You aren't ready to ride alone."

"I'll be busy, too. The cleaners will be here for quite a while."

Derek swung into his saddle. "I'll take the horses home and bring Wilson back."

"You don't have to do that," Kennedy protested. "He would much rather stay with you."

"Maybe, but *I* want him here at night. I'll pick him up every morning; he's a big help rounding up cattle. See you in a bit."

He lifted the reins, nudged his horse in the side with his feet, and rode away. Kennedy went inside and opened the windows so the house would cool. She carried two chairs out on the porch, and when Derek returned, she invited him to sit down. She could tell by his expression that he wanted to stay, but he shook his head.

"No, I won't stay. But be sure and call if you need anything."

"I'll try not to be a nuisance until after you finish roundup. Good night."

He swung into the saddle and waited. She knew he wouldn't leave until she'd locked herself in. She took Wilson inside and locked the door and then leaned back against the wood. It had been a good day, but Kennedy felt like crying, and she didn't know why.

* * * * *

The next week passed quickly for Kennedy. She spent the first three days walking around the property close to Riverside and looking through more old photo albums and papers that had belonged to her grandfather before the cleaning team came.

When the cleaners left Riverside, Kennedy couldn't believe the miracle that had transformed her neglected home into an architectural showplace. Two women and one man had worked the rest of the week. While the women cleaned inside, the man had trimmed the shrubbery, mowed the lawn, and planted flowers in the window boxes on the front porch. He had even found a ladder and cleaned debris from the eaves and spouts as well as replaced several shingles on the gazebo roof.

The faint scent of pine permeated the interior of the house, and the furniture shone like new. One of the women had spent most of the two days washing linens, curtains, towels, and washcloths. The hardwood floors were waxed and the carpets were cleaned.

Kennedy had worked alongside the others, concentrating on the kitchen and dining room cupboards. Crystal and china gleamed brightly in the newly waxed cabinets. If there was a speck of dirt or dust in the house, Kennedy couldn't find it.

The man she'd hired had found some wooden outdoor furniture in an outbuilding, and it had been washed and placed on the gazebo and the porch area. When she wrote a check for the work, Kennedy added a generous tip, and the workers went on their way smiling, insisting that they were available to work for her at any time.

As he had predicted, Derek hadn't been around, and she had missed him. When the cleaners left, Kennedy called the ranch house and June answered.

"I've got a beautiful house now, and I want to share it with somebody. Is Derek still busy? If he isn't, why don't the two of you come and take a look at the transformation?"

"He's coming in for supper now, but sometimes he goes out again. Hold on. Let me ask him," June said. Kennedy heard muffled words as June talked to Derek. "He still has some work to do tonight, but he says he'll come early in the morning."

"I'll get up early so he can come when he wants to. But you can visit this evening if you have time. I'm as excited as a kid with a new toy— I just have to show the house to someone."

Laughing, June assured her, "I'll be there as soon as we've had supper."

* * * * *

Derek didn't stay long the next morning, for they were driving some of the cattle to summer pasture that day. As the ranch owner, she knew she should be thankful that he was so conscientious in his work, but she had missed seeing him. Kennedy watched wistfully as he drove away. He obviously approved of the changes at Riverside, as June had the night before.

After her busy life in California, Kennedy wasn't accustomed to having much free time. Now she had a long day ahead of her and didn't know what to do with it. When the phone rang while she was making her bed, she answered it eagerly.

"Kennedy," a deep voice said, "this is Tony Morgan. I'm going to be visiting out your way this morning. Is it all right if I stop by?"

"It sure is. What time will you be here?"

"Midmorning."

"Sounds good to me," she said. "I'm looking forward to talking with you."

Tony came two hours later, and Kennedy gave him a tour of the house right away.

"As you might have guessed," Tony said, smiling as they ended the tour in the living room, "this is the first time I've set foot in this house. A Morgan visiting a Blaine in her ancestral home! What would our ancestors think?"

Kennedy laughed with him. "It doesn't matter to me what they think," she said, "and I have a feeling you feel the same."

Kennedy motioned Tony to a chair, while she sat on a nearby love seat. She pointed to the electric coffee urn and tray of cookies she'd prepared before he arrived.

"Would you like a cup of coffee? Or I can make tea if you'd prefer that."

"Coffee is fine, and I drink it black. I learned to do that in seminary when I was studying for exams. My friend Daniel and I shared an apartment. We spent more money on coffee than we did on food."

Kennedy handed a steaming cup to Tony and pushed the tray of cookies toward him. "Help yourself," she said.

"So, tell me, Kennedy, how long do you expect to stay in Nebraska? I had assumed this was a visit, but you seem to be settled in for a while."

She explained about her impulsive trip to the Circle Cross and how the land, the people, and especially Riverside had fascinated her. "When I left Los Angeles, I had no intention of staying. In fact, I had no plans at all concerning the ranch."

"But it's rumored that the ranch is going to be sold."

"I suppose that's the real reason I came. Dad's death was so unexpected that I wasn't ready to handle his estate. When my attorney received an offer to buy the ranch, I decided I wanted to see the property before it was sold. But after being here a few days, I'm not sure I will sell. This land has been in the Blaine family for a long time."

"Does our mutual grandfather know you're here?" Tony asked with a grim smile.

"I don't know."

Tony laughed slightly. "As I mentioned yesterday, my grandfather and I don't see eye to eye."

"Mind telling me why?"

"There's no secret about it. He's controlled my father's life, but I was determined he wouldn't rule me. It's still a sore subject to me so I won't give you all the facts, but he prevented me from marrying the only woman I've ever loved."

Kennedy could tell by the bitterness in Tony's eyes that he felt as she did about Gabriel Morgan.

"Matti Gray and I dated all through high school," Tony continued, and his eyes seemed clouded with visions of the past. "We were in love and got engaged when we graduated. Grandfather didn't approve. Matti's father worked for the Morgans and the Grays were poor. Grandfather thought I could do better.

When I refused to give her up, he apparently took matters into his own hands."

Tony put the coffee cup on the table, stood up, and, with clenched fists, walked around the room. "I don't know what he did to Matti, but while I was away on a camping trip, she left town. She didn't leave a note for me, her parents wouldn't tell me where she had gone, and I haven't heard from her since then. I don't know what happened, but I've never doubted that Gabriel Morgan was responsible for it."

"You don't think he had someone harm her, do you?" Kennedy asked.

"Oh, she's alive somewhere. She returned to Valentine when her parents died, but I wasn't here so I didn't see her. I've considered trying to find her, but I'm angry at her, too, for not contacting me."

"But if he was successful in breaking up your relationship with Matti, I'd think he would be happy that he'd gotten his way."

"Oh, there's more. He doesn't approve of my profession. He expected me to take over the Morgan Corporation when he couldn't control it any longer. He demanded that I prepare for that when I went to college, but for once, my parents refused to bend to his will. They supported my calling to the ministry. And our grandfather didn't want me to return to Valentine, either. If I was going to be a preacher, he thought I should try to get a prestigious church in a city. I've been back in Valentine for a few months, and he hasn't sent for me."

"I'm sorry, Tony. He never sent for my mother, either. I believe that she would have come home if he'd only asked her."

"Although I find it difficult to do, I pray for him daily. He has to be a miserable man to carry these grudges all his life. And all this just because our mutual ancestors loved the same woman and chose to start a feud over it. God willing, I intend for the enmity to stop with this generation. Will you help me?"

Kennedy hesitated. "I can't make that promise yet. I'm ashamed to admit that I don't feel charitable toward Gabriel Morgan, and I'll have to get over that feeling before I can help you mend fences."

"At least talking to you has helped me. I'm glad you came back to Nebraska, Kennedy."

"Me, too," she agreed, as she walked to the door with him. Before he left, she asked him for directions to Smith Blaine's office.

"He was Dad's manager of the Circle Cross," she explained, "and I want to see him and find out more about the offer to buy the ranch. I'm going shopping in Valentine this afternoon. I believe that today is when he's supposed to return from his vacation, so while I'm in town, I wanted to drop by the office to make an appointment to see him."

Tony gave her the directions she needed, and she thanked him.

"Will I see you at church tomorrow?" Tony asked.

"Yes, I'm planning to be there."

She waved to Tony as he drove away, her heart full of pleasure because she was connecting to her relatives. It was the right decision to spend the summer at the Circle Cross.

Chapter Seven

....

Kennedy drove into Valentine soon after Tony left to buy some clothes more suitable to ranch life than the ones she'd brought from California. She had previously had a conference with June about what to buy. Kennedy parked in front of Young's Western Wear store, which covered a large portion of the city block. Acting on June's advice as well as the help from the store's friendly staff, she left the store with a Rodeo King felt hat, a pair of cimarron–brown-and-beige boots, a straw hat from Larry Mahan's hat collection, two pairs of Cinch jeans, and two Wrangler shirts. Not that she believed all this Western attire would turn her into a cowgirl, but Kennedy figured she wouldn't be as conspicuous in these clothes as she was in her designer jeans and blouses.

Tony had told her that Smith Blaine's office was located on West Third Street not far from City Hall, and she had no trouble finding the office. There was one car in the parking lot, even though it was Saturday, so she wondered if Smith had returned home on schedule. She tried the office door, found it unlocked, and walked into the reception room.

"I'm Kennedy Blaine," she said to the secretary. Kennedy looked at the nameplate on the desk. "We've talked on the phone several times, Naomi."

"Well, of course, Miss Blaine. I recognize your voice. This *is* a surprise. Mr. Blaine didn't tell me you were coming."

"Is he back from vacation?" Kennedy asked, not inclined to tell the secretary that Smith didn't know she was in Nebraska.

"Yes, they returned late last night. I had a message on the answering machine that he'd be in the office this afternoon."

"I didn't expect to see him today, but I want to make an appointment when he has an opening," Kennedy told her. "I'm sure he'll be swamped with work that's piled up while he's been away."

"The office has been closed. I was on vacation, too. I only came in myself because of how much catching up there is to do," Naomi explained.

"When will he have time to see me?" Kennedy persisted.

When Kennedy had talked with Naomi on the phone, she had appeared to be competent and friendly, but she seemed flustered now as she leafed through the appointment book. "Will Monday afternoon at two o'clock be convenient?"

"Yes. But since Cousin Smith will be here soon, I'll wait and say hello. It's been a few years since I've seen him." Kennedy sat on a leather couch and picked up a magazine from the end table. "Don't let me interfere with your work."

Naomi excused herself, went into the adjoining office, and closed the door. Kennedy heard her talking. Was Naomi calling Smith to tell him that she was waiting? Perhaps she *had* been inconsiderate by just dropping in like this, but why could it matter? She wasn't expecting to consult with him about the ranch on the spur of the moment.

Before his secretary returned to her office, the outside door opened and Smith entered the office. He swept Kennedy with a cursory glance and walked by her with a nod. But he stopped suddenly, turned, and stared at her.

"May I help you?" he asked, as Naomi returned to the office.

Kennedy stood and, with an apologetic laugh, said, "I know it's been a few years since we've met, but I supposed you would recognize me. I'm Kennedy Blaine."

Smith's face flushed, and he hit his forehead with his palm. "Well, of course you're Kennedy. I just wasn't expecting to see you." He extended his hand. "It's good to see you. I didn't know you were coming to Nebraska. How long have you been here?"

"About two weeks. "

"That long! I thought you knew I was on vacation."

"I did know, but I had taken care of all the estate decisions in California. So I made a sudden decision to come to Nebraska. I'm glad I did."

"But where have you been staying? Eleanor and I will want you to stay with us while you're here. You can move your things to our house today." He lifted the phone from Naomi's desk. "I'll call Eleanor and let her know you're here."

Laughing, Kennedy said, "I'd better tell you what I've been doing before you make any arrangements for me."

He replaced the phone and appraised her with a skeptical glance. "Perhaps we'd better talk. Let's go into my office."

"I wouldn't presume to bother you with my affairs today. Naomi's made me an appointment for Monday afternoon. I'll leave now and come back then."

"But…"

"When I arrived in Nebraska, I went directly to the Circle Cross and met the Sterlings. June and Derek welcomed me, and Derek has been showing me around the ranch. I've always wanted to see the place where I was born, and when Derek took me to Riverside, I decided to stay in Nebraska for the summer." Excitement lifted her voice as she continued, "I've had the whole house cleaned and the lawns tended, and I'm at home for visitors. I hope you and Eleanor will come to see me."

"But what about the offer to buy the ranch?" he asked, and Kennedy didn't know what to make of the concerned look on his face. "That offer is only good for thirty days."

"We'll talk about that during my appointment time," Kennedy said. "I need to know a lot more about that offer before I make a decision.

And I'm not sure that I *will* sell the Circle Cross."

"Well, that's your choice, and I think you'll make a big mistake not to accept the offer." Smith shrugged his shoulders. "But it's your property."

With a smile, Kennedy said, "That's true, it is!" And from the expression on his face, she wondered if her cousin had suddenly realized that he was dealing with a client who wasn't as easygoing as her father had been.

Back at Riverside, Kennedy hoped that Derek would go to church with them the next day, but he and Sam had gone to a neighboring ranch to pick up a tractor he'd lent to a rancher to help him catch up with his work, and he wouldn't be back until late on Sunday. It was a long weekend for Kennedy instead. She went to church and had lunch with June as usual and spent the rest of the day sitting in the gazebo thinking of the changes in her life since she'd come to Nebraska.

* * * * *

Derek's eyelids popped open, and he wondered what had wakened him until the phone rang again. He realized he was still in the living room, fully clothed. He'd gone to sleep in his chair after he and Sam had unloaded the tractor. Apparently his mother had covered him with a blanket and hadn't disturbed him. As he reached for the phone, he glanced at his watch and saw that it was two in the morning. He released the footrest and sat up quickly when he saw Kennedy's number on the ID.

"Derek," Kennedy answered his quick hello, "I'm sorry to bother you…"

"What's wrong?"

"I don't know, but Wilson is just having a fit and I can't get him to stop barking."

"I'm leaving right now."

He disconnected the phone and rushed to his mother's room. "Mom, are you awake?"

"Yes, I heard the phone. Who was it?"

"Kennedy." Even in his fear for her, he thought of Kennedy's reputation. "She's okay, apparently, but something's wrong. I'm on my way, but I shouldn't be over there alone with her in the middle of the night. You get dressed, tell the men where you are, and follow me as soon as you can."

He didn't wait for her answer but ran toward his truck. In the five minutes it took him to drive to Riverside, dozens of scenarios of what might be happening flashed through his mind. The lights were on in Kennedy's bedroom as well as the front porch, and he hit the porch on a run. Wilson was still barking.

"It's Derek!" he shouted. "Let me in."

She must have been standing beside the door, for it opened immediately. He pushed his way inside, slamming the door behind him. She threw herself at him, and he gathered her close. Her body was trembling, and he detected a deep sob in her throat.

Wilson stopped his guttural barking and curled himself around Derek's legs, whimpering.

Derek held Kennedy close and tenderly rubbed her back until the trembling lessened. She seemed content to stay in his arms, so he didn't release her. "Now tell me what happened."

"I don't know! I was asleep when Wilson started barking. He was tugging at his leash, and he finally broke loose. He ran from one window to another, leaping up on the panes—just carrying on. I shouldn't have called you, but I was so frightened."

"Yes, you *should* have called me! Wilson wouldn't act like that unless he sensed danger of some kind. You didn't hear anything?"

She shook her head against his shoulder. "I couldn't hear anything except Wilson."

She stirred in his arms, and after kissing her on the forehead, Derek released her reluctantly. Automobile lights flashed through the glass pane in the door. "Oh," she said and clutched his arm.

"That's probably Mom. I told her to follow me."

June walked into the room, and her competent and calm presence seemed to soothe Kennedy. With his mother there to care for her and with Wilson tagging at his heels, Derek moved throughout the house, checking for forced entry and to see if anyone was hidden inside. When he came downstairs to report that no one was in the house, Kennedy and his mother were in the kitchen. Kennedy was sitting at the table, her head in her hands, and June had a pot of water heating on the stove.

"Everything is all right here," he reported, "but I'm going to check outside."

Kennedy's head shot up. "Be careful," she said.

This was the first time that Derek had seen Kennedy when she hadn't looked as if she'd stepped off the pages of a fashion magazine. Tonight she wore a knee-length robe tied at the waist. She was barefoot. She didn't have on any makeup and her hair was disheveled, but Derek was more conscious of her natural beauty than ever before.

He turned away before she caught him staring. "There's an iron bar on the back porch. I'll take it for a weapon and look around to see if you've had any visitors."

Carrying a flashlight, Derek walked around the house and the other outbuildings without seeing anything that should have alarmed Wilson. The dog walked beside him, and when he didn't seem upset, Derek decided that whoever or whatever had bothered Wilson was long gone. When he entered the kitchen, Kennedy looked toward him expectantly. She and June were sipping hot tea, and June poured a cup for him.

"I didn't find anything out of place," he reassured her. "Wilson might have heard a coyote or another wild animal to set him off."

"Does he do that very often?"

He hesitated. "I've never known him to," he admitted.

Her shoulders seemed to slump a little lower. "I'm sorry I bothered you. Go on home and try to get some rest."

"We're not leaving. I'm going to stay outside and keep watch."

"If you've got an extra blanket, I'll curl up on the couch in the living room," June said.

Kennedy nodded. "There are several in the closet of my room. I'll find one for you."

She walked out of the room, dragging her feet, and Derek glanced anxiously at his mother, whose eyes were wide with concern.

* * * * *

After Derek and his mother were settled, Kennedy went back to bed, but she didn't go to sleep right away. She shouldn't have been so headstrong. Derek had lived in this country for years, and he hadn't wanted her to stay at Riverside. She should have listened to him. But she hadn't, so what options did she have now?

She didn't think she slept but she must have dozed off, for when she woke up, she smelled coffee brewing. She hurried out of bed and dressed in a pair of her new jeans and a flannel shirt before she went to the kitchen. June was at the table drinking coffee.

"Where's Derek?" she asked

"Outside, looking around," June told her.

Kennedy went to look for him and saw him in the field between the house and the river, intently studying the ground. He looked up, saw her standing on the porch, and hurried toward the house.

"Didn't you sleep at all?" she asked.

"No. I'd gone to sleep watching the evening news. I'd had about five hours before you called, so I wasn't sleepy," he assured her. "I watched all night, but I didn't see or hear anything unusual."

"Did you find anything suspicious?"

Derek hesitated briefly. "I don't want to tell you, but you have to know. There *was* somebody here last night. I found fresh tracks in some muddy spots between the house and the river. A man—I'm assuming it was a man—had walked toward the house and then backtracked. I suppose Wilson's barking scared him off."

Through stiff lips, Kennedy said, "But why?"

"You've been in Nebraska for two weeks now, and I figure about everybody in Valentine knows you're living here alone," Derek answered. "Most people in this community are good moral citizens, but every area has its lawless element. I don't intend to scare you, but someone might have intended to break in on you."

"And that's the reason you didn't think I should live here in the first place?" she questioned.

"Partly," he admitted. "But you don't know who wants to buy the Circle Cross yet. They might be trying to scare you away. Now that you've fixed up the house, the potential buyer may have decided that you're staying."

June joined them on the porch with a cup of coffee for Derek. He took a big swallow of the coffee, and Kennedy noted the weariness in his face. He'd been working long hours, and she knew he was tired.

"I haven't had a chance to tell you that Cousin Smith is back in town," Kennedy said. "I saw him on Saturday and have an appointment with him this afternoon to discuss the Circle Cross. He mentioned selling the ranch. I told him I wasn't ready to make a decision but that I might not sell at all."

June nodded. "News travels fast in Valentine. That word could have spread and someone may have decided to give you a nudge to get out. Probably didn't mean you any harm."

"I should just go home and forget the ranch, but I'm happy to have the house restored and was really looking forward to staying here all summer." Looking intently at Derek, she said, "I wouldn't take your advice before, but I'm ready to listen now. I'll go back home if you think that's best."

With a grin, he said, "I accused you of being stubborn, but I'm stubborn, too. I'm determined that no one is going to force you off land that belongs to you until you're ready to leave."

"I'll come and stay at night," June offered.

Derek shook his head. "I know you would, and we may have to do that for a few nights, but that's no solution for the rest of the summer." To Kennedy, he said, "Would you object to hiring someone to stay with you at night? You would have the place to yourself all day and evening. There are a few retired women in Valentine who live alone and would probably jump at the chance to make some extra money. You could prepare a room for the woman and have her come about bedtime and stay until morning. As long as there's someone else in the house, I don't think anyone will break in."

Kennedy smiled broadly. "That would be the perfect solution. I have a housekeeper at home. After Dad died, she stayed with me at night, so I'm not accustomed to staying alone." Turning to June, she asked, "Do you think that's a good idea?"

"I do," June said emphatically. "Derek and I will put our heads together and come up with somebody reliable."

Kennedy told them what she paid her housekeeper in California. "Will that be a reasonable salary for the woman?"

Derek whistled. He and June exchanged amused glances, and

Kennedy deduced that Los Angeles's salary scale was a lot higher than Nebraska wages for the same kind of work.

"That will be a big boost for several of the women who attend our church and don't have any income except Social Security," June said. "I'm sure we'll find someone to work for you."

"Oh, that relieves my mind so much," Kennedy said, and she couldn't stop smiling. "I couldn't go back to sleep last night for worrying that I would have to leave Nebraska."

Derek's eyes locked with hers. "I worried about that, too."

His face flushed, and Kennedy noticed June's amazed glance at her son.

"I'll ask around today, if you want me to," June said, "and see if we can find someone quickly."

"Please do. I don't even have to talk to her, although she might want to meet *me* before she agrees to stay here," Kennedy said with a light laugh. "Make any decision you think is right."

"It's not likely anyone can come for a day or two, so what about tonight?" June asked. "I can come here, or you can stay at the ranch house again."

"I'll do whatever is the least trouble for you."

"Why don't you come to Riverside, Mom?" Derek suggested. "This house has stood vacant for several years without being bothered, but since Kennedy has fixed up the place, one of our local hoodlums might have decided it's a good place to burglarize. It might be better if the house isn't vacant."

"That's fine," June agreed. "I'll be here before dark, Kennedy."

Derek smiled with satisfaction, as if a big load had been lifted from his shoulders. "The men are going to move a herd of cattle today; is there anything you need me to do for you?"

"The mechanic called and said the car is ready," Kennedy said, "but he wouldn't have anyone available to deliver it until tomorrow. You can take me in to pick it up, if you don't mind."

Nodding, Derek asked, "Ten o'clock suit you?"

"Yes, and I'd just as soon you drove the car home, so let's take my car." She laughed lightly. "I've never driven a car without automatic transmission, and I don't want to make a spectacle of myself in Valentine. I can get used to it by driving around the ranch."

He nodded. "And will you want to take your rental car back to Omaha on Sunday afternoon?"

"Not yet. After I had decided to stay here awhile, I called the rental company and extended the length of time I had the car, so I won't have to return it for a couple of weeks. We'll wait until then just to make sure I'm comfortable driving Grandfather's car."

She followed the Sterlings out on the porch, thanking them again for their help.

"June," Kennedy said, "I wish you'd pray about my meeting with Cousin Smith this afternoon. My father was rather easygoing, and I have a feeling that my cousin made all the decisions and Dad agreed." With a sidelong glance at Derek, she said, "I'm not like that."

A wide grin spread across his face, and he nodded. "A Morgan trait!"

She ignored his comment and continued, "After working with Dad's lawyer in settling the estate, I've learned quite a lot about finances. I'll be asking Smith some pointed questions he may not want to answer. I don't want any trouble in the family, but I intend to make my own decisions about what goes on at the Circle Cross." Looking at Derek, she demurred, "With advice from certain people, of course!"

"Sure, I'll pray for you." June gave Kennedy a friendly hug. "I've been doing that every day since you showed up on our doorstep. That was a happy day for me."

Kennedy met Derek's eyes over his mother's shoulder, and he winked at her.

What was she going to do about *him*?

June said good-bye and drove away and Derek walked toward his truck, but he turned around to look directly at her. "By the way, I like your clothes—you look like a sure 'nuff cowgirl now."

"But I won't be one until a certain cowhand gives me some more lessons on how to ride a horse," Kennedy retorted.

His lips widened in a leisurely smile. "Soon," he promised.

Chapter Eight

....

Driving her rental car, Kennedy followed Derek closely as they traveled from Valentine to the ranch. She was happy she'd kept her grandfather's car. The waxed maroon surface radiated the sunshine, and the car looked like new. The mechanic had assured her that it would be as serviceable for her needs as a new car.

"What do you think of it?" she asked Derek immediately upon reaching Riverside.

"I like it so well that I'll take it off your hands for the cost of restoring it," he said, his deep chuckle that she'd come to recognize as his trademark of humor following the remark.

"No, thank you," she said pertly, "but I will let you drive it once in a while."

"Like to Omaha when we return your car?" he asked.

"That's a good idea," she agreed.

"Do you want to drive it before I leave?"

She shook her head. "I won't delay you any longer. Just so you have time to show me how to drive it before I turn in the other car."

"Then I'll park it in the garage until we both have the time."

* * * * *

Promptly at two o'clock Kennedy entered her cousin's office building. He met her with a smile and took her into his private office. Before he closed the door, he said, "Naomi, please hold my calls until we finish."

"Nice office," Kennedy commented, idly noting that the furniture was of high quality and that a cabinet near the window held several green plants. The carpet was thick and plush, and Kennedy felt as if she were walking on velvet as she crossed the floor. She sat in the roomy leather chair in front of his desk.

"I spend so much time here that I like to be comfortable," Smith said.

"Your sign outside indicates that you handle income tax returns as well as being an accountant for businesses in the area," Kennedy said. "That should keep you busy."

"The first four months of the year are hectic, but income tax work is seasonal," Smith answered. "I'm also a licensed real-estate agent and especially busy with that during the summer, so I'm busy all year long."

"So the reason you received an offer to buy the ranch is because you're a real-estate agent as well as the accountant for the Circle Cross?" Kennedy asked.

"I'm sure that's the case," he said. "And since you've brought up the subject, I hope you will consider the offer. In general, ranches are poor investments now—the price of machinery and operating a ranch gets more expensive every year. It's hard to make any money."

"Doesn't the potential buyer intend to operate the land as a ranch?" Kennedy asked directly.

"Why, I can't comment on that!"

"Can't or won't?" Kennedy answered quickly.

Smith eyed her, and his manner puzzled her. He arched his fingers and looked out the window. Kennedy was aware of the hum of traffic on the street while she waited for his answer. "I have to protect a client if he or she wants to remain anonymous."

"Don't you consider me a client?" Kennedy questioned.

"Well, yes," he said, looking quickly at her.

"Smith, I've lived under the cloud of family dissension all of my life," Kennedy stated, "and I don't want any trouble between us, but I won't be pressured into a hasty decision. I've been at loose ends since Dad's death, and I came to Nebraska looking for something. I'm not even sure what it is yet, but when I set foot on the Circle Cross ranch, I felt a tie to my past that I'd never felt before. Can you understand that?"

"I suppose so," he said reluctantly.

"My parents lived in exile for years because of family differences," she continued. "Although I may change my mind in the future, right now I wouldn't sell the Circle Cross for a billion dollars. So if your client has to know in a week or so, tell him or her that I'm not interested in selling."

"That puts me in something of a bind," Smith said in a husky voice. "Your parents didn't seem to have much interest in the ranch, and I had no idea that you would, either. I assured my client that you would sell."

Kennedy's eyelids narrowed. "You had no right to do that. Tell whoever it is that the ranch *is not* for sale." When he opened his mouth, she assumed that he was going to argue with her, and she said firmly, "That's final."

"Very well," Smith said, and he fiddled with some papers on his desk.

"Dad's attorney has notified me that he doesn't have any reports on the ranch's expenses and income for this year. I need all of that information before we can settle the estate. When can you have it ready?"

Smith looked at his watch as if he was suggesting that it was time for her appointment to end. "I'll ask Derek to send his accounts to me, and I'll try to have something ready for you by next week."

"Derek and I have already gone over the ranch records on his computer," Kennedy said. "His records are up-to-date, and he sent you a report at the end of April."

Smith fidgeted in his chair and pulled at the collar of his white shirt. He was obviously agitated at her persistence, and Kennedy knew that her father would have been displeased at her high-handed ways. But it was important for Smith to realize that he was dealing with her now, not easygoing Kenneth Blaine.

"Well, perhaps so," Smith said. "I've been very busy and may have missed some of his posts."

"Will you be able to get everything together within a week?" Kennedy insisted.

"I'll try my best," he said as he stood up, apparently dismissing her.

"In the meantime, I would like for you and Eleanor to visit me at Riverside. After all, it's your ancestral home, too, and I think you'd enjoy seeing the house like it used to be."

"Thank you," he said. "We'll call before we come."

Kennedy was troubled when she left her cousin's office, and she sat in her car for several minutes just thinking. She was troubled because she had the uneasy feeling that Smith wasn't being up-front with her.

Checking her watch first to be sure he would be in his office, she called Mr. Talbot, her lawyer in California. She identified herself and reported briefly on what she had accomplished since she came to Nebraska.

"But I'm troubled about something and want your advice. The ranch manager has gone over his accounts with me. He has them computerized, and I have access to his computer. His records show that the ranch *has* made a profit in the last few years, although Dad's accountant here says that the ranch isn't profitable. What should I do?"

"E-mail the manager's records from the past few years directly to me," Talbot said immediately.

"He's been in charge for fewer than three years," Kennedy explained.

"Send what he has, and I'll compare them to the records Kenneth had from his accountant. When am I going to receive the report for this year?"

"I gave Smith a week. I've gathered that he hasn't been consistent with his reports and that Dad didn't push him because he was a relative."

"You know that Kenneth wasn't himself after Grace died. He lost interest in lots of things. I looked after his other investments and kept them up, but he took care of the ranch."

"Which may have been a mistake," Kennedy said, adding, "I'll be in touch."

She pulled out into Main Street's slow traffic and stopped in a drugstore before she went home. She was loading her purchases into the trunk of the car when someone called her name. She turned to see Robin Donovan, the Blaine cousin she'd met in church, approaching.

"Oh, hello, Robin," she said and extended her hand. "I've finally gotten settled in at Riverside and had intended to call you. When can you come to visit?"

"I'm free tomorrow morning," Robin said.

"About ten o'clock?"

"Fine, I'll be there," Robin accepted. "I have several things to talk to you about."

Rather than bypass ranch headquarters, Kennedy drove in and parked in front of the house. She waved to Derek, who was working on a piece of machinery, and went into the house. She opened the screen door.

"June?" Kennedy called.

"I'm in the laundry room," June responded. "Come on in. I'll be out in a minute."

Kennedy leaned against the sink cabinet and continued the conversation. "I'm on my way back from town."

Wiping perspiration from her face, June came into the kitchen. "It's a hot day to be doing laundry."

Looking around the room, Kennedy said, "Don't you have an air conditioner?"

"Why, no!" June said, amused. "We don't need AC in Nebraska."

"You do today, and I'm sure there are lots of times in the summer you could use it." Kennedy made a mental note to have an air conditioner installed in the house.

"I'm glad you stopped by," June said. "Sit down and visit with me."

After Kennedy took a chair near her, June said, "I think I've found a companion for you."

"Great! When can she start?" Kennedy asked.

June started folding a pile of towels on the table. "I told her I'd have you call and make arrangements to meet her," June answered.

"Tell me about her," Kennedy said, as she picked up a towel to fold.

"Miranda never married. She grew up in Valentine, but she's worked away from here during most of her adult life. Her last job was as a security guard in a women's prison."

Kennedy gasped, and June smiled broadly. "She retired two years ago and came back to Valentine to live. She has some married siblings in the county."

"I'd almost hire her sight unseen," Kennedy said. "She seems like the perfect aid. I believe she'll be more help than Wilson."

June agreed. "Derek is the one who suggested her."

"I met Robin Donovan in town," Kennedy said, "and she's coming to see me tomorrow morning. Would you ask Miranda to come tomorrow afternoon?"

"I'll see if that's all right with her, and if so, I'll bring her over about two o'clock," June said. "But I'll spend tonight with you."

On her way to the ranch, Kennedy kept wondering how she could repay the Sterlings for the way they'd helped her. She suspected that she'd insult them if she offered them money, but she was determined to do something to show her appreciation. The air conditioner might be a good way to start.

The house seemed quiet when Kennedy let herself in, and it reminded her of how lonely she'd felt in her home after her father's death. She hadn't fully comprehended the disadvantage of being an only child until she'd lost her last parent.

Kennedy wandered into the living room. She picked up her grandfather's well-worn King James Bible from the coffee table. With time on her hands, she took the Bible and went to the gazebo. She leafed through the Book, noting the family records between the Testaments. Tears came to her eyes when she read the account of her parents' marriage and the date she was born.

Kennedy tried to recall what God's Word said about loneliness. She couldn't remember much except that Jesus was alone when He prayed in the Garden of Gethsemane before His crucifixion. She checked the concordance for references and was surprised that all of the verses she turned to had been highlighted, causing her to wonder if her grandfather had often felt lonely during the long illness of his wife.

She stroked the gold letters—HOWARD BLAINE—on the cover and felt very close to him. They had become good friends when he lived with them in California, and it made her feel more family-oriented when she read verses she knew he had cherished.

She read aloud the account of the beginning of mankind in Genesis chapter 2: "*And the Lord God said, It is not good that the man should be alone; I will make him an help meet for him.*"

Then she turned to the Sixty-eighth Psalm, to verse 6, and read: "*God setteth the solitary in families.*"

Kennedy was particularly interested in what the writer of Ecclesiastes said in chapter 4: "*Two are better than one; because they have a good reward for their labour. For if they fall, the one will lift up his fellow: but woe to him that is alone when he falleth; for he hath not another to help him up.*"

Kennedy closed the Bible but held it in her lap as she considered what she had read. She hadn't thought much about marriage until Steve Martin had proposed to her. And when she didn't feel any inclination to say "yes," she had thought the single life was for her.

But according to what she had just read, God had put His approval on the union between man and woman since the beginning of time and had even created Eve for Adam to marry. If God had created someone for her to marry, she couldn't believe that Steve was the one, or she would know. Automatically her mind turned to Derek, and she remembered her reaction the first time she'd met him. Had God directed her path to Valentine to bring her together with Derek? It was a sobering but precious thought. But surely she couldn't be having serious romantic notions about someone she'd only known less than a month.

* * * * *

The next morning Robin arrived at Riverside promptly, and as Kennedy took her on a tour of the house, she realized that they shared many of the same values. She experienced an immediate kinship with Robin.

"Let's sit in the living room and talk about family," Kennedy invited. "Dad wasn't one to discuss his extended family, but Mrs. Sterling told me that you're involved in historical research. I hope you can tell me about my relatives."

"Yes, I know a lot about your Morgan relatives as well as the Blaine family. I'll answer all of your questions, but I've come with another purpose this morning. I belong to the Nebraska State Historical Society. Over the past few years, we've been canvassing the state to prepare a list of historic sites that are in danger of being destroyed. We'd like to try to save them."

"That's seems like a rewarding thing to do," Kennedy said, suddenly interested.

Robin nodded. "We think so. And we need your help."

Kennedy didn't answer, but she lifted her brows inquiringly.

"Not only are we dedicated to preserving actual historic sites but also in preventing urban sprawl from eating up our best rangeland, and we're attempting to have vast acres of land put on the National Register of Historic Places. You've heard of that?"

"We studied something about it in one of my law classes on land management cases, but offhand I don't remember much about it."

"There's a great deal of criteria to be considered before this can be done," Robin said. "But here are the basics. If there's historic significance to a particular piece of property, in many cases the land surrounding that site can be included on the National Register."

"Which means?" Kennedy prompted.

"It means that the land is set aside only for rangeland or farmland to keep it from being used for industrial or commercial purposes," Robin explained. "Once a property is on the Register, it stays there in perpetuity. I'd like you to consider doing that with the Circle Cross and Riverside."

"It sounds like something I might want to do," Kennedy said thoughtfully, "but it isn't a decision I'd make on the spur of the moment."

Robin nodded. "And you're right to be cautious. But with your law background, it seems to me that you will able to weigh both sides of the situation. If the ranch is placed on the Register, you would be tying up the property for your heirs. Many children won't like that. It sometimes causes hard feelings in families, and you should consider all of those options before you make a decision."

Kennedy glanced around the room. "But unless you consider its age, I can't see any reason that this house would be considered a part of history. I've never heard that any of the Blaines were great statesmen or political figures."

Robin shook her head. "The age and architecture of the house would make it eligible for review, I think, but there is something else that makes the ranch itself of extreme historical value. There's an old cemetery on the Circle Cross that has recently been authenticated as holding the remains of pioneers who were caught in a blizzard as they traveled in a small wagon train toward the Black Hills of South Dakota."

"Really!" Kennedy said. "I didn't know that."

Robin nodded, and her eyes gleamed as she continued, "There are fourteen graves, and the word was handed down from generation to generation that the bodies were of pioneers who died along the trail. A couple of years ago, experts exhumed the remains from one grave and learned that the bodies had been buried there about 1870, and that they had died from cholera."

"Poor people," Kennedy said. "They thought they were headed for a new life, only to be struck down by that dreaded disease."

Smiling, Robin continued, "And your property *may* have the dubious distinction of once being a hideout of the robber Doc Middleton."

Kennedy laughed, and Robin said, "I'm serious. Of course, the outlaws were part of history, too."

Robin opened the briefcase she'd brought with her. "I don't intend to pressure you one way or another, for it's a weighty decision. But I'll leave some literature for you to read."

Robin laid the papers on the table and then stood and embraced Kennedy. "It's such a pleasure to meet you. My mother loved your father and mother, and she felt so badly when they went into exile. Uncle Kenneth didn't have much interest in the Circle Cross, but you may be like Grandfather Howard."

"I immediately felt an affinity with the land and the house," Kennedy said. She paused and continued. "Have you heard that Smith has an offer to buy the Circle Cross?" she asked.

"Yes," Robin said slowly, and she organized the papers in her hand without looking directly at Kennedy.

"Smith is insisting that I sell, but I don't intend to let go of the property until I know who's going to buy it." She laughed lightly. "I suppose that pretty well indicates that I'm interested in preserving the land. I'll ask Derek to take me to the cemetery."

"That's a wise move, in my opinion," Robin stated. "Give plenty of thought and prayer to what should be done with the ranch."

As they continued talking, Kennedy agreed to visit Robin and her family at a later date and then waved as Robin drove away. Kennedy walked over to the gazebo and sat down to think. Who would have thought that becoming the owner of the Circle Cross would require so many decisions? Since she was the only heir, her father's investments in Los Angeles had been transferred without any delay, and his holdings had involved large corporations with many stockholders. Being the sole owner of a ranch was apparently a different proposition.

* * * * *

Glancing at her watch, Kennedy stirred from her reverie and went inside the house. When she heard June's car, she hurried out on the porch to meet her guests.

After June had told Kennedy that her potential employee had been a prison guard, she had envisioned a large, brawny woman. Rather, the woman walking up the sidewalk beside June was of medium height, with gray hair and a slender build. She looked like a sweet little lady, and for once, Kennedy doubted June's wisdom.

When June introduced her to Miranda Pratt, Miranda pumped Kennedy's hand with a steel grip and fixed her with a magnetic look from blue, intelligent, assessing eyes. Obviously, there was more to Miranda Pratt than met the eye.

"Let's sit in the gazebo, shall we?" she invited.

Once they were seated, Kennedy said, "I suppose June has told you the terms of my proposal and that I want a companion only at night. Are those terms satisfactory to you?"

"They are," Miranda said, "except that nothing was said about a day off."

Momentarily, Kennedy was put off by her brusque manner.

"Derek and June have convinced me that I shouldn't be here alone, so if there's any point in hiring a bodyguard at all, I need someone *every* night, not five or six nights a week," Kennedy said. "It isn't necessary for you to stay awake all night. And since you'll be sleeping while you're here, it seems that you will have *every* day to take care of your own personal interests. However, if you need the time off, I can no doubt find someone to fill in those nights, but I would deduct that amount from the salary I offered you in the first place."

Kennedy had a feeling that June smothered a smile, and she was embarrassed at herself. Until the past few days, she'd had no idea she would be hardheaded in business deals. Saturday she had held her own with Smith Blaine and had laid down an ultimatum about when she wanted the ranch records. Today she was setting her own terms, like it or lump it, with a potential employee. She had better learn to curb her tongue, or the natives *would* think she was following in Gabriel Morgan's footsteps.

"I don't know that I *will* need any nights off," Miranda backtracked, "but if so, I have a friend who will be glad to fill in for me. I can start tomorrow night if that's convenient for you."

Kennedy nodded her agreement. "Let's go inside so you can see the house, and I'll show you where you'll be sleeping."

She pointed out the kitchen, where Miranda could have breakfast before she left each morning. And upstairs, Kennedy took her into a spacious bedroom across the hall from the bathroom. Miranda seemed impressed and said that she would return the next night before nine o'clock.

When they started to leave, Kennedy said to June, "I need to talk to Derek. Is he at home this afternoon?"

"Yes, it so happens that he is," June said. "He's training some young horses in the corral."

"I won't interfere with his work," Kennedy assured her, "but I will come over and talk to him when he's finished. I need his advice on something new that's come up."

Chapter Nine

....

When she arrived at ranch headquarters, Derek was in the small corral near the barn, working with a black horse. The horse tugged on the rope around his neck, and his silver mane shifted from side to side. Derek kept a heavy hand on the taut rope and steadily but slowly walked toward the animal.

After she peered through the wooden palings of the fence for several minutes, Kennedy climbed to the top, sat down, and hooked her shoes over a lower board to keep from falling. She waved to Joel, one of the ranch workers, who was perched on the fence opposite her and holding a coiled rope.

Kennedy watched in fascination as Derek grasped the horse's bridle and walked around the corral with him several times. Then, carefully and slowly, he saddled the animal and walked the length of the corral, talking softly to the horse as he walked. When he finally climbed into the saddle, the horse bucked several times, and Kennedy held her breath until the horse settled down and circled the enclosure at a slow trot. After riding the horse for about a half hour, Derek unsaddled the animal and turned him over to Joel.

Wiping his sweaty, dusty face on the sleeve of his shirt, Derek sauntered toward Kennedy.

"Sorry to make you wait, but once I started working with the horse, I had to keep at it," he said, looking up at her and tilting his hat to keep the sun out of his eyes.

"I was spellbound at the way you handled him so patiently. Besides, I'm not in a hurry. I have time on my hands right now. Can you take a breather?"

"Yeah, but you'd better keep your distance," he advised, climbing to sit on the fence not close to her but within speaking distance. "I smell of horse and sweat, which aren't very pleasing aromas."

Dirty or clean, he still had the power to provoke a tingling sensation in the pit of her stomach, and Kennedy didn't like it. Always before, she had been able to control her emotions. What could she do to build a wall of defense against Derek?

"How'd you like Miranda?" he asked.

"Very much. I think we'll get along fine," Kennedy answered.

Amusement flickered in his dark eyes. "Mom said you held your own with her."

"I don't know what's come over me," Kennedy admitted, and she sensed that her face colored. "On Saturday I got tough with Cousin Smith when I found out he hadn't sent the necessary reports to my lawyer. I told him he would have only one week to prepare them. Give me another month in Nebraska and I'll have a reputation like my grandfather."

"Some men try to take advantage of women in business deals," Derek commented, "so be as tough as you want to be."

With a sidelong glance at him, she said, "When you get tired of hearing my problems, tell me, and I'll stop pestering you."

"I haven't complained yet, and you aren't pestering me. But let's find a more comfortable place to sit." He motioned to a weathered bench beneath a cottonwood tree. He jumped down, lifted his arms, and helped her to the ground. When they were seated, he put his left elbow on the back of the bench and turned to face her. "What is it now?"

"I also got pretty sharp with Smith about the ranch sale," she admitted, "and I know Dad wouldn't have approved. But I told Smith in no uncertain terms that I would not be pushed into a sale, and if his clients had to have an answer in a matter of days to tell them no."

"I can't see any problem there," Derek approved. "That's what you should have done."

"But I need advice about something else. Robin Donovan came to visit me this morning to discuss placing the Circle Cross, or some of its properties, on the National Register."

When Derek said he wasn't sure what that involved, Kennedy explained what Robin had told her and what she had also gleaned from scanning the papers Robin had left. "Do you have any advice for me?"

"I'd have to think about it awhile, but my first impression is that if *I* owned the Circle Cross, I would jump at the opportunity to preserve the land that way. I realize that progress is important, but it makes me mad to see a large ranch turned into an amusement park or a shopping district. And as for tying it up for your children, you'd be doing them a favor, although they might resent it at the time. God created just a certain amount of land surface, and we need to be good stewards over what we have left. You're the one to make the decision, but I'd suggest that you give it a great deal of thought before you do anything."

Kennedy nodded. "I will. And the fact that Smith is so insistent on a quick sale makes me suspicious. I'll be praying for guidance, too."

"I know this isn't any of my business, so don't answer if you don't want to. But who will your heirs be when you pass on?"

"Don't spread this around," she said in a resigned voice, "but I don't have a will, and my attorney is pushing me to make one immediately. I've never given it any thought because I didn't own much before Dad died. I've been concentrating on graduating from law school, and I've never had a full-time job, so I haven't accumulated any money of my own. Dad paid for my education, but I worked for my personal needs and bought my own car."

"That was good for you."

"It sure was—it taught me the value of a dollar. But about my estate—the problem is, I don't have any close relatives, and until now I haven't known the extended family. I don't know what to do."

She appreciated Derek's compassionate glance, and she wondered if he had finally realized that her familial situation in some small way resembled his own.

"I'm leaning toward giving my estate to my church and to several charitable organizations," she said. "But I wouldn't include the ranch in that. And until I make up my mind, it's just as well that my scattered relatives in this country don't know I haven't made a will."

"I won't mention it to anyone," Derek assured her, "but I agree with your attorney; you should make a will right away."

"I will. Thanks for listening to me." She smiled at him. "Now I need another favor. When you have time to take me, I'd like to go to that cemetery Robin mentioned. Do you know where it is?"

"Yes, but it's too far away for you to ride on horseback when you haven't had much experience. It's located in a rocky stretch of land, and I can't drive to it. The best plan is to drive the truck as far as we can and then walk the rest of the way. It's a half-hour walk. Do you have walking shoes with you?"

"No, but I asked Rosita to pack a pair when she sends my other clothes. They may not be here for several days." Smiling fondly, she said, "Rosita doesn't move very fast. There's something else, too," she said hesitantly. "This is another matter that will have to stay between us. My lawyer wants a copy of your computer records from as long as you've been the manager. He wants to compare them with what Smith sends him."

"Who do you suspect? Him or me?" Derek said directly.

"Certainly not you," Kennedy said quickly, "or I wouldn't have told you. It may just be carelessness on Smith's part, but I've looked at your records and know that the ranch has been in the black all along. If there *is* anything wrong, I want my lawyer, not me, to approach Smith."

"How do you want to send them?" he asked.

"I'll fax them in a few days, if you don't mind."

"That's fine with me. I have nothing to hide, and you know how to access the ranch's records."

"It'll be tough to find out that Smith is dishonest, especially when Dad trusted him." She stood, saying with a grin, "Only one more thing. I'd like to install air conditioning in your house. June says she doesn't need it, but I know she does. If you don't have any objection, I'll contact someone to take care of it."

"That's good of you. I'll check out the best firm for you to contact. I think there's only one outfit in Valentine, but I'll let you know."

"Thanks for helping me."

"Anytime." He smiled. "I'll have to take the horse I was training back to pasture, unless there's something else you want to talk about."

"No, that's all. I'll go back to Riverside. Your mom is going to stay tonight, and then Miranda will be coming tomorrow night."

When she headed toward her car, Wilson left the shade of the barn where he'd been resting and ran toward her. She stooped down and patted his head.

"You don't have to look after me now," she said. "I've hired a bodyguard." She glanced toward Derek. "I'm sure he'd rather stay with you."

A smile tugged at Derek's lips when he answered, "I doubt that. I think Wilson has changed his loyalties, but I'll keep him here."

When he whistled at the dog and pointed back to the barn, Wilson whined piteously, but Derek said, "Stay." With his tail between his legs the dog obeyed, but he turned and glanced at Kennedy as if it was her fault.

Laughing, she said, "Now I know what the term 'a hangdog expression' means."

* * * * *

The next two weeks passed without incident as Miranda Pratt settled into the bedroom at Riverside. Because Miranda came in the late evening and most times left without her breakfast, Kennedy didn't spend much time with her. Just knowing that she was upstairs was comforting. She had a feeling that Miranda carried a gun.

But on the first day of June when Kennedy went out onto the front porch to get a breath of fresh summer air and saw a sign nailed on a porch post, she realized that having Miranda in the house was not the safeguard against danger that she had wanted.

Leave Nebraska Now or You'll Be Sorry.

Alarmed more than she'd ever been in her life, Kennedy rushed back into the house, slammed the door, and leaned against it. Miranda was ambling down the steps and stopped short. "What's wrong?" she asked.

Kennedy couldn't speak, but she opened the door and motioned for Miranda to look.

"Well, what on earth!" Miranda said. "Who's responsible for that? We'd better call the law."

Kennedy shook her head. "No. I've got to think about it. What have I done that would cause people to order me out of the state? It's just a practical joke of some kind."

"I don't think so. I'll call Derek."

"No, please don't. He would insist on me leaving, and I don't want to go."

"I'd sure hike out of here in a hurry if I got a note like that," Miranda said. "I don't like to leave you alone. It's hard to tell who's after you."

Kennedy heard a vehicle approaching. By the sound of the engine, she recognized it as Derek's truck. She ran out on the porch and snatched the sign off the post, holding it behind her when he hurried up the steps.

"Look what I found tacked on the barn," he said.

TELL YOUR LADY BOSS TO LEAVE TOWN!

When Kennedy showed him the sign she'd found, his face whitened and anger turned his eyes to dark cauldrons of concern. Throwing the signs out in the yard, he slumped down on the top step and put his face in his hands.

"God, help us," he muttered. "What are we going to do?"

Kennedy sat beside him. "Please don't ask me to go home."

He raised his head, and Kennedy had never seen such misery in a man's eyes.

"No, I won't."

"Do you think Cousin Smith is responsible for this? This has to be connected with the offer to buy the Circle Cross."

"I don't believe he's stupid enough to call attention to himself, but the warning could be from whoever wants to buy the ranch. That could be anyone. I have a notion to pay a call on Smith and see if I can scare the information out of him."

Miranda came out of the house carrying her purse, and she said, "You ought to call the police."

"Not yet," Derek said. "And please don't mention this to anyone, Miranda. Wilson can stay with you at night, and he will sound an alarm if anyone comes on the porch again. He has a sore paw and I kept him in the house last night, or he'd have barked when someone strange came around the barns."

After Miranda left, Derek said, "Will you stay with Mom during the day?"

Kennedy shook her head. She didn't want to add to Derek's

problems, so she said lightly, "I'm a big girl now."

Derek unwound his long frame and stood up. "I know," he said grimly. "That's the problem. I have to go to work, so be careful. What are you going to do today?"

"I have an appointment to see Smith tomorrow, but today I'm going to carefully read through all of that material Robin brought me about the National Register. I'll keep the doors locked, so don't worry about me."

* * * * *

With some misgiving, Kennedy kept her appointment with Smith the next day. Because she had experienced the trauma of strained family relationships all her life, she had hoped to avoid that with her cousin. He greeted her amiably and said that he had sent the requested papers to her lawyer in California.

Kennedy thought of mentioning the signs that had been placed on the Circle Cross to see if she could tell by his attitude whether Smith had been involved. She stifled the urge, for Derek had suggested that they might learn more if they didn't tell anyone about the posters. However, watching Smith closely, she did mention that she was considering placing the Circle Cross on the National Register of Historic Places.

It didn't surprise Kennedy that he was violently opposed to the idea. "Why can't Robin tend to her own business? She's always been meddlesome. Even when she was a kid, she was a bothersome brat."

Kennedy thought she remembered that Smith's father and Robin's mother had been siblings, so no doubt they had seen lots of each other. Humorously, she decided that it might have been a plus to grow up without childish rivalry and bickering with her cousins.

"Surely you won't be foolish enough to tie yourself to such an agreement," Smith continued. "Even if you won't consider selling now, you may want to sometime. But I think you're making a mistake by refusing the sale offer. At least why not find out how much money you'd be offered for the ranch?"

"Smith, we're at an impasse. You know that money isn't the issue. I won't consider the offer until I know who wants to buy and why." She gathered up her purse and a copy of the report he'd sent to California. Standing, she fixed him with a direct stare. "Is my grandfather the one who wants the ranch? Is that the reason you won't tell me?"

"Of course not!" Smith protested, but his expression was like a stone mask, and Kennedy couldn't tell if he was being truthful. "And what difference would it make? Gabriel Morgan's money is as good as anybody's."

"Not to me it isn't!" Kennedy retorted. She turned on her heel and left his office. As she drove out of town, she saw Tony Morgan coming down the steps of the church. He motioned to her and she pulled over to the curb.

"I tried to call you and didn't get an answer," he said.

"I've been in Smith's office and I left the phone in the car. What's up?"

He came around the car and sat in the passenger seat. "I had a strange request yesterday, and I thought you might be interested in it. I don't want to interfere with your vacation, so don't hesitate to refuse—but it's something you might want to do."

Grinning, she said, "Stop beating around the bush! Tell me what you want."

"I had a call from the supervisor of a community outreach center in Omaha asking if I could recommend a ranch in the Valentine area where a group of inner-city kids could camp for a week. According to the man who called me, these kids have never been out of the city. Would you consider inviting them to the Circle Cross?"

Kennedy hesitated. "Well, I don't know," she said slowly. "I'd need to think about it and get Derek's opinion. It will really be up to him."

"You depend on him a lot, don't you?" Tony said, in a teasing tone.

"Oh, don't get any ideas. After all, he *is* the manager of the Circle Cross. I wouldn't make a decision like that without his approval."

"I was just kidding you," Tony said. But chuckling, he added, "Judging from the fit Grandfather threw about my love affair with Matti, I can imagine his reaction if you and Derek got together."

"It wouldn't be any of his business."

"I'd be the first to agree to that, and it would be unjustified if he did object. Derek and I were in school together. He had a rough time when he first came here, but he's a smart guy and soon caught up with the rest of the class. Derek is sensitive about his past, but from what I know of him, I'd guess that he came from good stock somewhere along the line. We've always gotten along, and I intend to visit him and try to get him involved in our church activities." He opened the door and stepped out of the car. "Let me know in a few days, okay?"

Kennedy nodded and drove away.

She wouldn't see Derek for several days, for he and the men were mending fences on the range farthest from ranch headquarters, and they were camping out. Most of the time they didn't have cell phone access, and the time seemed endless without hearing from him every day. When he called upon returning home, a warm glow filtered through her body.

"Want to go try your horseback riding skills tonight?" he asked.

"Sure, but aren't you tired of riding?"

"Yeah, but I couldn't think of any other excuse to spend the evening with you," he said, and she knew he was smiling.

"You don't need an excuse, but I'd like to take a ride. June has been helping me with saddling. I've ridden around the ranch yard a few times, but I'm still tense."

"See you in a few," he said.

It seemed to Kennedy that she'd just existed while Derek was away. When he rode into the yard and bounded up the steps to the gazebo where she waited, folding her in a tight embrace, she knew he'd missed her, too. But the embrace was brief—too brief for Kennedy—before he released her.

"What trouble have you gotten into while I've been away?" he teased.

"That's for me to know and for you to find out," she retorted, recalling a remark she hadn't heard since she was a child.

He took her hand and held it while they walked toward the horses. "Mom says you can get in the saddle all by yourself now."

She nodded, mounting without too much awkwardness, and they headed up the river trail. "Tell me what you've been doing," she suggested. "I want to know everything about the ranch."

"We've been fixing the fences, and it's what I like least about ranching. I like roundup time, branding new stock, even haying and planting new crops, but repairing fences is boring. Still, it's an important part of ranching and has to be done."

Savoring the deep tone of his voice as he talked, she learned that in spite of the hard work, Derek loved every part of ranching. "We shift the cattle from pasture to pasture, and we always check the fences when we take the stock to new grasslands. Once a year we go around the whole ranch and check that the fences aren't down."

"And you still want to be a rancher?"

"There's no other life like it, at least for me, and I like camping out. You and Mom might go along with us sometime. She used to go when Dad was living. I know you would like spending the night on the range as much as I do. I feel closer to God when I'm sleeping under the stars than at any other time."

His statement surprised Kennedy, but she was pleased to know that he wasn't insensitive to God in his life.

"That's one of the things I enjoy about being on the ranch," Kennedy agreed. "I sit on the porch after dark a lot, listening to the insects and the sound of wind through the grass and trees. It's an experience I hadn't known until I came here."

"I know that feeling. Growing up in inner-city Chicago, I'd never seen the moon and stars. After we moved to Valentine, I slept outside as much as Mom would let me. It was awesome for a kid who'd lived in a city all of his life."

Kennedy laughed. "I'm glad to hear that, because I have something to ask you."

He looked at her, a question in his eyes, and she told him about the request Tony had gotten from the community center in Omaha. "As far as I'm concerned, it sounds all right, but I told Tony you'd have to make the decision."

"Since I know what it's like to be poor and living in the city, I'm all for it," he said readily. "We can take them horseback riding, on hayrides or canoeing, and do lots of fun things."

"When would be a good time?"

"Let me think about it. We usually have a slow time in mid-summer. Maybe the last week in July. The other men and I would have time to help with some of the activities, because I know how green I was about ranch life when we moved to Nebraska. Those kids wouldn't know anything about rural living."

"Then I'll call Tony and he can contact the center in Omaha and tell them we will host the kids. We can let him know more in a few days."

The horses' gait was slow and steady, and Kennedy found it more comfortable than her first ride. She glanced sideways at Derek just as he yawned. He did look tired, and she said, "You should be home resting. Or at least let's go back to Riverside and sit on the porch."

"I'm all right. We can ride a little farther before we turn around."

"Do you think I'm riding well enough now to go alone when you're busy?"

"Yes, if you're confident you can handle the mare. I'll leave Santee in the pasture beside the barn, and if I'm not around, Mom can help you get her ready to ride. But stay in sight of ranch headquarters."

When they reached Riverside, he followed her up the steps into the gazebo and stretched out on a lounge chair.

"I'll bring something to drink," Kennedy said. "Do you want Coke or iced tea?"

"Tea."

When she came back, he was lying with his eyes closed, and Kennedy paused. If he was asleep, she didn't want to bother him.

"I'm awake," he said, "but I won't be for long if I sit here with my eyes shut."

She handed the frosty glass to him and took a chair close to him where she could see his face in the dusk. "Tony said the two of you were in school together."

"Yeah. I was a scared kid from the city, didn't know anyone, and was really miserable. Tony befriended me the first day, and I'll never forget it. Having a Morgan for my friend paved the way for me to do lots of things. I got invitations to parties, made the football team, and was happier than I'd ever been in my life. We lost track of each other when he went away to college and seminary."

"Have you ever heard him preach?"

"No." He took a long swallow of iced tea. "And that's a poor way to treat him after he was so good to me."

"I've been going to church all of my life, and after hearing him speak a few times, I consider him one of the best preachers I've ever heard."

Derek didn't comment, saying instead, "Have you heard about the way his girlfriend jilted him?"

She nodded. "He stopped by to visit one day and told me. He's in the bad graces of Gabriel Morgan, too. Maybe he'll find another girl to love."

"I hope so," Derek said as he stood up. "He deserves some happiness. So long. I'll let you know about the camping trip."

She walked beside him to where the horses were tethered, and after he swung into the saddle, he said, "Isn't it time to take your rental car to Omaha?"

"We won't have to go to Omaha. I found out that we can drop it off at North Platte."

"Great! North Platte is straight south of here and much closer than Omaha, so we can go on Sunday afternoon. Do you have enough to keep you busy until then?"

"I received a packet of estate papers from Mr. Talbot last week, and I need to study them."

"Then I'll see you Sunday morning, if not before. If you'll bring one of your cars to our house Saturday evening, I'll bring you home, and then you can drive the other one to our house the next morning."

Chapter Ten

....

As planned, on Sunday morning Kennedy took her grandfather's car to ranch headquarters, realizing that she hadn't asked Derek if he would pick her up at church, or if she would ride back to the ranch with June and leave from there for North Platte. When she drove into the ranch yard Derek was sitting on the porch railing, but he jumped to the ground and walked toward her.

Kennedy stared in amazement. "Oh, my!" she murmured.

He was dressed in a tan suit, a white shirt, and a brown tie and wore a white Stetson. She considered him handsome in his work clothes, but it was nothing compared to the way he looked today. Surely he hadn't dressed up just for the drive to North Platte.

She hadn't made any move to get out of her car when he stopped beside her and opened the door. From the mischievous gleam in his eyes, she sensed he was aware of her astonishment. She blinked, feeling unnerved.

"I'm impressed," she said breathlessly.

His lips parted in an amused smile. "I thought you would be—that's what I had in mind. Let me drive. I want to try out the car again before we head south from Valentine."

When she stood beside him, Kennedy demanded, "Derek Sterling, are you going to church?"

"Yep," he said. "And if you don't mind, Mom will drive your rental car into town. She and a friend are going to spend the afternoon together, and her friend will bring her home. We can leave from the church. It will save us a little time rather than coming back to the ranch first."

Kennedy slid into the passenger seat, wondering what June thought about Derek's sudden notion to attend worship. Although she was trembling inwardly, Kennedy clenched her hands to keep them from shaking. Avoiding Derek's eyes, she looked out the window. She didn't want him to guess how his appearance and actions this morning had unsettled her.

Every time she was with him, she was acutely aware of the intangible web pulling them closer and closer. She *could not* fall in love with Derek. He'd made it plain that he never expected to marry, and neither of them would consider any other kind of a relationship. After she'd lived this long without giving her heart to anyone, it would be unthinkable to love a man who wasn't interested in commitment.

They were halfway to Valentine when she felt Derek's tender touch on her shoulder. "Is anything wrong?" he asked softly.

Kennedy shook her head, blinking back the tears that blinded her eyes and choked her voice. Determined to prevent him from knowing how his presence affected her, she looked over her right shoulder. "I see your mother catching up with us. Do you think the Buick is up to the trip to North Platte?"

"It seems that way to me, and when the mechanic says it's as good as new, I figure we can rely on that."

"That's great," she said, still unable to look at him. "It should be a fun drive—everybody will be looking at us and our antique auto."

* * * * *

Derek was mystified. While he had dressed for church, he had anticipated how pleased Kennedy would be that he was going. He knew her well enough by now to know that she wanted him to go to church. So if that hadn't upset her, what had? He had deliberately dressed up so she wouldn't be ashamed to be seen with him as they traveled. He pulled into a parking place beside the church and got out and had opened Kennedy's door by the time his mother arrived.

Although he'd attended this church until he'd gone away to college, Derek felt like a stranger when he entered the sanctuary. And it didn't help that many people turned and stared at him, looking away quickly when he noticed their interest. But noting the smile on his mother's face and knowing how much his presence meant to her, he wasn't sorry he came. He sat between Kennedy and his mother, and after several uncomfortable minutes, he felt more at ease. When his shoulder touched Kennedy's during the service, he was elated that she was sharing his first time attending church in several years.

When the service ended, people he'd known all his life rushed to welcome him, and as Derek started to shake hands with Tony, his hand was pushed aside as Tony folded Derek into a bear hug.

"It's good to see you this morning, old buddy," Tony said fondly. "I've hoped you would worship with us. I knew you couldn't be pressured, but that didn't keep me from praying for you."

Derek's throat tightened when he realized how much he'd missed by not attending corporate worship for so many years. Meeting Tony's glance squarely, Derek said, "It won't be the last time. I'll be back."

He followed his mother and Kennedy out of the church, and when they reached the parking lot, June said, "Be careful, and have a good day. You won't find many places to eat until you get to Thedford, and that's almost an hour away. I packed a light lunch for you; it's in the rental car."

"Thanks, Mom," Derek said. He waited for Kennedy, who was chatting with Robin Donovan and her husband. When she joined him, he explained about the lunch, adding, "There are picnic tables at the headquarters of Valentine National Wildlife Refuge, which is just a few miles south. We can eat there on the lakefront. I'll take the lead, but I'll keep you in view. Blink your lights if you want to stop."

She smiled her thanks, so apparently she'd gotten over whatever had been bothering her. This pleased Derek, for he'd been looking forward to this time with her, and he wanted her to be happy. He watched carefully to be sure she followed him as he picked up speed on U.S. Rt. 83, which would take them directly to North Platte.

* * * * *

This was new territory to Kennedy, and she watched with interest as they drove southward. Because traffic was almost nonexistent, she glanced around frequently. She didn't see many dwellings, and she remembered June saying that the residences and barns on many ranches weren't located near the highway. Kennedy smiled when she saw a small herd of deer grazing in a field.

They drove about a half hour before Derek pulled off on a side road. They passed several lakes populated by ducks or geese of some kind. On her mental to-do list, Kennedy noted that she must buy some books on the wildlife and local flora. She couldn't keep pelting Derek with questions about the rangelands, although she didn't think he minded too much. The road ended at the refuge headquarters, where two picnic tables were located.

White lacy clouds were mirrored in the rippling water of the lake. Two white herons lifted from the water, and Kennedy was thrilled at the grace of their departure. A brisk breeze blew her hair around her face, and she reached into her purse for an elastic band before pulling her hair into a ponytail.

Derek parked the Buick and came toward her carrying a picnic basket. He'd taken off his coat and tie and loosened his shirt collar.

"You choose which table you like," he said.

"Let's take the one in the sun. The breeze off the water is a little sharp."

They talked about the morning service as they ate the sandwiches, fruit, and cookies June had provided.

"Boy, these oatmeal cookies are good. The way June cooks, I can't imagine why you haven't put on the pounds." She shamelessly surveyed his sinewy body that many athletes would covet.

"But you've also seen how much I work! I'm too active to gain weight."

When Derek filled containers with coffee from the thermos, he said with a grin, "I asked you once and you didn't answer. Can you cook?"

"Is my answer going to be held against me?"

"No. I'm just curious."

"I'd never had to cook until I came to Riverside, and I've been snacking most of the time I've been here. Mother did the cooking, and after she died, we had a full-time housekeeper who took care of everything. I concentrated on studying. The few times I've had to fend for myself, I've bought pizza, carry-out food, or whatever took the least amount of time. I know I can never cook as well as June, but one of these days I'm going to prepare a meal for you. Will you be brave enough to eat it?" she asked mischievously.

"Sure thing," he answered without hesitation. "No doubt in my mind but what you can do anything you set out to do—and do it right."

Kennedy looked away from the deep admiration in his eyes. "Don't rate me too highly, Derek—you might be disappointed."

"Never!" he said, and when he stood and started repacking the basket, Kennedy noted that a melancholy frown had sharpened his features.

* * * * *

When they exited the airport where they'd left the car, it was late afternoon—but returning the rental car seemed to be an important step in her determination to settle her roots at least partially in Nebraska. When they headed north on the highway, Derek tugged on her arm.

"Seems a shame to waste this space between us."

Without answering, Kennedy scooted across the seat until their shoulders touched.

"That's better," he said. "You've seemed a mite thoughtful today. Anything bothering you that you want to share with me?"

"No, but I have been wondering if you've decided what we can do to entertain the kids from Omaha. They'll be here before we know it."

"How many will there be?" Derek asked.

"Since this is a test project, they're only bringing twelve kids—six boys and six girls—ranging between the ages of twelve and sixteen. There will be three supervisors along—one woman, two men. Since Tony and I both intend to help with them, we thought that would be enough."

"Unless we have ranch trouble of some kind, I'll intend to spend a lot of time with them, too. I've decided on a good place for their campsite. Do you remember that plot of ground west of the river I showed you when we took our first horseback ride?"

"The land with a building?"

"Yeah, the West Eighty. The building isn't finished inside, so they will need to bring tents, but that will be more fun for them anyway. Along that stretch of the Niobrara, there are good places where they can fish and one sandy beach area where they can swim. Also, there's a wooded area for trail rides and a cave or two for them to explore."

"The one that was Doc Middleton's hideout?" Kennedy asked with a grin.

"No, that's farther away. These are just small caves that show the different layers of rocks and soil, but they'd be interesting to the kids. Does that sound good to you?"

"Yes, it does. We don't have to furnish anything except a place to stay. The campers will bring their own food, tents, bedrolls, and other supplies."

"I'll have Al and Joel cut out twenty horses and start riding them so they'll be ready for the campers."

The miles passed quickly as they discussed plans for the camping experience, and dusk was falling as they reached the ranch. Derek drove to Riverside first. "I'll make sure that Miranda is there, and I'll bring back your Buick in the morning."

Miranda's pickup was parked in front of the house, and a light was on in her upstairs bedroom.

"Thanks, Derek. I've enjoyed the day," Kennedy said when he stopped the car.

"I'll step inside and you can call to Miranda to make sure everything is all right."

Kennedy didn't think it was necessary, but she unlocked the door and called, "Miranda, we're home now."

Miranda came to the head of the stairs. "I was just checkin' to see who'd come. I wanted to know you were home before I went to bed. Everything is all right."

"Good. I'll talk to you in the morning."

Derek stood behind her in the hall, and when she turned, he drew her into a brief hug. "See you tomorrow," he said. He stepped out on the porch, leaving Kennedy with conflicting emotions. She always wanted more from Derek than he seemed willing to give.

* * * * *

It was the first week in July before Derek called about the campers. After greeting her, he said, "If you're free this afternoon, I have time to take you to see what I'm proposing for the kids from Omaha."

"I'm cleaning the stove and refrigerator now, but I'll finish in time to go with you. I'm getting excited about their coming, and I want to see what we can offer them."

"I'll bring the horses. This will be a little longer than you've ridden before, but I think you're up to it. And if you don't mind my bossing you around, be sure to wear long sleeves and your new hat. With your fair skin and blond hair, you could easily burn in this wind and sun."

"I'll be ready," Kennedy assured him. She didn't tell him that she liked his bossing, that his interest made her feel more protected and loved than she had since her mother's death. She had plenty of bossing from Rosita, but her housekeeper bossed everyone. Kennedy sensed that the attention she received from Derek was something special he reserved for her alone.

When they left Riverside, they turned south along the river rather than take the trail they usually did. "There's a shallow place in the river down this way," Derek explained. "The trail is narrow, so we'll ride single file. I'll go first, but call if you need anything."

Kennedy judged that they'd traveled about a half mile before they reached the ford where Derek intended to cross the river. He waited until she was beside him before he instructed, "Follow me, but not too close. Hold the reins tight and keep Santee at a walk. I'll keep my eye on you."

There was a gradual downward slope down to the river, and Santee easily followed Derek's horse across a gravel bar. The horses slowly picked their way through the two feet of water flowing over the gravel. Derek looked backward more than he looked ahead, and Kennedy decided he probably knew these trails well enough that he could travel them with his eyes closed.

After they climbed the bank on the other side, Derek stopped and said, "You're doing great with your riding." His eyes lighted mischievously. "Just shows you were born to be a rancher."

"Maybe. But there's more to ranching than riding a horse."

He pointed upstream to a secluded area where numerous trees extended well-foliaged limbs above the water to form a canopy over a wide sandy area.

"This will be a good place for the kids to swim. There aren't any deep holes, the sandbars make a good beach, and it's in walking distance of the campground I have in mind. I haven't asked, but I assume you have a waiver so you won't be responsible for any accidents with the kids."

Kennedy nodded. "Yes, before I told Tony to go ahead and invite them, I contacted Mr. Talbot, and he forwarded forms that have to be signed by the children's guardians and the supervisor of the community center. Mr. Talbot called yesterday to tell me that he's received proof that the center carries adequate liability insurance. Individual waiver documents for each child and adult have to be in his hands a week before the children arrive."

"Good. I hadn't thought about it until right now," he said, and she saw laughter in his dark eyes when he added, "but I should have known that *you* would."

She knew he was kidding, but she said, "And don't call me Gabriel Morgan, or I'll…"

"Or you'll what?"

"I don't know yet, but it will be something terrible."

He lifted the reins and said, "Let's go."

The campground Derek had chosen was in a grove of cottonwood trees on the west bank of the Niobrara near the unfinished conference building on the West Eighty.

"I've arranged for sanitary facilities and bottled water to be brought from town," he explained, "but otherwise the kids will be roughing it. That means their baths will be in the river or as sponge baths. They'll be sleeping in bedrolls in tents, and their food will be cooked on a campfire. I've worked this out with Tony, and he's relayed all of the information to Omaha."

"I like your plans, and I trust your judgment. As I told you, I've never camped, so I don't have any suggestions. Can we look inside the building while we're here? It seems a waste for such a sturdy building to stay unused."

"Oh, we store grain and hay here to feed cattle that range on this side of the river, but I agree that it should be put to better use."

The two-story brick building with one-story wings faced the river. The windows were protected by boards, and the doors were padlocked. "We don't keep the electric power on here, but I'll open a couple of doors so you can see inside—though there isn't much to see. A few partitions were installed, so you can get an idea of the general layout of the building. I've heard that the investors went bankrupt before they could finish the building."

Kennedy followed him inside. Sacks of grain were piled in the entryway, and several pieces of farm machinery were inside. Derek pointed to the left wing. "That was supposed to be the meeting, dining, and kitchen area. And the other wing was for guest rooms."

"How long has the building been here?"

"About ten years, I think. As I understand it, your grandfather leased the land to the contractors, but when their plans failed, the building became his."

"Surely it could be utilized for a good purpose," Kennedy speculated.

"Yeah, I think so, too. That's the reason I suggested you might want to sell just this part. You receive some income from it, but you'd probably make more money if you sold the property and invested the proceeds."

"I'll give it some thought after we see how the camping experience works out."

When Derek went to the back door, he said in astonishment, "Well, would you look at this!"

"What is it?" she asked.

"Somebody's been in this building. Come here," Derek called, "but watch your step."

She could see his shadow in the distance, and she walked slowly in that direction.

A McDonald's container lay on the floor along with several aluminum cans.

"I check this building every few weeks," Derek said angrily, "and these things weren't here the last time I stopped by."

A cold chill ran up her backbone, and Kennedy looked around nervously, wondering if the intruder was still in the building. A bale of hay had been broken apart and scattered to make a bed. Several empty grain sacks had been folded to make a pillow.

"Whoever it is made himself right at home," Derek said. "I'd better find out how he got in. Stay close beside me."

He walked outside and checked the windows. The wooden panels nailed across the window appeared to be intact, but on closer inspection Derek pointed to a window, showing Kennedy that the nails were loose. He easily removed the barrier, and they saw that the lower window sash had been removed.

"Pretty neat," he said. "This wasn't just a bunch of kids snooping around. It looks like a professional job to me. I'd better call the sheriff."

"Oh, I hate to have the police around with the children coming in a couple of weeks."

"That's the reason I think we should notify them. We must have a safe place for the kids. We have a lady sheriff, by the way. Her last name is Morgan, so she's probably your kin."

This incident upset Kennedy more than she would have expected, for she had never been involved with the authorities in any way. She hadn't gotten as much as a driving citation. It bothered her, too, because she wanted the children to have a good time. But she figured Derek was right—the best way for them to be assured a good vacation was to keep them safe.

After Derek called the sheriff and made an appointment to meet her at six o'clock, he locked the doors and they rode upriver. He stopped at one place, saying, "This is a good place to fish. The bank is low and the water is deep. I'll arrange for at least one of the ranch hands to be with them at all times. If I don't sleep here, I'll ask either Al or Sam to stay."

After they'd ridden over two short trails where he proposed they take the campers, Kennedy said, "Your plans are wonderful, Derek, and I appreciate the time you've taken to make this happen. But I'm getting tired."

"I'm sorry. I haven't been very considerate. That break-in distracted me. I'll go home with you and still have time to come back before the sheriff arrives. You don't want to talk to her?"

"No. I want to go home and spend the rest of the evening in the gazebo. I'm not as good a cowgirl as you thought."

Derek didn't dismount when they returned to Riverside but promised to stop by and tell her what he learned from the sheriff and loped away. Kennedy went inside and filled a glass with ice and Coke and picked up the mail that Derek had brought earlier from the mailbox near the highway. She stretched out on the lounge and took a drink of the beverage. The fact that Derek was calling in the authorities about the break-in also indicated that he was worried about the warnings she'd received as well as the trespassings on the West Eighty and earlier at the ranch. Momentarily she wished they hadn't invited the young people to the ranch. It was causing more work for Derek, and he already had enough to do.

Idly glancing through the mail, Kennedy opened a letter postmarked at Omaha without a return address. She immediately recognized the bold, printed letters of the warnings that she'd first seen several weeks ago.

You're Running Out of Time.

"God," she whispered, "how much more of this can I take? Am I foolish to stay here?"

She lay with her eyes closed while fear and anger twisted around her heart. With trembling fingers, she folded the message and put it in the envelope. Should she tell the police about these warnings as Miranda advised her to? Would the harassment stop if she returned to California? Probably not, if she left without selling the ranch, since that seemed to be the problem in the first place.

As she often had, Kennedy tried to sort out the major reason she didn't want to leave the Circle Cross. Was it stubbornness—not wanting to be told what to do? Was it reluctance to give up Riverside? Although those things contributed to her determination to stay put, she knew these issues were only secondary. Honestly searching her heart, she knew she didn't want to be separated from Derek. But remaining in Valentine could easily result in her death or a broken heart, and at this moment, she couldn't decide which she dreaded more.

Chapter Eleven

....

Darkness was rapidly settling over the Niobrara Valley when Derek rode into Riverside's yard. Kennedy met him at the door, and he immediately noted her worried expression.

"Come in," she said, unlocking the screen door. "I'll put a frozen pizza in the oven."

"No thanks. I called Mom to tell her I'd be late, and she has my supper ready to heat in the microwave. I wanted to tell you what I found out. Let's sit on the steps. I'm too dusty to sit on your furniture."

"What did you learn?" she asked languidly as if she really didn't care.

"The sheriff had a detective with her, and they checked out the place. But there weren't any fingerprints on that window except mine, so whoever pulled the job was a professional. Or someone wearing gloves."

"So what now?"

"The sheriff said to leave the window as it is and watch the place to see if this was just a one-time thing—somebody passing through and looking for shelter to sleep. She also says they'll patrol day and night while the kids are here from Omaha."

Kennedy didn't answer, and her silence disturbed Derek. He'd been sitting two steps below her so he could watch her face as they talked, but spontaneously he moved to sit beside her. Taking her hand, he said softly, "What's happened?"

"I got another warning. It was in the mail today. It's apparently from the same source, but this was a new message—'*You're running out of time.*'"

Anger almost choked Derek. How could he find out the origin of these letters?

"Where was it mailed from?"

"Omaha."

"Now that the sheriff is involved in this break-in, it might be time to clue her in on these warnings. I'll do anything I can to help you; you know that."

"I could use a hug more than anything else," she said quietly. "I feel so alone."

Derek didn't need a second invitation. He drew her into the circle of his arms, and she put her head on his shoulder. He rubbed her back and kissed her hair softly, hoping she wasn't aware of his caress. More than anything else, he wanted to protect Kennedy from whoever was badgering her—but above all, he had to protect her from himself.

Her body was stiff with tension, which gradually lessened as he rocked her gently. Against his cheek, she whispered, "Go on home, Derek, and eat your supper. I'm always imposing on you. Miranda will be here soon."

"I'll stay until she comes."

Except for the dusk-to-dawn lamps, the glade was completely dark when Derek heard Miranda's pickup approaching. He released Kennedy, stood, and pulled her upward beside him. Before she stepped away from him, she stood on tiptoes and kissed his cheek.

* * * * *

When they didn't discover any more evidence of a vagrant on the West Eighty, Kennedy believed things would turn out well for the campers. That is, until Tony called the night before the campers arrived on July 20.

"Hi, Kennedy," he said. "I've run into a problem. One of our church members has been airlifted to Omaha in critical condition. I'm leaving right away to take his wife to the hospital to be with him. Their children live out-of-state and can't get here for a couple of days, so I'll have to stay until one of them arrives."

"But, Tony, you won't be here when the campers come tomorrow."

"I know, coz, but I have to look after my congregation when they're in trouble. I feel badly about it because I was sort of responsible for bringing the kids here."

Kennedy had grown to like Tony very much, and he seemed almost like a brother. She knew that the welfare of the members of his church *should* be his first responsibility. She respected him for his dedication, but it put more responsibility on Derek and her.

"Oh, I understand, of course. But that leaves me to greet them and make them feel welcome. I've never had much experience in that sort of thing. Since you won't be here to stay overnight with them, do you think I'd better stay?"

"It would make our visitors feel more at ease, I'm sure, but that's asking quite a lot."

"Derek or one of his men will stay with the campers all of the time, too."

Since they'd tried to keep her harassment a secret, Tony didn't know how much danger there could be, and she didn't see any reason to tell him about their trouble. He had enough stress with his pastoral responsibilities. He was just as well off not to know why Derek was keeping constant vigil for the campers.

"We're leaving right away," Tony said, "but I'll keep in touch by phone."

"God go with you, Tony. I'll be praying for you and the man who's ill."

"Good. His name is Gerald."

Tony's absence did put more responsibility on Kennedy's shoulders, but she preferred having enough activity to occupy her time. She was beginning to wonder if she would ever find the time to study for the bar exam until she went back to California. It wouldn't matter whether she took the exam this fall anyway, for she hadn't even thought about applying for a job. At the present she was too involved with happenings on the ranch and settling her business affairs to study. When she returned to California, with only Rosita for company, she could go through her notes, concentrate on the exam, and look for a job.

Derek called soon after she finished talking to Tony. "We've been working on the campsite all day," he said. "Do you want to go inspect it?"

"I'm sure it's all right, but I'll go with you." She told him about Tony's trip to Omaha, adding, "We had planned that he would stay with the campers at night and I'd be with them all day. We thought that our visitors would feel more comfortable if *one* of us was there all the time, so I'll stay day and night until he gets back."

"I don't know about that," Derek said slowly. "You're safer at home with Miranda guarding you."

"But if a Circle Cross man is there at night, I should be all right."

"I suppose so, but it's still risky." He paused. "I'll pick you up in the truck right away. I want to get to town before the grain store closes."

Kennedy waited on the porch for him, for she didn't want to delay him. It was a short drive to the campsite, and she was surprised how Derek and his men had transformed a cow pasture into a perfect campground.

The whole area was neatly mown. Wooden benches had been built facing the river, and rocks from the creek bed had been laid in a circle to make a place for a campfire.

"This will be where their evening services will be held," he explained. "I went to 4-H camp when I was a kid, and that's the way they did it." He pointed to another set of wooden benches and tables where a tripod hung over stacked wood. "Here's the cooking area. We've got a tent to put over the fire if it rains." A flatbed wagon stood nearby, and Derek said, "This wagon will be handy for the cooks to store their pans and skillets. They can put their supplies in the building."

"You've done a neat job in preparing for them," Kennedy assured him. Glancing at the building, she said, "I see that the window is still barricaded. Has there been any more trouble?"

"We haven't caught anyone snooping around," Derek said. "I'm hoping it was just a tramp looking for a dry place to stay overnight before he headed on his way."

Kennedy sensed that Derek really didn't think that, but he wanted to ease her worries if she was concerned about the incident.

"So you think the place is all right?" he queried as they got in the truck and headed toward Valentine.

"I've never been camping, remember, but I'd rate it as super."

"Tony said that the campers will bring tents, cooking utensils, and all the food supplies, but when they get here, I'll bring a couple of men to help them unload and set up their tents. The well water is pure so they won't have to worry about that." He pointed to a windmill on the crest of a small hill and then to a tank close to a large, weathered building. "That's the source of their bathwater. They plan to use bottled water for drinking and cooking."

"Thanks for taking this on, Derek. You already had enough to do without Tony and me disrupting your summer."

He shook his head. "I wanted to do it. With my background, you know that helping these kids will be a labor of love."

As they left the ranch property and drove on the county road, Kennedy swiveled in the seat and pointed. "I've not seen that barn before. Is that Circle Cross land, too?"

"Yes. That's where the windmill is. That might be a good place for the kids to hike for a picnic while they're here, so I'll keep it in mind. It's a high point with a great view of the river valley and the ranch headquarters."

Derek slowed down when they were almost to Valentine. "Have you seen where your grandfather lives?"

"No," Kennedy said coolly. "I haven't looked for it."

He made a right-hand turn on a narrow paved road. "This is a county road that comes into Valentine from the north, and his home is located about a mile north of town. You might as well see the house. I suppose it's where your mother spent her childhood."

Derek's foot touched the brake when they came in sight of a two-story red brick house in a secluded creek valley facing south along the Niobrara River. Two wings made the house seem larger than Riverside. A grove of tall evergreens formed a shelter belt northwest of the house.

Kennedy nodded. "It's a beautiful setting for a home, isn't it? Mother was sick a few months before she died, and during that time she talked more about Valentine than she ever had before. She often mentioned the view. It seems she had a happy childhood and loved this house. One of her cherished childhood memories was about the times she and her cousins had sleighing parties."

Derek moved on at a crawl, knowing that Kennedy wouldn't hesitate to tell him if she wanted to stay longer.

"So now I've seen the places where both of my parents were born as well as my own birthplace." She took a last look at the house before it was lost to view as he picked up speed. "I've often wondered how I'd feel when I saw Gabriel Morgan or his home, but I don't feel anything. I don't hate him as much as I thought I did. Now that Mother and Dad are both gone, it doesn't seem to matter. He can't hurt them anymore, and I'm determined that he won't hurt me."

"I knew you might resent stopping here, but I thought you might as well know where he lives."

"I'm surprised I haven't run into him someplace," she said.

"He doesn't get out much; he rules his domain from his home," Derek commented. "I don't see him more than two or three times a year, and that's when he's out riding with his housekeeper. I don't believe he drives anymore."

"You think I ought to try to see him, don't you?"

"I know you'll do the right thing," he answered. "But when I'd give a lot to know what kind of family I had, it seems sad for you and Tony to live in the same town with your grandfather and not have anything to do with him."

"It's his own fault," Kennedy said tersely.

Derek chose his words carefully. "Maybe it's his fault for driving your mother away and for interfering with Tony and Matti. But he's an old man now, and I figure he's lonely. I'll quit meddling in your family affairs now. It's only that I don't want you to be sorry later on that you didn't forgive and forget."

Kennedy turned to look out the window so Derek couldn't see her eyes. He hoped he hadn't offended her, but her alienation with Gabriel Morgan concerned him. Besides, he had a feeling that Kennedy wanted to see her grandfather.

* * * * *

Kennedy stayed in the truck while Derek took care of his business in the grain store. To keep her mind off Derek's advice, she determinedly thought about their visitors. They were scheduled to arrive about midafternoon tomorrow, and she wondered if the kids were excited or afraid to be coming to the Circle Cross.

Derek loaded several cartons in the truck bed. When he stepped up into the truck, he didn't start the engine right away. She raised her eyes to find him watching her.

"Mad at me?"

She laid her hand on his arm. "It'll take more than that to make me mad at you," she said. "I don't doubt that you're right. It bothers me that I can't forgive him, but I'm not ready to deal with it now."

"You know I'll listen if you ever want to talk about it, but I won't mention it again." He turned the key in the ignition. "Let's go home and settle in for the night."

* * * * *

Otho Steele, the director of the community center, had notified Kennedy that he would telephone her when they were a short distance from Valentine, and she made it a point to be ready by noon. June had provided a sleeping bag for her, and although Kennedy intended to come home to shower and change clothes every morning while the campers had lessons and craft time, she also packed a small overnight bag to take with her.

The phone rang shortly after two o'clock, and when she answered, a booming voice said, "This is Otho Steele. We've just passed Ainsworth, Nebraska, and our GPS indicates that we're forty miles from Valentine."

"That's probably right," Kennedy said, laughing slightly. "I grew up in California and have only been in Nebraska a short time, so I'm sure the GPS can direct you better than I can. We've put up a large sign to show you where to turn off of Highway 20 to reach Circle Cross land. After you make that turn, you'll see arrows to guide you to the campsite we've prepared for you."

"We've got a busload of excited kids," Otho said, and she detected laughter in his voice.

"Yes, I can hear them in the background. We're excited, too. I'll be at the camp with some of the ranch's cowboys when you arrive to help you settle in."

"Wow!" Otho said. "Kids, she says there will be cowboys waiting to greet us!"

Kennedy heard loud applause, exaggerated whistles, and shouting. "I believe they *are* excited," she said. "Call again if you have trouble finding us."

She dialed Derek's number and told him she was leaving Riverside.

"We're already on the way," he said. "Two of the guys are on horseback, hazing horses for the campers, and I'm following in the truck."

"The campers are excited because they're going to see *real* cowboys. Don't disappoint them. Make them think you're tough cowpunchers."

"As if I could act any other way! I'll tell the guys to pretend they're romantic heroes of the Wild West, too.

"Don't overdo that romance part," she answered. "I might get jealous if the girls get a crush on you."

"You have reason to be. After all, these girls, although a bit young, are in my social class. I grew up in the slums, too."

Angrily, she said, "You know I don't want you to talk like that."

"I know, but it's the truth. Besides, I couldn't be romantic if I tried. I have to hang up now. I stopped to answer the phone and the remuda is getting ahead of me." He said good-bye and disconnected the call.

"Couldn't be romantic if he tried!" Kennedy said aloud as she hung up the phone. That was the understatement of the year. She was sorry she'd lost her temper with him, though. She knew Derek had a stubborn streak just like she did, so she would have to accept it.

* * * * *

COMMUNITY OUTREACH CENTER was painted across the side of the gray bus, which had obviously been a yellow school bus at one time. Kids hung out of the windows, waving and yelling as their bus pulled into the campsite.

A man of average height and probably in his forties stepped out of the bus, and the door closed behind him. Kennedy and Derek stepped forward to greet him.

"I'm Otho Steele," he introduced himself. "I wanted to talk to you before I turn them loose." He extended his hand to Kennedy. "I assume you're Kennedy Blaine."

"Yes," she said, and touching Derek's arm, she added, "This is Derek Sterling, the ranch manager, and"—indicating the cowboys, "Al, Sam, and Joel are full-time employees at the ranch. All of us welcome you to the Circle Cross and will do whatever we can to make this a good experience for you."

"It was difficult to choose which children to bring," Otho said. "We had a great many more who wanted to come, but our budget wouldn't permit us to bring everyone. Of course, this is a pilot project, so we needed to start small."

One by one the twelve young people stepped out of the bus, with Otho introducing each member of the multiracial group separately. "We don't expect you to remember all their names right away—that's why they're wearing name tags. Their personalities are as varied as their names, but you'll soon learn who they are."

The bus driver appeared to be a man in his sixties, and Otho introduced him as Tim Spencer. "Tim is one of our volunteers, and he has nerves of steel or he couldn't have gotten us here safely with all the noise behind him."

A red-haired woman was the last one to leave the bus. She hesitated on the top step and glanced around as if she was looking for someone.

Kennedy heard Derek's sharp intake of breath before he muttered, "I don't believe it!"

Kennedy glanced at Derek, who looked as if he'd seen a ghost, and her heart plummeted. A quick and disturbing thought pierced her heart. Was this beautiful woman someone from Derek's past?

"And this is Matti Gray, the financial secretary at the center," Otho continued his introductions. "She's one of the center's full-time

employees and she has tons of work to do, but we had to bring her along at the last minute. Matti isn't a stranger to Valentine. In fact, she's the one who suggested the Circle Cross as a possible campsite."

Perhaps noting Kennedy's distress, Derek turned his head and whispered, "Tony's girlfriend. The one who jilted him."

Matti Gray! Kennedy experienced a flood of relief in knowing that the woman hadn't been romantically involved with Derek, but at the same time her heart clenched for Tony.

Kennedy nodded that she understood. Caught off guard by this turn of events, she stared at the beautiful woman. She was too shocked to say anything, but she quickly thanked God that Tony had gone out of town. Matti walked deliberately toward them, and Kennedy sensed desperation in her dark brown eyes.

"Welcome to the Circle Cross," Kennedy stammered.

"I hadn't intended to be one of the campers," Matti said in a low, silvery voice, and her lips trembled slightly. "The female volunteer who was scheduled to accompany the campers got sick at the last minute. No one else was available to come on such short notice, and we had to have a woman chaperone. I didn't want to disappoint the children, and after I'd helped set up the program, I felt I had to come."

Matti turned to Derek. "Shouldn't I remember you?"

"Derek Sterling," he said, extending his hand.

"Oh, yes," Matti said, as she shook hands with him. "My life in Valentine is so far in the past that for a moment I couldn't remember your name."

Derek was spared having to answer when Otho shouted, "Let's get our gear unloaded. Somebody tell us where to put everything."

Kennedy motioned for Derek to take charge, which he did without hesitation. Matti began detailing duties for the group, and Derek answered questions and made suggestions to Matti when she seemed unsure of what to do. Within a few hours, the whole area had been transformed. Tents were erected and clotheslines strung beside each tent. Boxes of groceries had been carried into the building. Three of the kids helped Tim prepare the evening meal.

"I'm going to stay at night, so I'll put my bedroll in the girls' tent," Kennedy told Matti. "I grew up in Los Angeles, so this is a new experience for me, but I thought there should be someone local camping with you. One of the men from the ranch will be here all the time, too. Derek thought you needed someone who's familiar with the country if there's an emergency of some kind."

"We appreciate that, too."

Apparently the campers had strict orders regarding their individual duties and behavior, for moving into the tents and preparing and serving supper went like clockwork. No doubt the kids considered it a privilege to attend the camp, and they would be on their best behavior.

After supper, the campers and staff members started preparing for evening worship and laying wood for a campfire afterward. Derek motioned for Kennedy to come to him, and when she did, he said, "Al is going to stay in the camp all night. I'm going home now to rest before coming back around midnight. I'll park at the entrance to the driveway, so you won't see me, but I'll be here. Don't be afraid."

She laid her hand on his forearm. "I'm too upset about Tony to worry about myself. Should we let him know that Matti is here? It will be horrible for him to come home and find her without warning."

He covered his hand with hers. "I've been wondering about that, too. I've tried to figure out if I'd want to be warned, if the situation had happened to me. When's he coming home?"

"As soon as the patient's children come to be with their parents. Tony will probably be here on Wednesday."

"That gives us a couple of days to decide," he said. He squeezed her fingers.

"What should I say to Matti?" Kennedy asked quietly.

"Nothing for a while. Give her a chance to talk to you."

"She seems like a nice girl," Kennedy said.

"She was when she was in high school, and it wasn't like her to treat Tony the way she did. They were the sweethearts of our graduating class, and no one could understand why she dumped Tony. I'll wait until I hear her story before I pass judgment on her."

"Wouldn't it be neat if this camping trip brought them together again?"

"Let's hope," Derek said. "Try to get some rest. But if it's like any other camp I've been to, nobody will sleep—especially the first night."

* * * * *

Derek was right, for the girls seemed determined to stay awake all night. Kennedy didn't sleep, either, so when the campers' schedule of Bible study, crafts, and nature lessons began the next morning, she went home and took a nap. After she showered and changed clothes, she returned to the camp at noon.

Joel had relieved Al as guard for the day, and after lunch he guided the kids to the swimming hole. Matti and Kennedy went along, but they didn't swim. With the two men from the center and Joel on guard duty at the riverside, Matti and Kennedy sat alone underneath the spreading branches of a giant hackberry tree.

Silence grew between them until in a quiet voice Matti said, "Do you know about Tony and me?"

"He's told me some things. You see, we both share the same grandfather. He blames Gabriel Morgan for what happened."

Matti swallowed a sob. "I was scared to step off the bus yesterday. When I told Otho about the Circle Cross, I didn't know that Tony had returned to Valentine. When I found out, I was careful to keep my name out of any correspondence about this outing. I didn't intend to come here at all. Does Tony hate me?" she asked directly.

"I don't know. We talked about it once for a short time, but your name hasn't come up since."

"Otho arranged this camp through Tony, and I assumed he would be involved in the activities. In fact, Otho planned for him to present some of the worship messages."

"Tony intended to be here every day, but he had to go to Omaha to be with a member of his church who's in the hospital. I haven't heard from him, but I imagine he'll be coming home tomorrow."

"It would be better if he'd stay away all week."

"I don't think so. Derek and I talked about it last night. Both of us think Tony should be told that you're here. He's never forgotten you, and it isn't fair for him not to know you've returned. "

"I don't want to hurt him again," Matti said, tears brimming in her dark brown eyes, "but I just can't call him."

"But you don't mind if Derek or I do?"

"I don't think so," Matti said hesitantly. "He should have the opportunity to decide if he wants to see me."

Kennedy sensed that Matti still loved Tony, and she felt sorry for her. "There hasn't been anyone else?" she asked quietly.

Matti swiped at her tears and she shook her head, apparently unable to speak for the moment. Kennedy took her hand and held it tightly until Matti conquered the emotions she was experiencing.

"Even if Tony won't have anything to do with me, it will be worth the heartache just to see these kids having such a good time. All of them come from broken homes, living with only one parent or with grandparents. Most of them are on welfare. The only recreation they have is through the community center, and our finances don't allow us to do as much as we'd like."

As Matti talked about her work at the center, Kennedy sensed the compassion she had for others and found out the scope of the center's need. She decided that she would talk to Mr. Talbot about donating some money for their work. Her father had always been generous with charitable contributions, and Kennedy wanted to continue his policy.

"Where did you go when you left Valentine?" Kennedy asked. "Or don't you want to talk about it?" Tim and Otho were in the water with the kids. Joel lounged not far from the edge of the water, ready to take over if an emergency occurred, so Kennedy knew she was free to listen to Matti.

Matti nodded woodenly. "I went to college in Illinois, but I wasn't content to be living out of Nebraska. I couldn't come back home, but after I received my degree, I moved to Omaha. I could have gone to work at several places where my salary would have been much higher, but I hadn't had many advantages when I was a kid, and I wanted to work where I could make life better for other disadvantaged children."

"Do you have any relatives in Valentine?" Kennedy asked.

"Only cousins," Matti said. "I kept in touch with my parents by telephone until their deaths. I came home for their funerals, but I left soon afterwards."

"Have you ever thought of coming here to live?"

"Valentine is still home, and I have considered it, but now that Tony is living here again, I know I can't. It would hurt too much to see him often when I still love him. And it will be easier for Tony if he doesn't have to be reminded of how I treated him."

The campers came trooping out of the water and interrupted them. As they walked back to the campsite, Kennedy considered this strange turn of events, wondering if there was any way she could help reunite Tony and Matti.

Chapter Twelve

....

Derek joined them while they were eating supper. Noticing the lines of fatigue around his eyes, Kennedy wished she could share some of his worries. She took a cup of coffee to him, but when she offered to fill his plate, he held up a hand and said, "Mom had supper ready when I finished work."

"Haven't you slept at all?" she asked.

He shook his head and rubbed the muscles in the back of his neck. "My truck cab is a mite small for a bedroom, so I didn't sleep last night. I had intended to take a nap today, but one of the horses was sick, so I stayed with the vet and let Al sleep. It's only a week—we'll manage. Any trouble here last night?"

"Not as far as I know. The girls were so excited that they couldn't settle down. Their attitudes are good, although Matti says that all of them have terrible family situations."

"I see Sam coming to relieve Joel, and I'm going home, too. But I'll have my cell if you need anything."

When she walked with him toward his truck, he asked, "Did you talk to Matti?"

"Yes. She admits that she treated Tony badly, but I think she still loves him. There's never been anyone else."

"It's too bad she had to show up now."

"She didn't intend to, but the woman who was supposed to come with the girls suddenly took sick, and there was no one else to fill in. Either Matti had to chaperone or the girls would have had to stay home."

"But what about Tony? He doesn't deserve to come to this camp without a warning that Matti is here."

"She was a little reluctant, but she agrees that Tony should be told so he can stay away if he chooses to. Will you call him?"

Shaking his head ruefully, Derek said, "I sure hate to be the one to tell him, but I will. Do you have his cell phone number?"

Kennedy reached into her pocket for the phone and checked her directory, and Derek put Tony's number in his address book. "I'll call him early tomorrow morning. Will you pray for me? I want to cause him as little grief as possible."

* * * * *

Dreading Kennedy's inevitable return to California, Derek had a pretty good notion of how Tony had felt when Mattie deserted him. Wondering how much longer it would be before Kennedy left him, he looked at her as if he'd never seen her before.

Her eyes weren't as sparkling as usual, she didn't have on any makeup, and the strong prairie breeze blew golden hair around her face and shoulders. She wore his flannel shirt that his mother had altered for her. He'd seldom seen her when she didn't look as if she'd just been outfitted in one of those high-end designer boutiques. But today she could easily have been a ranch girl rather than the multi-millionaire that he figured she was. For a blissful moment he wondered if she might actually fit into life on the Circle Cross, and he lifted his hand and caressed her cheek. He immediately realized he'd made a mistake, for her eyes brightened and she moved closer to him before he stepped backward.

"I'll be here again tonight," he said tersely.

Turning quickly from her wistful eyes, he wondered if he'd imagined that her longing was the same as his, for her voice was steady when she said, "They're planning a big Western-style campfire tonight. Why don't you come for that and bring June? Although he doesn't seem like the type, Tim Spencer is quite a banjo picker. He played some variety pieces last night and had the kids roaring with laughter."

"I'll tell Mom, and she'll probably drive over. I'll catch some sleep if I can."

"Some of the women from Tony's church are coming tomorrow night with food for supper. Don't miss that."

* * * * *

Even though Kennedy kept busy on Wednesday, she was anxious about how Matti's return would hurt Tony, and time seemed to drag. She enjoyed going with the kids on a short trail ride and was even proud of herself that she'd learned enough about riding to be helpful. Al, the cowboy on duty for the day, bragged on her when she taught two of the girls how to saddle their horses and shared with them some of the riding tips she'd learned from Derek.

"You're doing great, Miss Kennedy," Al said. "You stick around the Circle Cross for a few months and we'll be asking you to help us rope and brand the cattle. We can always use another cowhand."

Kennedy cast a dubious glance in his direction. "Are you just saying that to make me feel good?"

"No, ma'am!" he said, and his black eyes blazed with sincerity. "I never did learn how to flatter women. You're doin' good, and don't let anyone tell you different. The boss has taught you right."

"Well, maybe if I'm still here during the next roundup, your boss might let me help."

With a sly look at her, Al guffawed. "I've not noticed that the boss man has kept you from doin' anything you want to do yet."

Kennedy knew that her face had turned beet red. "That's because I'm hardheaded and used to having my own way. No doubt I'd be better off if I *had* taken Derek's advice about a few things."

"Maybe. But you've been good for Derek, Miss Kennedy," Al said seriously. "We'd like it if you stayed here all the time."

* * * * *

The campers stared in wonder at the abundant fried chicken, baked beans, potato salad, and cakes that the women from Valentine placed on the table.

"That's just for starters," one of the women said. "We've got hand-cranked ice cream and cookies for your evening snack."

Derek arrived while the kids were still in line filling their plates. Although he first talked with Otho and Tim, Derek soon moved to where Kennedy stood. She ignored Al when he lifted significant eyebrows, wondering how much the cowboys teased Derek about their relationship.

After only a few hours' separation from Derek, Kennedy was as hungry for his company as if she hadn't seen him for a week. What would it be like to be in California and not see him for weeks or months? Would separation make the heart grow fonder, as the old adage was, or would they soon forget one another?

He reached her side and stuck his hands in his pockets. She suspected that the gesture was necessary so he wouldn't touch her in front of the others.

"Hey," he said, and she felt a tender affection coming from him.

"Hey, yourself. Everything all right at the ranch?"

He nodded. "Are the kids still having a good time?"

"It's fantastic," she said. "Most of them have taken to horseback riding like they've lived in the country all their lives. One of the guys caught a foot-long fish today and you'd have thought he landed a whale. We'll have to do this every year, Derek. I've been having some pretty lofty ideas about what we can do with this building and section of land."

His eyes were tender when he said, "Do you think that surprises me? You're always having lofty ideas."

"I'd need your help."

"Always having lofty ideas," he repeated, "and drawing me into them. I'm a sucker for punishment where you're concerned."

"Complaining?"

"I refuse to answer on the grounds that it might incriminate me."

They laughed together, and then Derek's face sobered. "I talked to Tony."

"Poor guy! How'd he take it?"

"He was so stunned at first that he couldn't talk. He told me he'd have to call back. It was several hours before he called, and I was really worried. I haven't been praying as much lately as I should have been, but I was so concerned, I went off by myself and fell on my knees asking God to give Tony the strength to deal with seeing Matti again."

Not even caring what the others thought, Kennedy put her hand on his arm, and Derek drew his hand out of his pocket and covered her fingers. "But it's all right?" she asked.

"Yes. Tony said he's often wondered what he would do if he saw Matti again, and he believes that perhaps God is giving him the opportunity to set things right between them. But he went through some awful hours before he got to that place. He's forgiven her, and he's determined to find out why she deserted him."

"They must have some time alone, but Matti is on a tight schedule here."

"I've talked with Otho about taking the kids to the Circle Cross headquarters tomorrow morning to let them see what a working ranch is like, and we also want to take them for a short canoe ride on the Niobrara River. Perhaps you and Matti can stay at camp, and Tony can meet her here without anyone looking on. I'll keep everybody away all morning—that should give them enough time."

"Count me in," Kennedy said eagerly. "I'll guard the camp, and they can be alone."

"I'll tell Tony to padlock the gate when he comes in, so there should be complete privacy."

* * * * *

The next morning when Kennedy saw Tony's truck approaching, she hugged Matti.

"You're on your own now. I don't want to be here when you first meet. You can tell me about it later if you want to. I need to explore this building, so I'll use the spotlight from our tent to take a good look inside. I'll be praying for you."

"I'll need it," Matti said, and her expression was tight with strain.

Kennedy went into the building through the door that had been open since the campers had arrived and splayed the light around the interior of the building. She slid back the bars on all of the doors and opened them. The day was sunny, and more light shone through than the day she and Derek had looked inside.

Still wary about the break-in they had discovered, she shone the flashlight around the place where the intruder had made himself at home. Everything was just as they'd left it, so she continued her inspection without concern.

By the time an hour had passed, Kennedy had made a fair assessment of the inside of the building. The architect had planned well, or so it seemed to her. She could envision the central, two-story area as an entrance hall with an auditorium that would seat at least one hundred people. Although she hesitated to try the steps, she found them stable enough. The upstairs had been separated into six areas. There were no partitions, but she estimated that this spot was intended for conference rooms.

In the wing to the left of the entrance hall, provisions had been made for a large kitchen and a dining hall. The other wing was divided into spaces for twenty rooms, which would provide sleeping accommodations for two persons to each room. Kennedy had been in enough conference centers to know that this building would be perfect for that purpose. Her only question—was Valentine too small a place for such a facility? She'd never make a move without Derek's advice, but she had a fantastic idea rolling around in her head.

She'd been in semidarkness for so long that the sun almost blinded her when she went outside. Shading her eyes, Kennedy noticed that Tony and Matti were strolling toward the campsite from the direction of the river. They were holding hands—which seemed like a good sign to her. *Thank You, God,* she whispered. She sat on one of the picnic tables to wait for them.

Their smiles, reflecting the happiness in their hearts, caused a bittersweet moment for Kennedy. Apparently they had reconciled, and she was happy for them, but she also wished that she and Derek could find the same happiness. She stepped off the table when they came close, and Matti rushed toward her.

"He's forgiven me," she said, and tears ran like rivulets down her red cheeks.

Kennedy put an arm around Matti's waist and held out her hand to Tony. "I'm so happy for you."

"I didn't think I could ever forgive her, but the minute I saw her again, I knew I still loved her regardless of what she'd done." His face hardened. "By the grace of God, I pray that I'll be able to forgive our grandfather for driving Matti away, but right now, I can't. Let's sit down before the others come back, and we'll tell you what happened."

"Oh, no, you don't have to tell me anything," Kennedy protested. "What happened is between the two of you."

"But we want you to know," Matti insisted. "Then you can tell Derek."

"But we don't want anyone else to know," Tony said.

"I'm honored that you want me to confide in me. Derek and I will keep your secret."

"Well, the sordid truth is that Matti's dad worked for Grandfather," Tony said, and Kennedy noted the hardness of his voice. "He also owned the house her family lived in. He sent for Matti and told her that if she didn't stop seeing me, he would fire her dad, make them move, and see to it that he couldn't find another job in Cherry County."

"The trouble was that Dad had a weak heart," Matti said, "and I was afraid that the stress of losing his job would kill him. Mom and I discussed it, and I didn't feel like I had much choice." She choked up and Tony put his arm around her shoulders and held her close until she could speak again.

"Part of the bargain was that Tony wasn't to know *why* I left. Mr. Morgan also gave me a check for twenty thousand dollars with the stipulation that I wouldn't contact Tony or come back to Valentine. I'm ashamed to say that I let him buy me off, but I didn't know how I could make it on my own. I was only eighteen, and I'd never been out of Nebraska. I got a part-time job and used his money to pay for my college tuition as long as it lasted. I didn't even feel guilty about it because I figured Gabriel Morgan owed me something. I didn't promise him I wouldn't come back home, but of course he had the canceled check to show Tony if I didn't cooperate."

"I was away when her parents died and didn't see her the few times she came to Valentine. But Grandfather isn't going to win this one," Tony said sternly. "As soon as Matti can, she'll return to Valentine. Grandfather doesn't control everyone in this county, so we'll find a job of some kind for her until we get married."

"When will that be?" Kennedy asked.

"I'd marry her tomorrow if I could, but she wants to wait so we can be married on Valentine's Day. It's traditional for couples—locals and people from other places—to be married in our town on February 14. We thought it would be cool to get married then. That's what we had planned seven years ago."

"Oh, that sounds romantic!" Kennedy said. "It *will* be worth waiting for."

"I'll give the center two months notice, at least," Matti said. "I do a lot of things that aren't necessarily in my job description, and it will take time to find a replacement. I hope I can be settled in Valentine before winter. And, by the way, we aren't mentioning anything to Otho or the children. It's okay for them to know that Tony and I used to be friends, but nothing more for the time being."

"Your secret is safe with me," Kennedy assured them.

* * * * *

On the first day of August Kennedy watched with Derek as their visitors from Omaha loaded onto the bus and started their return to the city. It had been a busy week, and Kennedy felt as if she could go to bed and sleep around the clock. But it had been the most satisfying week she'd ever spent. At the closing service around the campfire the night before, all of the youths told how the week had changed their lives and pointed them in a new direction.

She had learned the family background of most of these children from Matti, but some of the kids had talked openly of how terrible their home lives were. Kennedy felt guilty that while she'd had so much, which she'd taken for granted, there were millions of kids worldwide whose lives were as bad or worse than the way these children lived. Throughout the week, she'd asked God more than once what He wanted her to do about it.

And the hours with Matti had brought about a close relationship with her. When she told Matti good-bye, she said, "Matti, I know that you're my sister in Christ, but how about becoming my sister in the flesh? I've never had a sister, and I think you'd make a good one."

"I don't have a sister either, so you're it," Matti said, and her brown eyes sparkled with pleasure. "Let's keep in touch."

"Count on it," Kennedy assured her.

When the bus passed out of sight, Derek said, "What a week!"

"I'm so pleased that we asked them to come. But I am tired. Sleeping on the ground isn't comfortable."

He cuffed her playfully on the shoulder. "You're too soft, City Girl. I thought you might go with us the next time we fix fences. You'd have to sleep in a bedroll then, too."

"I'll take you up on that, Cowhand. Let me know when you're going, and I'll be there. But right now I'm going home, taking a shower, and going to bed."

"The kids did a good job of cleaning up everything, and we'll just leave the benches for now. Tony asked if he could bring the young people from the church here for a wiener roast some night. I was sure it would be all right with you."

Kennedy yawned and headed for her car. "I told you that all decisions about the use of the ranch are your responsibility." She opened the door, got inside, and started the engine. "But I need your advice about something else, so when you have time, come and talk to me."

He nodded, and she added, "I haven't checked e-mail all week, so I'll come to your office this afternoon and see what I've missed. Maybe we can talk then."

When Kennedy arrived at ranch headquarters, June told Kennedy that Derek and the men were cutting out several cattle that he wanted to take to market. She spent an hour reading messages from her friends, deleting a lot of junk mail, and pondering over a disturbing message from Elliott Talbot. She downloaded the lawyer's post so Derek could read it later. She knew what she had to do it, but it wasn't going to be easy.

June opened the office door. "I'm going to town, Kennedy. Need anything before I leave?"

"No thanks. I've done all I intend to for today."

Kennedy was still sitting at the computer staring at the screen when she heard Wilson barking, cows bawling, and cowboys shouting. She closed her e-mail box, locked the door, and stepped out as Derek and the men hazed the cattle into a large holding pen not far from the barns. Dust swirled around the cattle as well as the men, so Kennedy didn't venture too close, but she did sit on the bunkhouse porch and watch. Al dismounted and closed the gate on the milling cattle, and the men rode toward the barns. Kennedy waved, and Derek lifted his hat to show that he'd seen her.

She walked to meet him, and he was brushing dust off of his shirt and jeans when he met her. Wilson raced ahead of him and jumped up on Kennedy. She petted him until Derek said, "That's enough, Wilson. Leave her alone."

The dog barked belligerently at Derek but moved away.

"Go ahead with your work," she said. "I was ready to leave when I heard you driving in."

"Let's sit on the porch steps," he said. "I told the men to take a half-hour break. We've been in the saddle for several hours."

"June said that you're going to sell these cattle."

"They're mostly cows that haven't calved for two years, so we culled them out of the herd. We'll keep them in the corral and feed them grain for a few weeks so they'll bring a better price. We sell cattle a few times in the year."

"Do you ever buy new stock?"

"Smith has discouraged it, so we haven't bought any stock lately. It would be good to buy some more purebred stock. I'd like to have a young bull from the Arrowsmith Ranch in Bassett, Nebraska. They have good stock, but they're expensive, too."

"Smith is no longer involved in this ranch, so if you need new cattle, go ahead and buy them." She lifted the paper she held. "I left a copy of this on your desk so you can go over it at your leisure. It's from my lawyer, and he says that Smith has been skimming money from the ranch for the last four years—amounting to about thirty thousand dollars."

Derek stared at her as if he doubted her word. "I've never heard a word against Smith Blaine."

"It's true. Mr. Talbot wouldn't make such an accusation if he didn't have proof. He even wondered if Smith might be embezzling from all his clients. I'll call and talk to Mr. Talbot about the situation and see what he thinks I ought to do about it. Family or not, if Smith stole that money, he's going to pay it back or I'll have him arrested."

"Wouldn't your dad have suspected?"

Kennedy shrugged her shoulders. "He was easygoing, and he probably wouldn't have said anything to Smith if he had noticed anything questionable. After Mother's death, he lost interest in everything."

"So you're going to accuse him of stealing from you?" Derek questioned.

"I'll have to see what Mr. Talbot says," Kennedy answered, "but I hope he'll press charges."

"Don't go to see Smith alone anymore. I'll go with you."

"I'd like that. I wouldn't put it past him to lay the blame on you, and I want you there to defend yourself."

Derek's attention seemed to wander, and he pointed to the lane, where a yellow taxi was stirring up a dust cloud. "It's unusual to see a taxi coming to the Circle Cross."

When it stopped, a dark-skinned man stepped out. Derek took a deep breath, his body stiffened in shock, and he muttered, "Impossible!"

Several tattoos were prominent on the man's arms, and an earring in his left ear jingled as he swaggered toward Derek and Kennedy. The man's dark, insolent eyes swept Kennedy's face before he faced Derek.

"I'm looking for Mr. Sterling," he said.

"What do you want?" Derek asked.

"I'm looking for a job, man, and I heard your spread was hirin' now."

His manner disturbed Kennedy. She turned to watch Derek, but he was poker-faced, and she couldn't tell what he thought about their visitor.

"What you heard is wrong," Derek said bluntly. "We only hire extra help during roundup in the spring and fall. We don't need any help now."

"I'm just tryin' to represent, man. I'll be hangin' around Valentine for a while, and I'll catch you later. I'm about to pearl."

The stranger returned to the taxi, and the vehicle drove away.

Derek stared after the taxi, and Kennedy wondered at the cold, resentful expression on his face. Or was it hopelessness she saw smoldering in the depths of his dark eyes?

"He didn't look as if he would know much about ranching," she said lightly, to break the somber mood that hovered over them. "And I couldn't understand half of what he said. What did he mean, he was about to 'pearl'?"

Derek looked at her as if he'd forgotten she was even there. "What? Oh, that's street gang talk. He meant he was leaving." He stood up. "I'd better get back to work. Are you going to stay and work in the office?"

"No, I'm finished for the day."

Kennedy's mind was troubled when she got in her car and turned toward Riverside. Why had Derek changed so quickly? Although he had tried to act unconcerned, she knew him well enough to realize that the man who'd approached them was not a stranger.

Chapter Thirteen

Although Derek had wanted to keep up a front for Kennedy's benefit, the bottom had just dropped out of his life. He should have known he couldn't live down his past. But why, after all these years, had Lazaro shown up in Nebraska? Time had changed his former associate, and at first Derek had doubted that he really was the man who'd enticed him into a Chicago street gang. But as he led his horse toward pasture, Derek knew he wasn't mistaken. It was Lazaro, or *Chill*, as he was known in the Chicago underworld. What should he do? Ignore him or try to find out what he wanted?

Derek was glad his mother hadn't seen Lazaro, and he wished Lazaro hadn't seen Kennedy. He gritted his teeth upon remembering the look in Lazaro's eyes when he'd glanced at her. When this old acquaintance had walked back into his life, any vague hope that he might have a future with Kennedy had flown out the window.

After supper Derek drove into Valentine, and although he searched all over town, especially in areas he thought Lazaro would frequent, he didn't see any sign of the man.

He finally returned to the ranch and sat up watching late-night television, hoping he would get sleepy. At midnight he finally went to bed, but he couldn't sleep. His mind was too full of the mistakes he'd made when he was a boy—which now might destroy his future. But if he went down, he was determined that he wouldn't take Kennedy with him.

She called him the next day to tell him that her lawyer was going to write Smith a letter about the shortage in the funds, and he'd also suggested that Kennedy not talk to Smith until he had an opportunity to review the charges. Derek thanked her, but when she asked him to come to Riverside when he had time to talk over some plans she had, he told her he'd be busy for a few days.

* * * * *

On Sunday, after seeing that Derek wasn't at the ranch when she stopped to get June, Kennedy knew that something was wrong. It had been five days since she'd seen him. She was convinced that his absence had something to do with the stranger who'd approached them at the ranch.

When she asked about Derek, June said, "I've hardly seen him all week. He eats his breakfast, goes out on the range, and doesn't come home until after dark."

Because she was so upset about the change in Derek, Kennedy hardly heard a word of Tony's sermon, and she found it difficult to even rejoice with him when he whispered, "Matti has given her notice. She'll be returning to Valentine in a couple of months."

"I'm glad, Tony. I'll call her soon."

June invited her to stay for lunch, but she declined, knowing that it would be too painful to be in Derek's company and think that he didn't want to see her. She was a little embarrassed to see him now anyway. She'd done everything she could to show him she cared for him and that the differences in their social and family backgrounds didn't bother her. Well, she had some Morgan pride left, and she was determined that the next step was up to him. She realized it was time for her to leave Nebraska, and she would go as soon as she settled matters with Smith.

However, any doubts Kennedy had that she was still important to Derek fled from her mind the second week in August when she found another warning. She hadn't heard anything unusual during the night, but when Kennedy went to the door with Miranda when she was leaving, a large cardboard sign was tacked to the front door. In large, bold letters was written:

Get Out of Nebraska, Rich Lady.
You Don't Get No More Warnings.

"Well, forevermore!" Miranda said. "I've never seen the like!"

Kennedy was stunned into speechlessness. Her breath seemed to be oozing from her body, and she felt dizzy. Miranda took her arm in a strong grasp and helped her to a chair.

"How do you suppose anybody tacked up that sign without one of us hearing?" Miranda asked.

Kennedy shook her head. Miranda took a phone from her purse and dialed.

"Are you calling Derek?" Kennedy mumbled.

"No. I'm calling the sheriff. This needs to be investigated before we mess with it."

In a short message, she stated what had happened and then severed the connection. "She'll be here shortly." Starting to dial the phone again, Miranda asked, "Do you know Derek's number?"

Kennedy told her, and Derek answered on the first ring. When he heard what had happened, he must have asked about her, for Miranda said, "She's okay now, but I thought you should know. I've called the sheriff—she said she'd come right away"

Kennedy was still in her nightclothes, so she went into the bedroom and changed quickly into denim shorts and a dark blue knit shirt. When she heard a vehicle speed into the driveway, she hurried out to the porch. It was Derek rather than the sheriff.

He parked quickly and leaving the truck door ajar, ran to the house and came up on the porch, taking the steps two at a time. Kennedy hurried to meet him ,and, apparently unconcerned what Miranda might think, Derek pulled her into a tight embrace.

"Are you *sure* you're all right?"

"Yes," she whispered into the soft flannel of his shirt. "Neither of us heard anything, so we don't know what time the sign was put there."

With his arm still around her shoulders, he walked to where he could read the sign, and his face blanched and then turned red in anger when he read aloud, *"Get out of Nebraska, rich lady. You don't get no more warnings."*

He released her and Kennedy stared at Derek, almost shrinking from him in his wrath, which she knew wasn't directed toward her but to whomever was threatening her. His hands knotted into fists, and his dark eyes blazed with anger.

He gripped the porch banister with both hands and bowed his head. His body shuddered violently, as if he was trying to get control of his emotions. Openmouthed, Miranda stared at him. A siren shrilled loudly in the morning calm, and when the squad car stopped and the sound of the siren had ceased, Derek shook his head and straightened.

"Kennedy, you've got to leave Nebraska and go back home," he said in a strained voice. "You're not safe here. You can come back after we learn who's threatening you."

"It might just be a crank message—you know, the Western custom of tormenting the greenhorn," she ventured hopefully.

Derek shook his head. "I don't think so."

The sheriff had reached the bottom of the steps, and Kennedy watched her as she looked over the area. Tricia Morgan was a tall, slender woman, and dressed as she was in the masculine uniform, Kennedy first considered her appearance ordinary. But on closer observation, she decided that Sheriff Morgan was a striking woman. Her short hair was dark brown. Her eyes were a clear hazel, and she had a smooth, flawless, rosy complexion. Although she must have been almost six feet tall, she walked with grace and strength as she mounted the steps and stood before the sign.

"Sheriff," Derek said, "this is Kennedy Blaine."

The sheriff shook hands with Kennedy. "Glad to meet you, Kennedy, but I'm sorry it had to be under such circumstances." She motioned to the sign. "Miranda says you didn't hear anything in the night."

"Nothing! And I sleep right there." She pointed to her bedroom, only a few feet from where the sign had been tacked. She explained about the night that Wilson had heard something. "Derek found some tracks that night."

"I don't see any tracks now. But if the sign was put up before the dew fell, it would be hard to find footprints. Did you notice anything, Derek?"

"I'd only been here a few minutes before you came, so I hadn't looked around."

"I'm not inclined to consider this a joke, Miss Blaine," the sheriff said. "I'm going to take this sign in for some lab work and send a deputy out here to look around a bit."

"I guess we're related," Kennedy said hesitantly, not knowing if the sheriff would want to acknowledge the kinship.

"Yes, your mother and my dad were cousins, and I've always been sorry that we didn't know you. There are a few other Blaines and Morgans who have intermarried through the years, but I guess your parents were the first who had the courage to try it."

"So I've been told," Kennedy answered.

"I'll be on my way now," Sheriff Morgan said. "But I'll be in touch. Are you going to leave Valentine?"

Kennedy shook her head and, with a sidelong glance at Derek, she said firmly, "It will have to get a lot worse than this before I go back to California."

"Then you'll have to keep Wilson with you at night," Derek said, a worried expression in his eyes. "At least you'll have a warning if anyone trespasses."

"That's a good idea, Derek," the sheriff agreed. She turned to Kennedy. "I urge you not to take this message as a joke. It's a warning, and although Miranda is very efficient, she can't watch you all the time. At the first sign of any problem, call me."

"I will. I'm honest enough to admit that I'm afraid to stay here, but," she added doggedly, "I'm also determined that I won't be a coward and let someone scare me off my property."

"I'll be working on every lead I have." The sheriff's probing eyes swept from Derek to Kennedy. "Both of you keep sharp eyes on what goes on around you and notify me at the first hint of trouble."

But in spite of Miranda's company and Wilson's protection, during the next two weeks, the intimidating signs kept appearing. One was nailed to a post near the gate between Riverside and ranch headquarters. June found one in the mailbox on two occasions. Another similar sign was stuck under the windshield wiper of Kennedy's car while she was shopping in Valentine. Both Derek and the sheriff were at their wits' end with trying to figure out who was responsible.

Kennedy insisted that Smith or the people who wanted to buy the Circle Cross were responsible, and she couldn't understand why Derek disagreed with her. What did he know that he wouldn't tell her? Although she trusted Derek implicitly, she was convinced he knew more about the threats than he was telling her.

* * * * *

Derek could understand why Kennedy wanted to stay in Nebraska, and he didn't want her to leave, either. He'd become so fond of her that he couldn't imagine how it would seem to not see her every day. But if his former acquaintance Lazaro was trying to get to Derek through Kennedy, he knew she wasn't safe. Although Lazaro was an educated man, he chose to use slang from the street. It stirred his warped humor to have people in authority, especially police, think he was dumb, while all the time he was laughing behind their backs about how stupid they were. So if Lazaro was responsible for harassing Kennedy, Derek wanted to find him before he did any harm to her or the Circle Cross.

Every evening he drove through the streets of Valentine looking for his former accomplice, but he didn't see him. Derek was almost to the point of believing that Lazaro had left the area when he received a call on the office phone.

"Just checking to see if youse hirin' now?"

"What do you want from me?" Derek demanded. "Stop this cat-and-mouse stuff and speak what's on your mind."

"I'm fo sho lookin' for a job, man."

"The Circle Cross doesn't need the kind of work you do, but we do have to talk. Where can I meet you?"

The line went dead, and Derek threw up his hands in frustration. He asked the sheriff to trace the call. She soon found that it had been made from a cell phone, but she didn't learn who the caller was.

Trying to guard Kennedy as much as possible, he went often to Riverside after supper to go riding with her. They took the trail along the river as they usually did, for in the evening the trail was shaded. Watching her as she rode, he complimented her. "You've come a long way, Kennedy. You don't even need me to ride along now."

Slanting a teasing glance toward him, she said, "Are you getting tired of waiting on me?"

"You have been a nuisance ever since you came," he said in a bantering tone. It was the first time in days he'd joked about anything.

"But I can't shirk my responsibilities until I take you to the old burying ground. I can do that the day after tomorrow, if you still want to go."

"I do," she said readily.

"I'm going to Ogallala tomorrow to an auction. They may have some machinery we can use, and I'll be gone all day," he said. "But I'll keep Saturday open for you."

"While you're gone, if you don't mind, I'll work in your office," Kennedy stated. "I want to download some files off the Internet."

"Sure, go ahead," he said readily. "You know where everything is. I may not get back tomorrow night until you're already in bed, so we ought to decide now what time we'll leave Saturday."

"I'll be ready when you say."

"Nine o'clock, then," Derek said. "It's quite a few miles, and since we'll be walking part of the way, I plan to make a day of it."

Before he left her at Riverside, Derek asked, "What about Santee? Do you want me to keep her in the corral close to the house?"

Hesitantly, Kennedy said, "No, I don't think so. You'll probably think I'm loco, but even when we're riding together, sometimes I have the feeling that someone is watching me. I'm not normally so paranoid, but I feel uneasy. Has that ever happened to you?"

He looked around the home site and across the river and shook his head. "No," he said hesitantly, "but if you feel that way, you shouldn't go riding alone. You're the most sensible woman I've ever known, and you won't give in to fanciful imaginations. If you sense you're in danger, you probably are. I still think you're safer to leave Nebraska."

She shook her head. "Don't forget I have the Morgan stubborn streak."

He frowned in exasperation. "Then I'll come as often as I can to take you riding. But I'm worried about you. I can't sleep at night, wondering what's happening to you."

She moved closer to him and laid her hand on his arm. Tears stung her eyes as she looked up at him. "I'm sorry. I don't want to be a burden to you. If you want me to, I'll go back to California tomorrow."

He captured her hand in his, held it to his lips, and kissed her fingers. "I didn't say I *wanted* you to go. If I had my druthers, you'd never leave Nebraska. You were made for this country, Kennedy, and it was a cruel string of circumstances that kept you from enjoying your birthright. You do what you want to do, and if you stay, I'll do whatever I can to protect you."

Her throat was too tight for words, and she nodded. In an effort to break the tension of the moment, she cleared her throat. "Don't worry about me tomorrow. I'll spend most of the day at your office. Or I could go with you to the auction if I had an invitation," she said hopefully.

"Not this time," Derek said, and his disappointment was obvious in his voice. "Joel is going with me to help drive. Besides, it will be a long day."

"Okay—just thought I'd ask."

Chapter Fourteen

....

When Kennedy arrived at the ranch office the next morning, she opened her e-mail first. She didn't anticipate a lot of mail, for she and her closest friends communicated by phone more than on the Internet. She scrolled through the inbox, noting several messages from Steve Martin, and she smiled wryly. Since she'd been in Nebraska she'd hardly thought about him, and she wasn't eager to read his messages. No doubt he'd noted on his list of "to-do" items, "Write Kennedy every Friday." Steve was very methodical, even in his courtship.

She scanned his messages. They were lengthy, writing about his experiences. At the end of each message, he wrote, "Love, Steve."

Steve's life was pretty much cut-and-dried. Although she hadn't bothered to analyze him before, she suddenly realized how self-centered he was. It was all about him and his activities. Did she want a lifetime of that?

On the last message, he had written, *I had expected to have a post from you before now. Don't forget, I'm looking forward to your "answer" when I get back in September.*

Kennedy's hands hesitated briefly over the keyboard before she hit the Reply tab and typed a message.

Dear Steve:

I'm pleased that your journey has met all your expectations. This is the first time I've checked my mail for several days.

On impulse, on the first of May, I decided to come to Nebraska to check out the family property here. We're trying to get Dad's estate settled, and I wanted to see the ranch where I was born. I didn't expect to stay long, but

I've learned to love the area and have stayed on. I'm living in the home my Blaine great-grandfather built more than a century ago. I'm not sure when I'll return to California.

Kennedy left the post unfinished and walked around the office. One of Derek's hats hung on a hook behind the door. A pair of work boots leaned against the filing cabinet. A framed picture of June and a man, whom she presumed to be Derek's father, occupied a prominent place on his neat desk. A collage of photos hung on the wall, and a signature and date on the matting indicated that June had given it to Derek for Christmas three years ago. Each picture was labeled.

There were no baby pictures, of course, but Kennedy assumed that June's collection portrayed Derek's life after they'd adopted him. She had mounted a few of his elementary school photos. In the large center picture Derek stood proudly, holding the reins of his first horse. In another photo he posed in his football uniform. Kennedy saw his high school and college graduation pictures. Another picture showed him holding Wilson as a pup. In another pose, Derek leaned against the corral fence in his everyday clothes, looking exactly as he had the first time she'd seen him.

Kennedy sat in a lounge chair that looked practically new, one she figured June had bought to entice Derek to exchange it for his father's well-worn chair in the living room area. She sensed Derek's presence so keenly that she felt as if his arms held her as his chair did.

Closing her eyes, Kennedy prayed quietly. *God, my life seemed so well-ordered until six months ago. Since then, I've had to make one decision after another. Right now, I'm probably facing the greatest decision of my life since the day I accepted Jesus as my Savior. Is it right for me to keep Steve dangling when I know my own heart? Should I tell him now that I won't marry him or wait until I return to California? In this environment,*

*my former life seems unimportant and far away. But when I return
to California, will I forget Nebraska and settle easily into my previous
schedule? Please, let me know what I should do.*

She stood, walked to the wide window, and looked out over the
Circle Cross rangeland. Several scenarios passed through her mind—
scenes of the past and what the future might hold. She had seldom
thought of Steve after he'd left on his trip. Wasn't this a good indication
that he wasn't indispensable to her future happiness?

Wondering if she would feel the same way if she hadn't met Derek,
Kennedy sat at the computer again and read what she had written.
Aloud, she said, "Regardless of what happens, should I settle for a
substitute when I *might* have a chance at the real thing?"

Believing that God was guiding her thoughts and hands, without
hesitation she wrote:

*The days we have been separated have opened my eyes to what I want
in a marriage. During the past two years, our college work has brought
us together quite often. What we thought was romance—on my part, at
least—is only friendship. And while I would like to continue as your friend,
I will not marry you. I believe you know me well enough to realize that
I haven't made this decision without praying about it, and that I won't
change my mind. You are a fine man, but marrying you won't give me the
sacrificial, fulfilling love I observed between my mother and father. I won't
settle for anything less, and I pray that you will understand.*

She read the message once more, hit Send, and leaned back in
Derek's chair, confident that she'd made the right decision. She wished
she could be as convinced that Derek might someday think about
sharing her future. But even if he didn't, she wouldn't marry Steve.

* * * * *

Derek picked up Kennedy the next morning soon after Miranda left. Much to Wilson's displeasure, Derek stopped at ranch headquarters and put him in the office so he couldn't follow them. Wilson's pitiful whines followed Derek as he got into the truck and headed northeast.

"It's a nice day to visit the cemetery," he commented. He was pretty much attuned to Kennedy's moods by now, and he was sure that something was disturbing her. She wasn't watching the countryside with eager eyes as she usually did.

"Did you have more trouble last night?" he asked.

She shook her head. "No. Wilson didn't bark, and I didn't hear anything all night."

"Does that mean you didn't sleep?" he persisted.

"I didn't sleep very well," she admitted, and he noted the lines of worry between her brows.

Derek hesitated to keep pressing her, but he sensed that she was bothered by something he should know about. "C'mon, tell Papa what's wrong," he needled her.

She hesitated, "Oh, lots of things kept running through my mind, but while I was in your office yesterday, I looked at the ranch records and compared them to the e-mail from Mr. Talbot. Smith's embezzlement was pretty shrewd, but it infuriates me that he treated my dad that way."

"How did he do it?"

"He doubled his commissions. For instance, instead of taking his commission regularly, he deducted it at various times, and occasionally it would be paid twice in one quarter. There were other more subtle things that I didn't understand."

"Your dad apparently didn't catch on."

"Now that I look back on the past several years, I realize that Dad had been going downhill mentally as well as physically since Mother's death. He hadn't been as alert as he used to be, but it happened gradually, and I didn't suspect how bad off he was. Or maybe I didn't want to acknowledge the change in him. Smith took advantage of him."

"This certainly puts you in a predicament," Derek sympathized. He stopped the truck and looked at her.

"I know," she said grimly. "Dad may have known and just let it pass. But I don't intend to. More than the money, it's the principle of the matter—that he would actually cheat my father! It's only a matter of thirty thousand dollars or so, but if he owes me that money, I intend to get it."

He drew a deep breath, and she looked at him, a frown on her face.

"Am I reminding you of my grandfather again?"

"Something like that," he said soberly. "But I was also thinking that thirty thousand dollars sounds like *tons* of money to *me*, which is another good indication of how much our lifestyles differ."

"Why do you keep talking about that?" Kennedy said angrily, her eyes blazing into his.

Shrugging his shoulders, Derek answered, "I'm just stating a fact." He took his foot off the brake and moved forward. "I'm glad your lawyer is going to confront Smith, but I'll still go with you if you have to meet with him. I don't want it to look like I took the money."

"Oh, it doesn't," Kennedy quickly assured him, her anger fading as quickly as it had appeared. "He juggled your figures and added some of his own, which altered the totals." She directed a keen glance his way. "I just thought of something! Since your father kept all his books by hand, Smith was probably taking money then and it didn't show up as easily. If you didn't have everything computerized, it wouldn't have been so easy to detect."

"Well, don't worry anymore about it today," Derek said soothingly. "You can't do anything until Mr. Talbot gives the go-ahead."

Smiling, Kennedy said, "I'll try not to. I feel better sharing my worries with you."

"I'm glad I'm some use to you," he said, and she sliced another cross look in his direction in response.

* * * * *

Kennedy noted that they were traveling in a different direction from the one they'd taken when he'd shown her around the ranch the first time. For a while they followed the meanderings of the Niobrara River and then turned due north. Derek pointed out the huge circular bales of hay covered with plastic that they had harvested recently. He readily answered any questions she asked about the ranch, although she realized that most of the things she didn't know were rudimentary to him. At length they arrived at an area several acres in size that was surrounded by a wooden fence.

"We'll walk from here," Derek commented. "Because some of this area still has the ruts of a trail that pioneers followed to the Black Hills, the fence keeps the livestock away. We're trying to preserve everything as it was. I'll show you some wagon wheel tracks in the clay that almost certainly were made by the immigrants."

For the next two hours they walked through the small acreage. Inside the gate was a mural showing the condition of the burial ground before protective barriers had been placed around the fourteen stone markers the pioneers had used to mark the graves.

"It makes me feel very insignificant when I realize what these people went through to make a new start in life," Kennedy said. "Even if they didn't reach the goldfields, they died trying to live their dream rather than just accepting the status quo. I'm not sure I would have had the courage to try it. Would you have gone?" Kennedy asked Derek directly.

"I haven't thought about it," Derek said slowly, "but as you know, I'm ambitious." His brow wrinkled in thought before he continued, "But if I had lived in the East and couldn't see any way of getting ahead and heard that gold was available in the West, I'd have risked a lot to go."

She nodded her head. "Yes, I believe you would have."

"Have you seen everything you want to?" Derek asked, as he knelt to pull weeds away from one of the markers.

Kennedy nodded. "Yes, enough that I'll do whatever I can to see that this area isn't torn up by a bulldozer and a plant or some other modern building isn't erected here."

Derek called her attention to a low range of hills on both sides of the cemetery. "The pioneers chose to go through valleys when they could. We can see the trail a lot better if we walk up a ways. If you're up to the climb, we can go a little farther."

"I'd like that."

He went to the truck and fastened a knapsack on his back. "Follow me, but watch where you're stepping. There are snakes around here."

Kennedy was panting by the time they reached the top of the knoll.

"I'm sure a tenderfoot," she mumbled.

Derek gave her a hand during the last several feet, saying, "The altitude is higher here than what you have in California. It takes awhile for your lungs to adjust to it."

They sat in a grove of oak trees, and Derek opened the knapsack. "I don't know what Mom prepared for us."

He spread a tablecloth on the grass and laid out roast beef sandwiches, sweet cherries, and chocolate cookies. June had put iced tea in the large thermos. They sat down shoulder to shoulder and leaned against a tree trunk while they ate.

Kennedy looked several miles in both directions, and it was easy to make out the route of the westward-bound wagons. "And you're sure I'm right in protecting this area for future generations?" she asked.

"Yes, I am. Perhaps it seems foolish to tie up a whole ranch because a few people were buried here long ago. But it's really more than that. The way technology is developing, we need to preserve our farms and ranches."

"I've been praying for wisdom to make the right decision," Kennedy said quietly. "I don't like to cause trouble in the family. If I make Robin happy by doing this, Smith and a lot of other relatives will probably be angry. He indicated to me that he and Robin fought when they were kids. From what I've heard about both the Blaines and the Morgans, I may have been fortunate to grow up without a family."

"Like me, huh?" She could tell by Derek's tone that he wasn't joking, and she was irritated at herself for touching a sore spot with him.

"I didn't mean to imply that." she said softly.

"I know you didn't," he replied apologetically. He held out his left arm and pulled her close. Kennedy settled against him, enjoying the feel of his arm around her. He kissed her hair, and she sighed contentedly.

"I shouldn't pick at you like that," he apologized, "but I can't stop thinking about you and how our worlds are so far apart."

She started to protest, but he kissed her softly and stifled the words. "Let me finish. You know that financially, in family background, and prestige I'm inferior to you.

There's nothing I can do to change that."

"You know that doesn't matter to me," she said quietly, lifting her hand to caress his cheek.

"Now it doesn't, but when you return to California, you'll see that I'm right," Derek said with finality. "No matter how much I'd like to think differently, I'm so far out of your world, I shouldn't even be holding you like I am now. It isn't just the money. I think I could deal with that, but I'm a nameless person from who knows what kind of background. If I had any backbone, I'd stay away from you."

"Have you ever tried to trace your ancestry?" she asked. "With all of the Internet research today, most people can find out about their background."

She felt his head shake against her hair. "I've never tried, and I won't. I'm afraid to find out. I'd feel even worse than I do now to learn that I came from a family of criminals—and considering the area of Chicago I was found in, it's a possibility."

Kennedy pulled away slightly and looked up into his eyes. "I don't believe that for a minute. I realize that June and your father had a lot to do with the way you've turned out, but heredity determines character, too. I'll check it out if you want me to. And if I find anything shameful, I won't tell you."

After deliberating for a moment, he said, "I'd rather you didn't. I've lived this long without knowing, so there's no point in finding out now."

She let the subject drop without saying anything else. She didn't want to be committed in case she decided to disregard his wishes and search for his roots. Kennedy knew how she felt about him, but she feared there was nothing she could do or say to change Derek's mind, so she would take what he was willing to give. Today she was content to relax in his arms and leave the future to God.

When they returned to the truck, they found a flat tire. Daylight was fading by the time Derek had changed it.

"I hadn't expected to be this late," Derek said, as he replaced the tools he'd used and threw the punctured tire into the truck bed. "Mom will probably be worried about us. I'd call her, but there's no satellite service in this section."

"She knows you can take care of yourself and me," Kennedy assured him.

"That's true," he admitted, "but I don't cause her any worry if I can help it."

"I'm sure you've never worried her," Kennedy said with confidence.

"Yes, I have," Derek said grimly, as he helped her into the truck cab. "But that's a part of my life I hope you'll never know about."

This wasn't the first time Derek had referred to his past with shame, and Kennedy tried to imagine what he could have done that was so terrible that he didn't want her to know about it. He'd been a teenager when his family had moved to Valentine, so what could have happened in his early years to distress him now?

Several miles from ranch headquarters, darkness overtook them while they were still driving across the rangeland. Before they came to the road that connected the various sections of the ranch, Kennedy had started to worry. Although she had confidence in Derek's abilities, she was somewhat apprehensive about whether they might get lost, for the unending grasslands all looked the same to her.

But soon they reached a stretch of land she recognized, and she knew they were only a few miles from home. There was something she wanted to tell Derek before the day ended, and she knew she had to speak soon.

"I told you when we first met that I'd been seeing someone for a couple of years and that he wants to marry me. I was supposed to let him know my answer when he returned from Europe."

She was staring straight ahead, but she was conscious that his piercing eyes were watching her. "So?"

"I had some e-mail messages from him yesterday," Kennedy explained, "and he reminded me that he was expecting an answer when he came home. I already knew the answer, and I couldn't see any reason to delay."

The silence in the truck was deafening. Derek stopped, turned off the lights, and waited.

"I answered that I wouldn't marry him at all."

"Why did you do that?" Derek asked, sounding surprised.

Kennedy's heart shouted, "Because I love you!" But her lips said, "I've never felt anything more than friendship for him, and there has to be something more than that before I marry anyone. He's a good man, with a family background similar to mine, and I hope he'll remain a friend. But I don't love him. It wouldn't be fair to him, and I'd be miserable."

Without speaking, Derek moved closer and pulled her roughly into the circle of his arms. Kennedy's heart danced with excitement when he leaned to kiss her, and she raised her lips to meet his. She didn't know how long the embrace lasted, but when he lifted his head, she breathed deeply, enjoying the feel of his arms around her.

Derek moved away from her and leaned his head on the steering wheel. She touched his shoulder, and he said, "Don't!" He took several deep breaths, obviously trying to control his impulses.

After a few tense moments, he continued, "I've tried so hard to keep this from happening, but it did, so we have to go on from here. In spite of what we're feeling tonight, it doesn't change anything I said a few hours ago."

"Not even if I think you're wrong?" Kennedy whispered.

He went on as if she hadn't spoken. "This has happened too fast. I've got to protect you from yourself. Maybe if we wait a year or two and you still feel the same way, it might work. But as soon as you're back in California, you'll understand that this was only 'a midsummer night's dream.' An interlude when you saw everything through rose-colored glasses before you decided to get on with your life."

She was somewhat surprised that Derek knew about Shakespeare's works until she remembered that he was a college graduate. "Do you honestly believe that?" she asked softly.

He didn't answer.

"Can we ever be happy after we've had a glimpse into paradise and wouldn't go in?" she persisted.

"I'm not expecting much happiness, Kennedy, but that's the way it has to be." In a resigned voice he added, "Don't think this is easy for me."

She leaned over to kiss his hand that lay listlessly on the steering wheel. "I know," she said. "I'll have to live with it until you admit you're wrong, but I won't make it any harder for you."

When they reached ranch headquarters, he stopped to get Wilson. In the light from the dusk-to-dawn light, she noticed when he returned to the truck that his shoulders were stooped and his expression wistful but determined, as if he was guarding his emotions with unyielding restraint. She wished she could remove the pain from his eyes, but she knew there was nothing she could do.

Miranda's car was at Riverside, but Derek walked to the door with Kennedy. When they entered the hallway, Miranda called from upstairs, "Is that you, Kennedy?"

"Yes. Derek just brought me home."

Derek walked out of the house without touching her. When Kennedy sat on the side of the bed, buried her face in her hands, and sobbed, Wilson ran to her and put his head on her knees. Without changing into her nightclothes Kennedy stretched out on the bed, not even objecting when Wilson cuddled up beside her.

* * * * *

Derek got up the next morning feeling as if he'd aged perceptibly overnight. As he showered, shaved, and dressed, he actually wondered if he was crazy. What man in his right mind would refuse when Kennedy Blaine practically offered herself to him on a silver platter? Both of them had stopped short of saying the words, but their mutual love was so strong that their emotions were bouncing off the walls of his truck.

Kennedy was a proud woman, and it wouldn't have been easy for her to humble herself to let him know how she felt about him. He'd tried to discourage her, but he didn't think it was a passing fancy with her. Surely after she went home she would realize that a relationship between them wouldn't work.

He didn't think anything could make him feel worse, but while he was in the office completing his weekly reports on ranch activities, he had a phone call. The caller didn't identify himself, but Derek recognized the voice.

"Tonight! Same time!" Lazaro muttered. "Behind George's Mule Barn."

George's bar was in Valentine, but when Derek had received similar calls in Chicago, the bar had been Smiley's Bar and Grill. The months he'd been active in a street gang had finally come back to haunt him. Derek still had nightmares about the time when Lazaro had been found guilty of murdering two policemen and he'd tried to implicate other members of his gang. The police had questioned Derek, but he had an airtight alibi because he had been out of town with his father that weekend. Lazaro had been indicted and sentenced to life imprisonment without mercy.

Except for petty theft, Derek hadn't been involved in any serious crimes during the six months he'd trailed the gang. Several years had passed, but he could still remember the face of the old lady, the victim of his first crime, when he'd snatched her purse. There was less than twenty dollars in the bag, probably all she had to live on. He'd tried to get out of the gang then, but Lazaro had threatened to harm his parents if he quit, so Derek continued with the gang rather than have his parents pay for his crimes.

Most of the things he'd done had involved shoplifting, and he remembered every item he'd ever stolen. Some he'd shared with the gang, but the DVDs and other minor things that he'd taken for himself he'd thrown away before they left Chicago. If only he could dispose of the memories so easily.

As soon as the authorities allowed him to leave Chicago, Derek's parents had brought him to Nebraska, and during those thirteen years he'd hoped he'd put the past behind him. It wasn't likely that Lazaro had been released, so he had probably escaped from prison. It would be extremely dangerous for Derek to meet Lazaro alone, but what choice did he have?

A few times Derek had been tempted to tell Kennedy about his youthful indiscretions, and he wondered if he should have done so. If she knew about his past she probably wouldn't have any trouble forgetting him, but he wouldn't decide whether to tell her until after he'd met Lazaro.

It was impossible for Derek to get his mind on the bookwork. He went into the house and told his mother that he wouldn't be going to church with them today, went to the corral, saddled his favorite mount, and started riding. Would he ever be able to live down his past? Should he start over with a clean slate, as he'd tried to do when he came to Nebraska?

He had been grateful to his parents for standing by him when they learned he'd been doing things they didn't approve of. To make up for all the heartache he'd caused them, he'd worked hard to get good grades and excelled in sports because his dad had wanted him to. College had been a struggle for him, but again he'd made his parents proud.

But the guilt was never erased. He had attended church regularly until he'd gone away to college. As Derek rode aimlessly around the ranch, he remembered the time he had gone forward in a worship service to accept Jesus as his Savior. He still remembered the pastor's text that morning from Isaiah 1:18: "*Come now, and let us reason together, saith the Lord: though your sins be as scarlet, they shall be as white as snow; though they be red like crimson, they shall be as wool*" (KJV).

The preacher had said that when a person turned his life over to God, He no longer remembered previous sins. The slate was wiped clean, and before God, that life was as white as snow. Derek recalled that the preacher had quoted a verse from the forty-third chapter of Isaiah, where God promised His people that when they repented, He would forget their sins and remember them no more.

Derek believed it then and he still believed that God had forgiven and forgotten the sins he'd committed as a teenager. The big problem was that *he* couldn't forget what he had done or forgive himself for causing his parents so much trouble. He didn't intend to taint Kennedy's life with his past, but now he was worried about what Lazaro might do to her.

He had stopped going to church during his college years. Although he had hated to hurt his mother, he felt like a hypocrite when he sat in the church. He had often longed to share how he felt with someone, but he'd kept it all bottled up inside. Somehow he felt that if anyone could understand his spiritual burden, it would be Kennedy. But was it worth unburdening his soul to make himself feel better only to see the disillusionment in her eyes when she learned what kind of a person he really was?

Derek stayed out on the range until late evening so he wouldn't be tempted to go to Kennedy. When he reached home, he unsaddled his horse, went in the house, showered, and prepared to go into town.

He made it a point to be late for his appointment with Lazaro. If he arrived early, the man would think he was nervous. He waited until almost nine o'clock before he left the ranch. He parked in a well-lighted spot, got out of the truck slowly, locked it behind him, and strolled into the alley behind George's bar. His nerves were as taut as a bowstring.

"God," he prayed mentally, "I deserve anything Lazaro hands me, but keep him from taking vengeance on me by harming Mom." Suddenly Kennedy's face infiltrated his mind. Surely, his former accomplice wouldn't have any reason to harm her—unless he was the one who'd been sending her messages. "Or Kennedy," he added to his prayer.

Derek leaned against the building to be sure Lazaro couldn't step behind him. Only a glimmer of light from the street filtered into the alley, and he couldn't see anyone. The waiting seemed endless, although it probably wasn't more than five minutes before he sensed that someone was standing near him.

"So you came," a deep voice said.

"Yes."

"Why?"

"To find out why you're in Valentine and what you want from me."

"Why, man, maybe I only wanted to see an old friend."

"All right, you've seen me, but I figure you're after more than that. What is it?"

"Money! What else?"

"Then you've come to a poor source. I'm a cowhand—I work for a living and I don't have any money. What are you doing out of prison?"

"Maybe the cops found out that they'd made a mistake when they nailed me. Maybe they're lookin' for somebody else now. Not that it matters. I'm out of prison for good and I'm needin' a stake to start a new life in South America. If you put fifty grand in my hands, you'll never see me again."

"Fifty thousand! I don't have that kind of money."

"Yeah, but you can get it. There's a lot of cattle on your ranch. You can sell some of them and grubstake me."

"I stopped stealing when I parted company with you. I won't start now. Forget it, Lazaro. I don't believe for a minute that you've been pardoned, so get out of town before I call the cops."

"You ought to know by now that I don't scare easy."

Derek turned to leave, but Lazaro's next words halted him in his tracks, and his nerves tensed immediately.

"Your pretty boss has megabucks," Lazaro said, and a warning hung on the edge of his words. "The rumor is that she's hung up on you, man. Don't you think she'd cough up some green stuff to keep you out of trouble?"

Derek reached for him, but Lazaro jumped backward. "Don't lay a hand on me," he snarled. "You'll hear from me again."

Lazaro took off at a run and soon disappeared into the gloom. Derek's heart was hammering, and he gasped for breath. He didn't know if he was capable of driving home. He'd never been in the bar, but he walked inside and ordered a cup of coffee. He slumped down in a booth to drink it, trying to figure out what to do next. He didn't doubt for a minute that Lazaro would harm Kennedy if he didn't do what the convict demanded.

Chapter Fifteen
· ·

Kennedy woke up when she heard Miranda stirring overhead, but she stayed in bed.

Sometime during the night, she'd changed clothes, put Wilson on his leash, and gotten into bed. She had finally gotten to sleep, and now that she was awake, she didn't have any inclination to get out of bed. Her eyes felt dry and swollen and her head was stuffy, and she didn't want Miranda to see her in such a state.

Wilson barked when Miranda tapped on her half-closed door. "Are you all right?" she asked.

"Yes, but I'm feeling lazy this morning. Lock the doors when you leave, please; I may take another nap."

"I made a pot of coffee, and there's some left for you. See you tonight," Miranda said.

After she heard Miranda's car leave, Kennedy turned on her left side, hoping to go to sleep again, but it was useless. After rolling from one side to the other for a half hour, she got up, showered, and dressed. She called June and, without giving any reason, told her that she wasn't going to church. As keen as June was, if she saw Derek and Kennedy together, she would know that something had happened. If Kennedy didn't go to church, perhaps Derek would come by this afternoon and they could deal practically with any future relationship. She refused to believe that they could separate in a few days or weeks and forget their feelings for one another. They had to have some relationship, even if it involved nothing more than discussing the affairs of the Circle Cross.

But Derek didn't call, nor did he stop by, and by evening Kennedy had almost lost her optimism that she and Derek could continue as friends and business partners.

Sitting alone on the gazebo, longing for him to be with her, she came to terms with what she must do. Just because her dreams practically died yesterday didn't mean that her life had ended. Derek may have been right in his assessment. Perhaps these weeks at the Circle Cross had been a summer interlude. When she went back to California, she would forget about Derek and continue the plans she'd made for the future before the death of her father.

* * * * *

After another restless night, by Monday morning Kennedy had accepted facing the future without Derek. She had enough Morgan willpower in her genes that she was convinced she could do anything she set her mind to do. But that didn't mean she would find any happiness in what she did. God had blessed her with good health, supportive parents, and no lack of money to do anything she wanted to do.

However, none of those things could win Derek for her. And strangely enough, she felt no bitterness toward him because he'd rejected her. If anything, she loved him even more for his ideals. If the tables were turned and she had nothing to offer him, she wouldn't have married him, either.

The most important thing she could do for Derek was to make sure that the Circle Cross wouldn't be sold away from him. The threats against her could be more than a hoax, more than an effort to drive her away from the ranch. If anything happened to her before the ranch was put on the National Register, she supposed her estate would go to her next of kin—and she suddenly realized that would be her grandfather, Gabriel Morgan. And as shrewd as he was, he would know that, too. Was she in danger from *him*?

Stunned at the thought, Kennedy's first consideration was for Derek rather than herself. She rushed to her grandfather's desk in the living room where, spurred by anxiety, she wrote in longhand, "I, Kennedy Grace Blaine, being of sound mind and disposing memory, do hereby make, declare, acknowledge, and publish this as my Last Will and Testament." She named Elliott Talbot as the executor of her estate before she added all other preliminary information that needed to be included in a will.

Without a moment's hesitation, she concluded, "I hereby give, devise, and bequeath to my friend, Derek Sterling, the Circle Cross Ranch located near Valentine, Nebraska, stipulating that all inheritance tax or closing costs pertinent to the transfer of the ranch to Mr. Sterling be paid out of my estate before the residue is distributed as follows."

After she had provided a sizable amount for Rosita, Kennedy divided the remainder of her assets between her church in Los Angeles, Tony's church in Valentine, the Community Outreach Center in Omaha, and several charities that her parents had always supported.

She signed her name and the date and sealed the will in an envelope, writing on the outside, "To be opened *only* in the event of my death."

Taking Wilson and his leash with her, she got into the car and drove to the Valentine post office located on South Hall Street. She'd promised Derek she'd be careful, and the dog was about all the security she had.

Kennedy bought a Priority Mail one-day-service envelope, addressed it to her lawyer, and, with an inward sigh of satisfaction, shoved it into the outgoing mail slot.

Thank You, God, for bringing that thought to my mind. I'll rest easier knowing that Derek will have the ranch if these people who are harassing me should take my life.

She went next to Robin Donovan's office and waited about ten minutes before her cousin could see her. She told Robin that she wanted to start proceedings to place the Circle Cross on the National Register. She made an appointment to meet with Robin later in the week for help in filling out the application form and to receive pointers on how to research the house to see if it was eligible for the Register.

Although she intended to wait on her attorney to initiate the embezzlement action, she drove by Smith's office on West Third Street. Only his car and his secretary's were in the parking lot, so she stopped. While she had been in Robin's office, she'd left Wilson in the car with the windows slightly open, but it was getting warmer now and she took him inside with her.

Derek had warned her against going to Smith's office alone, but that was only if she accused him of embezzling, which she didn't intend to mention. The connecting door between Smith's office and the reception room was open, and although Kennedy intended to present an air of calm and self-confidence, her heart was pounding like a jackhammer.

Forcing herself to speak normally, she asked Naomi, "Is your boss busy now?"

"Come on in, Kennedy," Smith called from his office. "I saw you drive up."

He greeted her suavely, apparently in a jovial mood. "I see you've acquired a guard dog," he said.

"This is Derek's dog, but he stays with me," she said, patting Wilson's head. "He seems to like my company, and I like his."

"What can I do for you, cousin?" Smith said with a smile.

She was tempted to say, "You've already done enough," but he was family, and her father wouldn't like what she was going to do. Besides, she had promised Derek, so she held back the accusation that hovered on her lips.

"Thank you for sending the report to my attorney and the copy to me," Kennedy said deliberately. "After all my years in college and law school, I've learned enough to handle my own business affairs, so I don't find it necessary to retain an accountant any longer. I've learned a lot about the Circle Cross this summer, and having seen how well Derek keeps records, I'll have him send his reports directly to me from now on."

Anger spread across his face, but he said civilly, "So you're not going to sell."

"Definitely not. That ranch has been in the Blaine family for a long time, and I intend to keep it."

"Are you moving to Nebraska?"

"I'm leaving for Los Angeles soon, but I don't intend to be an absentee landlord like Dad was. I'll take a personal interest in running the Circle Cross. I plan to keep a residence in both states, so I'll be here often." She stood up. "I'll keep in touch."

Smith didn't say anything as she left his office. Facing him hadn't been easy, and Kennedy's hands shook as she started her car.

Although she knew it would be easier for Derek if she stayed away from him, he should know that she was starting the process to put the ranch on the National Register and that he'd be reporting directly to her instead of Smith. Kennedy was disappointed when she drove into the ranch yard and saw that his pickup was gone.

June was sweeping the porch and waved to Kennedy. Wilson jumped out of the car and headed toward his food and water containers on the back porch. "Come in," June called.

"I can't stay long. I wanted to see Derek, but I see his pickup is gone."

"He and Al went to the northwest pasture to check on the horses. There's always something to do around the ranch. Let's sit on the porch. He'll be back soon."

Mentally and physically exhausted, Kennedy welcomed sitting in the rocking chair. June was a good companion, and Kennedy encouraged her to talk about Derek's childhood. "I know he's an adopted kid," she said, "but that's about all he's told me. Will you tell me how you came to adopt him?"

Derek's mother was too sharp to have missed what was going on between Kennedy and her son, but Kennedy knew she wouldn't become involved in their decisions.

June slowly rocked back and forth, gathering her thoughts. "John and I moved to Chicago after he found good work in a factory, but neither of us ever liked living in the city. We were young and expected to have a large family, but that didn't happen. I was volunteering at a city mission when Derek came up for adoption. He'd been in two foster homes before that, and they had been bad experiences. After I'd worked with Derek for a few weeks, I loved him and talked to John about adopting him, which we did. We felt that God had provided a son for us, and we loved him like he was our own."

"I haven't questioned Derek about his background, but he volunteered a little information. He said he was abandoned on the streets of Chicago when he was a toddler."

June nodded, and there was a faint tremor in her voice when she answered. "The director of the mission told me that he was a healthy baby, dressed well, and hadn't been abused. Because he'd been abandoned near the mission, they believed he'd been left there deliberately so he would be taken in. He must have been dropped off by someone out of town, but they could never find out where he'd been born. We figured he might have been adopted by someone who couldn't keep him for some reason or other, but whoever it was wanted to be sure that he found a good home."

Trying to swallow the lump that lingered in her throat, Kennedy stood and walked to the edge of the porch, her troubled eyes scanning the wide sweep of rangeland around ranch headquarters. Knowing how much this land meant to Derek, she closed her eyes, her heart aching for the pain she knew he experienced because of his family background.

She'd given him the Circle Cross, but what else could she do for him?

With her back to June, she said, "I asked him if he had tried to find his biological parents, but he said he didn't want to know. He's afraid he'll find out things that will make him feel worse than he already does about his heritage. I'm convinced he came from a good background. I told him I'd search for him, but he said he doesn't want me to. I may do it anyway."

June continued the talk by telling about their early days at the ranch, but she was vague about their lives in Chicago after they had adopted Derek. He'd told her that there were things in his past he hoped she'd never learn about, so Kennedy thought perhaps she should refrain from asking questions regarding that portion of his life. She loved the man he was today—his past didn't matter to her. But it did to Derek, and that was the hurdle they couldn't overcome.

After a while Kennedy went to the office, checked her e-mail, and downloaded some information she needed to review for the bar exams. After asking June to have Derek get in touch with her, she went home.

In the late afternoon Wilson started barking, and by now she could tell by the dog's tone when he was greeting Derek. She hadn't dared to hope that he would stop by so soon, and her heart beat a little faster. Smiling, she hurried to unlock the door when she heard his footsteps on the porch.

His dark eyes softened at the sight of her, and the very air around them seemed to be charged with an undeniable magnetism. After an interminable minute, he shook his head and looked away. "Mom said you wanted to talk to me."

"Yes, but I didn't expect you to come over until this evening. Do you want to sit inside or in the gazebo?" Kennedy questioned.

"Let's sit out here," Derek said, looking down at his clothes. "I'm not very clean. I still have some work to do, and I didn't change my clothes."

"You sit down, and I'll bring out some iced tea."

He had taken off his boots and hat and was relaxing on a chaise lounge when she returned with a pitcher of tea, two glasses, and a plate of cookies.

He seemed more depressed than she'd ever seen him, and there was a bleak expression on his face. She longed to sit beside him, smooth back his ruffled, sweaty hair, kiss his forehead, and tell him she loved him. But it would be cruel to talk about her emotions when it was painful to him. Whatever his problems, she wouldn't add to them.

"Bakery cookies," she said lightly. "I haven't learned to cook yet. There isn't much motivation when I generally eat alone."

"I like bakery cookies," he said, taking three of them and a glass of tea. He drained half the tea in one swallow and she refilled his glass before she sat on the lounge near his feet. A cool breeze wafted around the house, and they sat silently for a few minutes.

"Anything wrong?" he asked.

"No, everything is right, in my opinion," she said. "I told Robin today that I wanted to place the Circle Cross on the National Register, if possible. We're going to meet later in this week to work on the application. Of course, Robin says it sometimes takes a long time to review applications and that our ranch might not be approved, but we'll never know until we try."

"So that means you won't sell the Circle Cross no matter how much money you're offered?" he asked.

"That's right, and I feel content with my decision. There are some things that money can't buy."

"Yeah, I know," he said, with a pointed look at her.

She wasn't sure what he meant. Surely he didn't think she was trying to buy a husband! But she'd opened the door for his comment.

"I intend to get the papers ready before I leave."

Wistfulness clouded his eyes before he looked away and asked,

"When are you going?"

"I intend to make plane reservations this week." She poured more tea for him and said, "I also stopped by Smith's office today and told him that I didn't need his services any longer—that you'll be submitting your reports directly to me."

He glanced quickly toward her, obviously surprised.

"Well, why should I pay for a middleman I don't need?" she said. "I've looked over your system and can understand it a lot better than I could the reports Smith made to Dad. Besides the fact that he's an embezzler, I really don't need him."

"You didn't confront him with your suspicions?"

"No. I'm leaving that up to Mr. Talbot. I don't want Smith to sue me for libel."

"Only a lawyer would think of that," he said with a wry grin. Taking a deep breath, he sat up. She stood up while he pulled on his boots. "It's sure comfortable here, but I have some work to finish."

"Will you promise me something?" she asked.

His dark eyes were sharp and assessing. "Not until I know what it is."

"I want you to treat the Circle Cross as if it were yours. Together, I think we can make it the best ranch in Cherry County. After I'm back in California, anything you think of that will make an improvement, let me know about it, and we'll discuss it. Will you do that?"

"I'll think about it." He put on his hat. "Anything else?"

"Yes. I don't intend to mention this to anyone else before I give it a lot of prayerful consideration, but I'm considering turning the West Eighty into a conference center where we can have spiritual conferences for people of all ages. You said that it isn't very valuable to the Circle Cross. I looked over the building inside and out while I stayed with the campers, and I think we could easily have it in operation by next summer. I'd have to get a contractor to estimate what the cost would be to finish. It would have to be set up as a corporation, with a board of directors to advise me, and we'd have to hire someone to manage the place and set up a program that will provide adequate income to fund the operation. I thought it could be named the Grace and Kenneth Blaine Conference Center to honor my parents. Do you think it's a good idea?"

Derek shrugged his left shoulder. "I'm just a rancher, so I don't have a clue as to what would work and what wouldn't. But I don't know of anything else like that in Nebraska, so it probably is a good idea. Your lawyer and Tony could give you a better opinion than I can."

"But I wanted you to know before I mentioned it to anyone else. It's just an idea now, but I can't let go of it, if you know what I mean."

He nodded understandingly. "Give it a few more weeks, and if the idea won't go away, then go for it. My only help would be moral support, and you know you'd have that." He grinned at her, and for a moment his burden seemed to have lifted and he was the Derek she'd learned to love. "Do you realize how complicated my life has become since you showed up on my doorstep? Until then, all I had to do was worry about running a ranch."

She knew he was kidding her, so she retorted, "You haven't seen anything yet."

"That's what I'm afraid of. Sorry to leave good company, but I have to go."

Derek went slowly down the steps, and she noticed that his shoulders were bent as he walked to the truck. It wasn't his work that he loved but rather emotional stress that had caused the change in his demeanor. If only he would tell her what was wrong!

"Derek," she said. He turned dark and unfathomable eyes toward her. She stifled the desire to run and throw her arms around him and tell him that she loved him. Right now he looked like a man who needed a hug. Instead she said, "If there's ever *anything* I can do to help you, *please* let me know. You won't even have to give a reason—just tell me what you need."

"Thanks," he said. "I'll bring the horses as soon as I can so we can go riding."

He leaned down, pulled gently on Wilson's ears, and pointed to the house. Tail wagging, Wilson joined Kennedy on the porch, and Derek drove away without looking back.

* * * * *

When Derek drove into the ranch yard, Al ran toward him. "Boss," he said, "we've got trouble. Five of the cattle in the river pasture have been shot, and there's a big note on one of them. I didn't touch a thing."

Derek didn't waste any time questioning Al, who was a reliable puncher. But he was stunned at the news. Nothing like this had happened at the Circle Cross since he'd lived here. Was this Lazaro's attempt to get money out of him? Or did it have some connection to Kennedy's harassment? *If so, better the cows than Kennedy,* he thought.

"I'll phone the sheriff, and you bring her to the pasture when she gets here," he called to Al as he reached for his phone. "I'll get in touch with Kennedy, and as soon as she gets here, we'll go see what's going on."

He dialed the courthouse. A deputy answered, and Derek learned that the sheriff was out on a case. "Contact her right away and tell her that Derek Sterling called. We have some bad trouble on the Circle Cross. Have her come to ranch headquarters." He didn't go into detail, figuring that the sheriff would act more quickly if she was in doubt as to what had happened.

Kennedy didn't answer until the fourth ring, and Derek fidgeted from one foot to the other. He was on the verge of getting into the truck and going back to Riverside when she answered.

"Are you all right?" he asked quickly.

"Of course." Laughing, she said, "You've only been gone ten minutes."

"Several Circle Cross cattle have been killed, and I figured you'd want to go with us when we investigate. How soon can you go?"

"I'm on my way."

In spite of being worried, Derek had to smile. Kennedy was one in a million! Most people would have started pelting him with questions, wanting to know all the details. But she instinctively knew that they had serious trouble, and she wouldn't cause a delay by questioning him.

June must have realized that something was wrong, too, for she hurried out of the house. He explained what had happened, and she asked, "What was written on the sign?"

"I don't know." He walked to where Al stood. "What did the sign say?"

"Just some big letters with an *X* on top of them. Didn't make sense to me."

Derek heard Kennedy's car coming at breakneck speed, and he went to meet her. She parked quickly, and they got into the truck. She struggled to catch her breath.

"What's happened?"

He told her what the cowboy had found. "I've called the sheriff, and Al will bring her to the pasture when she gets here, but I want to get there as soon as possible."

They traveled the ten miles to the field quickly and almost in silence. To get to the field where the slaughter had occurred, Derek crossed the Niobrara River at a ford. About twenty cattle had gathered in the shade of a tree, bawling and looking at the dead animals. Derek turned off the truck's engine and stared with anger and sorrow at the five two-year-old heifers, among the best cattle on the ranch, lying dead in the sun.

He couldn't understand why anyone would take out their spite, whatever it was, on helpless animals.

"Oh, Derek," Kennedy whispered, and she turned tear-filled green eyes toward him. She moved closer and put her hand on his where it gripped the steering wheel. "I'm so sorry," she said, and he knew her grief was for him, not the loss of five valuable cows.

In spite of his good intentions to avoid touching Kennedy, he lifted her hand and kissed it.

"Let's get out," he said. "I don't want to mess up any evidence for the sheriff, but we can take a closer look. I'd like to see what's on the sign."

He stepped to the ground and raised his arms. She scooted under the wheel and he lifted her down. Holding hands, they walked closer. His first thought was that Lazaro was responsible, but if he wasn't mistaken, the killing had been done with a high-powered rifle, and Lazaro was a knife and handgun killer. Were there two different threats hanging over the Circle Cross? He halted abruptly when they reached the large cardboard sign leaning against one of the cows.

NRHP had been painted in bold strokes with a large *X* superimposed over the letters.

"NRHP," Kennedy said slowly, and then the significance of the letters must have hit home, for she whispered, "Of course! National Register of Historic Places. I can't believe it! Why would people go to such an extent to keep me from setting this property aside for historic purposes? I only decided yesterday. Who would have known?"

"You're used to L.A. The news travels fast in small towns," Derek muttered. "A lot of people could already know that you're considering it."

"Smith Blaine, for instance," Kennedy said angrily. "There has to be more going on here than someone wanting the property for a housing development. As big as Nebraska is, there must be a lot of land that would be more valuable than this. Could there be oil or gas on the ranch?"

Shaking his head, Derek answered, "Not according to geological surveys."

"I feel sure that my grandfather Morgan is behind all of this— still trying to punish my parents through me."

Derek put his arm around her, and she snuggled close to him. "Don't torture yourself with that idea, my love. Gabriel Morgan wouldn't have any part in destruction like this."

The minute the term of endearment was out of his mouth, Derek knew what he had done, and he felt heat starting from his neck and diffusing through his face. He had determined to never tell Kennedy that he loved her. Now he'd called her the pet name he had used for her hundreds of times in his mind and his dreams. He tensed for her reaction, but if she had noticed the slip of his tongue, she didn't say anything.

He heard the sheriff's cruiser approaching, and he moved away, careful not to make eye contact with Kennedy until he got his emotions under control. "We'll soon find out what the sheriff has to say."

* * * * *

Kennedy turned to watch the approaching cruiser. In spite of the tragedy around her, a warm, gentle glow spread through her body. Because Derek had been so careful not to tell her that he loved her, she didn't give any indication she'd noticed the slip of his tongue. But the easy way he had said "my love" told Kennedy what she longed to hear. He did love her, or the term wouldn't have rolled so easily off his tongue. But she wouldn't let on that she knew he loved her until the day he told her so.

The siren was turned off before the car got close to the cattle, but they were already spooked and quickly loped across the river. Another police vehicle followed close behind the other, which contained several men who quickly walked toward where the slaughtered animals were. Kennedy assumed they were a forensic team, although she was surprised that a small area like this would be that far advanced in detecting crime.

Sheriff Morgan parked the car and stepped out. Again Kennedy was impressed by the beauty and efficiency of the officer. Sweeping Derek and Kennedy with her extraordinary brown eyes, she said, "The Circle Cross is keeping me busy." She walked closer to the slaughtered animals. "When do you think this happened, Derek?"

"I didn't touch anything until you got here, but from the condition of the wounds and the stiff carcasses, I'd guess it was less than twelve hours ago. We haven't checked this pasture for two days."

She whistled when she saw the sign and looked significantly at Kennedy. "There's considerable opposition in this state to setting aside land for parks and historic places, but I've never known anyone to go this far."

"I didn't tell Robin until yesterday that I had decided to register the Circle Cross," Kennedy answered. "I can't believe that it's already common knowledge."

"But you've always lived in a big city where people aren't concerned about what their neighbors are doing." With a piercing glance from her large eyes, the sheriff continued. "I've heard that you've turned down an offer to sell the ranch."

"That's true," Kennedy admitted.

Shrugging her shoulders, the sheriff said, "Derek, let's walk around and see if we can spot any clues."

"Do you want to go with us?" Derek asked Kennedy.

"No, I wouldn't be any help. I'll stay here." Kennedy climbed into Derek's truck and watched as the forensic team moved among the slaughtered animals. The sheriff and Derek walked for more than hour, but Kennedy was content to wait.

A brisk wind was blowing, but the sun shone and she was physically comfortable. Her thoughts, however, were chaotic as she tried to sort out what steps she should take now. A reckless idea had popped into her head, but she wouldn't tell Derek, for he probably wouldn't approve.

Derek came to her as soon as they returned to the crime scene. "We couldn't find how the person or persons got here. There are horse tracks around, but Al was riding when he found the cattle, so that doesn't tell us much. No vehicles of any kind have been in the pasture recently. There's a county road a mile south of here, so someone could have driven that far and walked."

"What are you going to do with the carcasses?" she asked.

"If there was only one we'd bury it here, but with so many, I'll call a slaughterhouse and have them hauled away."

"That seems rather cruel," Kennedy commented.

His large hand pulled her close, and she hid her face in his chest. "But not any worse than burying them. Believe me, Kennedy, I feel as bad as you do about this, so I'm not insensitive to the way the cattle died."

"I didn't think you were," she assured him. "Is the sheriff about finished?"

"Yes. It's going to be dark soon, so they can't see anything more. I'll phone Mom and tell her that we're almost finished. I know she's worried."

They made the return trip to ranch headquarters without talking much, but Kennedy sat close to Derek, her hand on his shoulder. Sometimes gestures conveyed more than words anyway, and she wanted him to know she didn't hold him responsible for the death of the cattle. She turned down his invitation to eat with them. She had a weighty decision to make, and she couldn't be distracted by Derek's presence when she made it.

* * * * *

Kennedy spent most of the night considering what she should do. If she thought the ranch's problem would stop when she went back to

California, she would go right away. Her refusal to sell the Circle Cross seemed to be the contention, but she wouldn't sell the ranch no matter where she lived. At this point, all she wanted to do was make life easier for Derek.

After she heard Miranda leave in the morning, Kennedy put on her robe and, carrying her Bible, went to her favorite chair on the gazebo. A haze hanging over the river valley concealed the view of the countryside that she always enjoyed. It seemed as if she was in her own little world. She felt at home in this house and on the ranch, and she couldn't bear the thought of leaving.

God, just because I told Derek I would leave doesn't mean I can't return, but I can't wallow in sentiment now. I have a decision to make today. I want to do the right thing, but if I take the bull by the horns for revenge, then I'm not living worthy of my Christian beliefs. I won't ask Derek's advice. But I need Your direction in deciding what action to take.

Kennedy recalled one of God's promises that she'd relied on since the death of her father when she'd felt so inadequate to make decisions. She turned to the Thirty-second Psalm and found verse 8. " '*I will instruct you and teach you in the way you should go; I will counsel you and watch over you.*' "

She meditated on these words, trying to relate them to the visit she wanted to make to her grandfather. She didn't receive a definite *no* from God, and when the urge was still strong in her heart, she considered the promise God had made to David—also appropriate to her situation. She *would* go to see Gabriel Morgan. Remembering his treatment of her mother, she was afraid to see him, but Kennedy believed that God would be with her. She might never have approached him if she didn't suspect that he was the potential buyer for the ranch.

Kennedy would have preferred for Derek to know where she was going, but if he insisted that she shouldn't go, she would hesitate to go against his advice. She didn't want to stir up any more trouble for him, but she felt this was something she had to do. So she decided to make an effort to see her grandfather without telling anyone where she was going. But even as she reached the decision, she contemplated the wisdom of attempting this visit when no one knew where she was.

When she was ready to leave Riverside, she took the precaution of calling June to let her know that she was going into Valentine for a few hours.

Kennedy hadn't driven by the Morgan home since the day Derek had showed it to her. The gates were open, so she drove up the circular drive and stopped near the front portico. Panic like she'd never known before swept through her as she walked up the steps and clacked the old-fashioned knocker several times.

A woman with a stern expression, who was probably in her sixties, soon opened the door. Her speculative gaze rested on Kennedy, but she didn't speak.

Determined not to be intimidated by this woman, Kennedy said in a strong, cool voice, "I want to see Mr. Morgan."

"Do you have an appointment?" the woman asked.

"No, but I want to see him anyway," Kennedy said bluntly. "I'm Kennedy Blaine."

"Oh," the woman said, staring at Kennedy with obvious interest. "I'll check with Mr. Morgan," she added and closed the door.

Wondering what she would do if her grandfather refused to see her, Kennedy sat in one of the cushioned porch chairs and reflected on the numerous times her mother might have sat in this same spot. Momentarily, she missed her mother so much that tears misted her eyes. She swiped them away. This wasn't the time for melancholy.

The door opened behind her and Kennedy stood, again questioning what she would do if he refused to see her. But if Gabriel Morgan *was* the one trying to buy the Circle Cross, he was probably rubbing his hands in glee, thinking she'd been brought to her knees and had come to negotiate with him.

"You may come in," the woman said. Her voice was friendly, which encouraged Kennedy somewhat. "I'm Esther Holmes, Mr. Morgan's housekeeper."

"I'm glad to meet you, ma'am," Kennedy said.

With a sense of awe and some remorse, Kennedy stepped inside the house where her mother had once lived. She followed the middle-aged, gaunt woman down the hallway into a large, high-ceilinged room. The housekeeper closed the door behind her as she left the room.

A tall man with iron gray hair sat behind a massive walnut desk, staring at her from faded green eyes. He looked tough, sinewy, powerful. Although he was in his nineties, Morgan still had an overwhelming personality, for Kennedy sensed the strength of the man as soon as she entered the room. A mask of indifference covered what his feelings might have been as he stared at the granddaughter he'd never seen.

"Sit down," he said, motioning to a chair near his desk.

She shook her head. "I'll stand. This isn't a social call." Kennedy said, breathing a silent prayer of thanks that she didn't feel intimidated. "I want to know if you're the one who's responsible for the harassment I've had since I came to Valentine. Are you trying to buy the Circle Cross?"

Surprise lit Morgan's eyes for a moment, but his face was impassive again when he said, "Not that it's any of your business, but I did *not* make the offer. I wouldn't take the Circle Cross if you gave it to me. I don't want any property that once belonged to Alexander Blaine."

Strangely enough, Kennedy believed him. "Then," she persisted, "were you responsible for the slaughter of five Circle Cross cows yesterday with a warning not to place the ranch on the National Register?"

Morgan's mouth spread into a thin-lipped smile, and although

Kennedy had thought he might fly into a rage because of her accusations, his eyes registered a strange, indefinable emotion. Could it be pride?

"I'm not in the habit of explaining, or justifying, my actions to anyone, but I'll make allowances this one time. I had nothing to do with killing those animals. That's not the way I operate—but you'd better think twice before you tie up the Circle Cross by such a foolish move."

"I didn't come to ask for advice, thank you, only some information. I've learned what I need to know."

Kennedy turned to leave, when her grandfather's laughter stopped her in her tracks. She faced him again when he said, "You sound just like your mother did when she stood in that exact same spot and told me she was going to marry Kenneth Blaine and I could like it or lump it. You may have been born a Blaine, but you're a Morgan through and through."

Smiling in spite of herself, Kennedy nodded. "My dad told me that numerous times, and I've also been reminded of the fact since I came to Valentine."

Morgan stood up, and his vital power and self-confidence filled the room.

"You may not want any advice, but I'll give you some anyway. Smith Blaine is a crook, and he's probably cheated your father out of a lot of money. If you're going to keep the ranch, you'd better get rid of him."

"I've already fired him. From now on Derek Sterling will report to me."

He nodded approvingly. "Sterling is a good man."

She turned again toward the door but stopped suddenly when he said, "Did your mother ever forgive me?"

A tense stillness filled the room. Kennedy had come here expecting to dislike her grandfather. Instead she experienced a close filial connection to him, and she wished she could tell him what he obviously wanted to hear. Without turning, she said quietly, "No, she never did, and she passed the same loathing to me. I've tried to forgive you, but

I can't forget how lonely Mother was all of her life, wanting to return to Valentine and her family."

In a quiet voice he said, "If she had asked me to forgive her for marrying into a family I hated, I'd have relented."

Upon her deathbed, Grace Morgan Blaine had spoken of Nebraska, and Kennedy remembered anew the sadness on her face and in her voice during her last days. Facing her grandfather, she said, "Ah, but you see, it didn't work that way. She expected you to take the first step toward reconciliation. Remember, she was a Morgan, too!"

She turned on her heel, ran out of the room, down the hallway, and out of the house. Tears blinded her eyes as she left the estate grounds. She had never missed her mother more than she did at this moment.

* * * * *

Kennedy wanted Derek to know where she'd been before he learned it from another source, so she pulled into the ranch yard on her return. He was walking from the barn toward the house, and he came to meet her.

He started to open the door, but she forestalled him. "I'm not coming in, Derek, but you need to know where I've been this morning."

Looking up at him and hoping for understanding, she told every detail of her visit with Gabriel Morgan. He listened intently, and when she finished, he said, "I never did believe he was involved in what's going on out here. He's hardhanded and vicious sometimes, but whatever he does is always within the law."

"You aren't mad at me for going without telling you?" she pleaded.

Her hand was lying on the door, and he covered it with his warm fingers. His eyes were warm and gentle. "It was your decision to make, and I *wanted* you to see your grandfather. There are worse people in Cherry County than Gabriel Morgan. I'd give a lot if I had a grandfather to know, even one as ornery as yours."

"But we still don't have an answer as to who wants to buy the ranch and why," Kennedy said.

"I've been thinking that the quicker you complete your National Register plans and make it known that the Circle Cross is going to remain rangeland, your harassment might stop."

"According to Robin it's a slow process, and might not happen at all," Kennedy commented.

Tension spread across his face. "Just be careful until you can get a flight home."

"This is so frustrating to me. I thought I was settled for the rest of the summer. I want to stay here." When a grimace of pain crossed his face, she said, "I'm sorry. I know you wouldn't ask me to leave if it wasn't for my own good."

"I'm afraid for you, Kennedy. There's something wicked going on here, and I can cope with it better if I'm not worried about you all the time."

He whistled for Wilson. "I forgot to send him home with you last night."

When Wilson hopped into the car, Kennedy released the brake, saying, "Then I'll make arrangements to leave as soon as possible. But, Derek, I *am* coming back."

The expression on his face was unfathomable, so she didn't know if he wanted her to return to Nebraska. Had she been too pointed in her interest in Derek? Had she been pushing herself into his life? Perhaps his emotions hadn't been as deeply stirred as hers had been.

* * * * *

The next morning Kennedy walked to the door with Miranda and watched as she drove away. She took a broom from a cabinet and started sweeping the dust and cottonwood leaves that had accumulated near the gazebo.

She was thinking how much she would miss the ranch when Wilson started barking inside the house, and she suddenly had a feeling that somebody was standing behind her. Kennedy knew it was danger of some kind, for Derek would never slip up on her that way. She had started to turn when a strong arm grabbed her, and before she could cry out, a piece of duct tape was pasted over her mouth. A dark cloth was thrown over her head and her hands were tied behind her back.

Wilson's frantic barking echoed around the area, and Kennedy realized that she hadn't unhooked his leash yet. Hands fumbled at her waist, momentarily terrifying her until she realized that a rope was being tied around it.

A guttural male voice said, "Watch the steps." The man tugged on the rope. As she walked forward, a large hand held her arm as she eased her way carefully off the porch. Her captor walked close in front of her and Kennedy bumped into him, though he set a rapid pace. She lost all sense of direction, but she believed they must be walking through the woods because she occasionally bumped into solid objects that could only be trees. When she slowed down, the man tugged on the rope and jerked her forward.

Trees lined the Niobrara River along the trail she'd often ridden with Derek, so they might be heading in that direction. Once she got over her initial fright, Kennedy knew she must be alert to any opportunity to get away from this man. She was able to see slightly through the black hood. She made out the form of her captor. He was a man of medium height, but brawny. He seemed to be dark-skinned and with black hair, but the dark cloth over her face might have made him look that way.

Although she had dressed in slacks and a knit shirt when she'd gotten up, she hadn't put on any shoes. The terrycloth scuffs she wore provided little protection, and in a short time, Kennedy's feet were scratched and blistered. Her arms were numb from the tight string around them. It seemed as if they'd been walking for miles when her captor stopped suddenly and she bumped into him again. Unable to breath through her mouth, she inhaled deeply.

He stepped behind her and cut the cords that bound her hands, and she groaned when the blood started circulating through her arms. He continued walking, and when they started downhill, Kennedy realized why he had freed her hands. The ground was damp and slippery, and she could hear running water. They were crossing a stream—probably the Niobrara, but she was completely disoriented. When they reached the river, her feet flew out from under her, and she sat down in water that reached to her waist.

Her abductor snarled a curse and jerked Kennedy to her feet. She decided that there was a gravel bar at this point, for the water wasn't more than ankle deep as they crossed the river and climbed the opposite bank. Kennedy had lost her scuffs when she fell into the river, and walking across the rough terrain was torturous. She stifled a scream every time she stepped on a rock or a brier.

It seemed like hours had passed before a tall structure loomed before them. A door squeaked, and Kennedy was shoved into a building of some kind. It was dark inside, and she couldn't tell where they were. Without speaking, the man again tied her hands behind her back, took the rope from around her waist, and tied it to one of her legs. The interior of the building was pitch-black and she couldn't see anything, but she had a feeling that he was securing the other end of the rope to a large object. A door slammed. Kennedy listened intently. The only sound she heard was the whir of a windmill, and she knew instinctively that she was alone. Unable to stand any longer, she supported her back against a wall and slid to the floor.

Was this the kind of trouble Derek had feared for her? Was there any connection between her kidnapping and the man who'd come to the Circle Cross in a taxi a few weeks ago? Her kidnapper could easily have been that man. Since his arrival, Derek had been tense, morose, and burdened. Was he someone from Derek's past who was trying to get to Derek through her? Could that be the main reason he had insisted on her leaving Valentine?

Kennedy was still gagged, and she couldn't call for help. She had no idea what time it was or how long she'd been a captive. She was hungry and thirsty, and she wanted Derek. All during the long ordeal of plodding along, shackled to her captor, Kennedy had tried to keep from crying. But now she felt helpless; tears seeped from her eyes, and her nose started running. Without a tissue or handkerchief, all she could do was sniff.

Chapter Sixteen

....

Derek and Sam were saddling their horses near the stable when Wilson ran wildly through the pasture, scaling fences in giant leaps. The dog was dragging his leash, and when he jumped up on Derek, panting and drooling, Derek noticed at once that the rope had been chewed in two. Wilson looked into his face and barked loudly then turned and raced toward Riverside, pausing once to see if Derek was following him.

"Something has happened to Kennedy!" Derek shouted. He tossed his horse's bridle toward Sam and ran toward his truck.

"What's up?" Sam yelled back.

"I don't know."

"Want me to come with you?"

"No. Stay here until I find out what has happened."

He had expected to find Wilson at Riverside, but there was no sign of the dog. He rushed through the front door, which was hanging open, and called for Kennedy. Her bed hadn't been made, and the coffeepot was still warm. He shouted her name over and over, but there wasn't any answer.

He went outside and noticed the broom lying on the gazebo floor where Kennedy had probably left it. That's when he saw a note pasted to a porch column.

I'VE GOT HER, STERLING. DON'T CALL THE COPS!

"Oh, yeah, right," he muttered.

Lazaro! He should have alerted Sheriff Morgan days ago instead of trying to fight his enemy alone. Feeling as if he'd been sucker-punched,

Derek dropped into a chair and reached for his phone.

Fortunately, she answered on the first ring. "Sheriff, this is Derek. Kennedy Blaine has been kidnapped. I'm at Riverside, and I'll stay until you get here."

Derek felt as if he'd aged fifty years in the past fifteen minutes, and he slouched in the chair. Through the years he'd often mourned his youthful indiscretion—but never more than he did at this point. If the six months he'd strayed from the straight and narrow had brought disaster on Kennedy, he would never forgive himself.

God, don't make her pay for my sins. I love her more than my own life. I'll spend the rest of my life atoning for my sins if You will keep her safe.

But even as he prayed, Derek remembered that Jesus had atoned for the sins of all mankind. The supreme sacrifice had already been paid on Calvary more than two centuries ago. What God wanted from Derek Sterling was love, worship, and a committed life.

"You have it, God," Derek said. "I'm not bargaining anymore. No matter how this turns out, I'm going to serve You with my whole heart and life."

Now that his relationship with God had taken on new meaning, Derek found the strength to go out and meet the sheriff when he heard her cruiser approaching. He explained quickly what he knew about Kennedy's abduction.

Fastening her direct, brown-eyed gaze on him, the sheriff said tersely, "Anything else I should know?"

"Yes. Something I should have told you weeks ago."

He directed her to the gazebo where the sign was still in place.

"I grew up in Chicago and got mixed up with the wrong crowd. When I was a boy, I ran with a street gang for six months. I never got into drugs, but I was involved in several cases of petty theft. Lazaro, the leader of the gang, killed two cops. He tried to implicate me and some of the other boys in the crime, but there was no evidence against us. He was sentenced to prison for life with no chance of parole. Mom and Dad brought me to Nebraska, and you know I've lived straight since then."

The sheriff nodded.

"A few weeks ago, Lazaro showed up in Valentine. He came to the ranch pretending to be looking for work. I knew that was a sham—he wanted me to know he'd located me. I looked every place I could think of to find him, but Lazaro was always good at keeping himself hidden."

"Would this guy have mob connections?" Sheriff Morgan questioned.

"I'm sure of it, but I can't imagine how he got out of prison. He was sent up for life."

"Give me the facts, and I'll check him out," the sheriff said. She took notes as Derek told her all he knew about Lazaro. "I can soon find out if he's escaped from prison."

"I've been miserable, not knowing what to do and trying to protect Kennedy if he *was* responsible for her harassment. A week ago, I met him behind George's bar in Valentine. He told me that he'd been released from prison after he squealed on the rest of us who were involved in the murder. That's a lie; he did the job himself. The police records show that I wasn't involved, but if he's still trying to implicate me, I *may* be wanted for questioning in Chicago, even if it has been a long time since I was with the street gang."

Sheriff Morgan fixed him with her compelling eyes. "Better tell me all of it, and the sooner the better, for Kennedy's sake."

Derek took a deep breath and told her that Lazaro had somehow learned about Kennedy and that he had demanded that Derek get fifty thousand dollars from her so Lazaro could leave the country. "I refused, of course, but I've been worried about her ever since. She intended to go back to California in a few days. But she waited too long."

"Check to see if her car is here. Also, look around for any clues. I'm going to call the state troopers to get help in combing this county. I won't let some cheap crook cut up the peace of Cherry County."

The sheriff had opened the door of the cruiser when Derek noticed that Wilson was running across the field from the river. He was barking loudly, and when Derek started toward the dog, Wilson halted, barked again, turned, and ran the direction he'd come.

"Wait a minute," Derek said to the sheriff. "Kennedy is a favorite of Wilson's—he may have located her. I'll follow him."

The sheriff got out of the car and kept pace with Derek as they ran after Wilson. The dog stopped after a few yards to be sure they were following before he started running again. When he came to a ford in the Niobrara, Wilson jumped into the water. "Looks like he's heading toward Valentine," Derek said.

"I'll go back to the cruiser, cross the river, and keep in touch with you by phone." Turning, the sheriff said, "Be careful. If the convict did take her, he doesn't have anything to lose by killing someone who can identify him."

Derek nodded his understanding and plunged into the river, which brought him to the West Eighty. He thought Kennedy might be hidden in the unfinished conference center, but Wilson raced by the building without stopping. Derek panted for breath, wondering how much longer he could keep up this pace in his boots. When he reached the road, he vaulted over the gate and saw the sheriff's cruiser approaching.

When she stopped, Derek opened the door and nodded his thanks. Wilson stood waiting for them, but when the car eased close to him, he took off at a run. A mile down the road, he ducked under a fence and cut off across a Circle Cross pasture.

Derek groaned, but he got out of the squad car.

"I'm coming with you, Derek," the sheriff said, and she parked beside the road.

"There's a barn in this field where we store hay for emergencies when a blizzard hits the ranch," Derek said. "It's in a grove of trees, and the Circle Cross headquarters can be seen from that point. It would have been easy for Lazaro to hide there. We haven't been in this field for a month or so."

When they were within a few yards of the building, the sheriff laid her hand on Derek's arm and pulled him behind a large bale of hay.

"From now on, I'm in charge," she said. "You stay behind me and do what I tell you to do."

"No way! I'm responsible for this. I told Kennedy I'd look after her if she stayed here."

"Listen to me! Lazaro may be in the building with Kennedy. He's dangerous."

"But…" Derek began. The sheriff held up her hand.

"I can see your point, but Lazaro will be less apt to shoot *me*."

"He was sent to prison for killing two cops. One more won't matter to him."

The sheriff continued as if he hadn't spoken. "I have on a bullet-proof vest. I'm armed. You aren't. And even if you were, if you don't have a permit to carry a gun, you'd be in trouble if you shoot him. Stay behind me!"

Derek shrugged his shoulders in defeat. He knew the sheriff was right, but how could he stand by idly and allow Sheriff Morgan to risk her life for Kennedy? She was his responsibility.

Wilson was sniffing around the building, and the sheriff said, "Tie him up if you can't hold him any other way."

Derek whistled softly, and Wilson ran toward him. Derek cut a piece of twine from the bale of hay, connected it to the dog's collar, and tied him to a tree. When Wilson growled, Derek said, "Stop!" Wilson stared up at Derek with eager black eyes and whined piteously, but when Derek put a restraining hand on his head, the dog collapsed, panting, on the ground.

Unwillingly, Derek yielded to the sheriff's demands. He knew she was right, but he watched anxiously as she ran to one corner of the building and moved slowly toward the door. Staying undercover, she pushed the door inward. Derek held his breath, expecting a gunshot, but he didn't hear one. Moving quickly, the sheriff entered the building in one giant leap.

Derek crouched beside Wilson, agonizing over what was happening inside the barn. Although it seemed like a lifetime, it was probably less than five minutes before the sheriff stepped to the door and motioned for Derek to come.

"She's here alone and apparently all right. You take care of her, and I'll look around."

Derek thanked God that they had found her. Kennedy was tied to a wagon wheel. Derek rushed to her, dropped to his knees, and fumbled at the dirty tape on her mouth. His anger increased when he saw how the tape had bruised her lips. The joy in her eyes when he knelt beside her pierced his conscience. It was a miracle from God that she wasn't dead; he would have been responsible for it, yet she was glad to see him. Bitter tears blinded him as he worked to free her.

"Are you all right?" he asked as he removed the rope from her arms and wrists. She moved her lips, but she couldn't talk. By the time he freed her feet, she croaked, "Water."

"Just a minute. There's a windmill here. I'll bring some."

Sheriff Morgan entered the barn. "I've looked everywhere, and I can't find anyone else. Can she answer some questions?"

"She wants water. I'll get it."

A tin can filled with nails stood on a shelf. Derek emptied the nails and ran out of the building. He rinsed the can and filled it with water. He knew it wasn't sanitary, but there wasn't any other way to get water to her immediately. As he ran back to the barn with the water, Derek whispered, *Thank You, God, that she's still alive.*

When he returned to the building, Sheriff Morgan had helped Kennedy to stand, and she was hobbling a few steps. "Look how her feet are bruised!" the sheriff exclaimed. "Apparently she walked all the way from Riverside."

While Sheriff Morgan supported her, Derek lifted the can to Kennedy's mouth, and she gulped a few swallows. He wet his handkerchief and wiped her swollen lips and tear-streaked face. Giving him a tremulous smile, Kennedy lifted her hand and wiped the tears from his cheeks.

"I've called for backup," the sheriff reported. "I told my deputies to come through the field. As soon as they get here, you can take her back to the Circle Cross, but I want to find out what happened first."

After she swallowed some more water, Kennedy licked her lips. "I can talk now," she said hoarsely.

The sheriff nodded. "Let's take her outside, Derek. There's a bench she can sit on."

He lifted Kennedy in his arms, and she put her arm around his neck. Moving slowly, he lowered her to the bench.

"Just tell us what happened." Sheriff Morgan said. "Take your time."

Derek went to the water trough for another can of water, and Kennedy took a few swallows when he came back. While she talked, he knelt beside her and sponged her bare feet, gritting his teeth in anger when he saw the lacerations caused by the rough terrain she'd been forced to walk over.

Kennedy gripped her hands in her lap. "I got up soon after Miranda left, and then I went outside to sweep the porch. Somebody slipped up behind me and jerked my hands behind my back. I was surprised into silence at first, and before I could call out, he'd gagged and blindfolded me. I don't know who it was."

The time for complete honesty had come. "It was Lazaro, the man who came to the ranch a few weeks ago asking for work," Derek admitted—but he couldn't meet her eyes. "He left a note for me."

The sheriff's phone rang. While they waited for her, Derek untied Wilson and the dog rushed to Kennedy, jumping up on her and licking her face. Derek pulled him away, and the dog settled beside her, his head on his front two paws, soulfully gazing up into Kennedy's eyes. Derek sat down again and rested Kennedy's feet on his legs.

Lifting her hand to his lips, he said, "Did he molest you? I want the truth."

"Oh, no," she assured him at once, "nothing like that."

"What time was it when the guy showed up?" the sheriff asked when she finished her phone conversation.

"Miranda leaves between seven and eight. It was probably around half-past seven. What time is it now?"

Derek glanced at his watch. "One o'clock."

"I didn't think you'd find me that fast. Or if you'd ever find me."

"Wilson broke loose and ran to the ranch, and I knew something was wrong," Derek explained. "It's a good thing the front door was still open so he could leave the house, or we wouldn't have known yet."

A vehicle approached, and the sheriff went to meet her deputies.

"Why did the man kidnap me?" Kennedy asked.

Derek drew a deep breath. "I should have told you this before, but I hoped you would never have to know. Lazaro is a convict and was also the gang leader I ran with for six months when I lived in Chicago. When he was arrested for a double murder, he tried to prove that I was involved." He explained about the alibi that had exonerated him, his parents' move to Valentine to remove him from further danger, and Lazaro's recent demands for money from him. "I told him I didn't have that kind of money, but obviously he had found out that you're rich.

I'm guessing that he intended to hold you for ransom."

"Why didn't you tell me?" Kennedy said quickly. "I'd have given you the money in a heartbeat."

Derek, still holding Kennedy's hand, squeezed it as he said, "I know you would have, but I'm not that low-down. Don't you realize now that you must leave Nebraska and go back to California? He's a hardened criminal. You're not safe as long as he's running loose."

Sheriff Morgan joined them, and she had apparently heard what Derek said, for she nodded. "I agree with him, Kennedy. Until we capture Lazaro, you're in danger."

* * * * *

Noting Derek's haggard face and the pain in his eyes, Kennedy decided she wouldn't cause him further worry. But how could she bear to be in California not knowing what was happening to Derek? He wasn't safe in Nebraska either as long as Lazaro was out of jail.

"I'll go," she said.

"Good," the sheriff said. "My deputy will take you and Derek to Riverside, and the detective and I will check this building for fingerprints and any DNA possibilities. We need something to tie this crime to Lazaro."

Derek picked up Kennedy and deposited her gently in the police cruiser. "I'll start to the Omaha airport with her as soon as we can get ready."

Derek called June when the squad car left the barn. "Kennedy is all right, Mom, except for some bruised feet. Will you meet us at Riverside with some ointment for those injuries? I'm taking her to the airport today so she can leave for California." He briefly explained about Lazaro's appearance at the Circle Cross and his actions since then. His face was grim when he hung up.

"I'll be ready as soon as I shower and dress," Kennedy said. "I'll leave most everything here, except for what I can put in my carry-on bag. I'm leaving to keep from worrying you, but I'm coming back, Derek. I'm coming back."

"But not until Lazaro is captured," he said, and she agreed by nodding.

June was already at Kennedy's home when they arrived, and, without asking any questions, she helped Kennedy into the shower then massaged her feet and applied ointment to the places where the skin was broken.

"There aren't any deep cuts, but your feet will be sore for a few days. What shoes are you going to wear?"

"The white tennis shoes. They're a little big anyway, so they'll be the most comfortable. I'll wear my brown sweat suit and carry my red jacket."

Kennedy sat on the bed while June packed her overnight bag. "I'll be surprised if I can book a flight out of Omaha tonight, so put in a nightgown, slippers, and a change of underthings." When June closed the bag, Kennedy said, "Derek told me this morning about his connection with a street gang."

"I'm glad he did. I thought you should know, but it was his story to tell so I kept my mouth shut."

Looking directly at June, Kennedy said, "Learning about his past didn't make any difference to me. I love him for what he is today."

"And surely you know that I'd welcome you as a daughter-in-law."

"I'd like to be a member of your family, but it isn't going to happen. That doesn't mean that I won't be here often. Maybe if I'm underfoot every month or so, Derek's defenses will break."

"I hope so," June said sincerely, "but I don't hold much hope, either. Derek sets his life by strict principles, and he doesn't bend very easy."

"Tell me about it!" Kennedy said with uplifted eyebrows. "Will you call Miranda and tell her that I had to return to California temporarily? I hate to lose her, but if she gets an opportunity for another job, she should take it."

Derek had gone to change clothes for the trip, and Kennedy heard his truck returning. June was teary-eyed, and Kennedy said, "Don't start that. I'm trying my best to accept this without being babyish about it. But one sniffle out of you, and I'll break down completely."

Kennedy hugged June tightly. June swiped at her eyes and carried Kennedy's bag to the porch. Although she tried to walk without limping, each step was painful, and she couldn't imagine how sore her feet would be tomorrow. Although she protested, Derek swung her up into his arms.

"I'll stay behind to lock up the house," June said.

Derek shook his head. "You lock the doors and follow us back to the ranch. It might be dangerous for you to be alone, too."

"You shouldn't try to come home tonight," June suggested.

"I'll head back as soon as I see Kennedy off on the plane."

"Be sensible, Derek," June said. "You're already worn out. I can see it in your eyes and in the way you walk. Stay in Omaha. The sheriff is on the job."

"But I'm responsible for the Circle Cross. Lazaro has already killed some of our cows. Who knows what he'll do next?"

"June is right," Kennedy argued, adding lightly, "I'm sure the Circle Cross owner won't hold you responsible for anything that happens while you're taking her to safety."

"I know, but I'll be back before morning," he said. "If I get sleepy, I'll pull off the road and take a nap."

Kennedy rolled her eyes at June. "And he has the nerve to accuse me of being stubborn."

Derek watched until June got into her car before he left Riverside. Kennedy turned her head to look at the house, wondering when she would see it again. Once she had returned to California and settled into her normal routine, would the enchantment this place held for her fade into the background?

Chapter Seventeen

....

Derek was quiet as he pulled away from ranch headquarters and accessed the road that took them eastward on Rt. 20. After driving in silence for several miles, he took a deep breath and grinned at Kennedy. "I feel we're safe enough now, so I can relax."

"I suppose I should call and make plane reservations," Kennedy said.

"A good idea," he agreed. "The sooner the better."

They traveled several miles before Kennedy could connect to a satellite, and when she placed the call, she learned that they would arrive in Omaha too late to get a plane for the West Coast that evening. She booked passage on a flight leaving at nine o'clock the next morning.

"I'd better reserve a motel, too. Can you suggest one? I don't know anything about Omaha."

"There are some motels near the airport, but I don't remember the names. I wish you could have gotten a flight tonight. I don't like for you to be alone in a motel."

She laughed at him. "I'm used to being alone. You don't think Lazaro could follow me this far, do you?"

"He could if he wanted to, even if he had to steal a car to do it. But, no, I don't think he will. When he realizes that you've escaped and that the cops are after him, he'll head west away from Chicago. He told me he wanted money to go to South America. You'll be safe in Omaha, but I just figured you were a little upset about leaving and that you'd be lonely."

"I am upset about it; I don't want to go home. I'm leaving because I'll be a distraction to you if I'm at Riverside. I've already caused you enough trouble this summer."

With an unfathomable glance toward her, he said, "You've brought me more happiness than trouble, and if I were thinking about myself, I'd want you here all the time. I don't know how I'll get used to not seeing you or talking to you every day. But for your safety, you should go home."

Kennedy didn't answer, for she didn't think she could speak without crying, but she wondered if she would ever think of California as home again.

After a few miles she said, "I've been thinking about Matti Gray. Since I can't leave Omaha tonight, maybe we could get together with her for dinner before you start home."

"Of course!" he said. "I hadn't once thought about Matti. You can stay overnight with her."

"You're being ridiculous, Derek. I won't invite myself to stay with Matti. She lives in a small apartment. What time will we make it to Omaha?"

Glancing at his watch, he said, "Probably not until seven o'clock."

Kennedy shrugged her shoulders. "That might be too late for dinner, but I will call. I have her number."

She dialed, and when Matti answered, Kennedy explained that they were traveling toward Omaha so she could take a plane to California. "Derek and I will have dinner together before he returns to Valentine. Are you free to eat with us?"

"I'd love to. I know it hasn't been, but it seems like a long time since I've seen any of you. Tell me where you are and what time you'll get here."

"We're passing Bassett now." She turned to Derek. "How long before we reach Omaha?"

"Over two hours, I'd judge. We can call again when we're closer."

Kennedy told Matti what Derek had said, and Matti asked, "What time does your plane leave? I need to know whether to choose a restaurant with a buffet and quick service or one that takes more time."

"Derek is returning to Valentine tonight, but my plane doesn't leave until tomorrow morning. I plan to stay in a motel near the airport tonight."

"What?" Matti said. "You can overnight with me. The sofa in my living room makes a fine bed."

When Kennedy protested, Matti said, "I *want* you to stay with me. My apartment is only fifteen minutes from the airport, and I can take you to catch your plane before I go to work. Please! It's as much for me as it is for you. It would make my day."

Laughing, Kennedy said, "All right. You've talked me into it."

"Tell her I plan to come into town on US 73," Derek said, "so I'd be close to a bridge that crosses the Missouri to the airport. She can choose a restaurant that's best for her."

When Matti heard their route, she said, "I'll meet you where Rt. 73 crosses Ames Avenue and becomes Thirtieth Street." She named a convenient restaurant. "I drive a blue PT cruiser, so look for it in the parking lot, but if you don't see it, call and we'll soon find each other."

"By the way, Matti, we left Valentine unexpectedly, and I didn't have time to tell anyone good-bye. I doubt if Tony knows I'm gone, so if he calls, don't tell him that I'm leaving. I'll fill you in on the details and then you can let him know."

Kennedy said good-bye and put the phone in her purse, wondering what else they needed to talk about before they met Matti.

"While you were talking to Matti," Derek said, "I've been thinking that we don't want anyone else in Valentine to know that you're leaving. Until you're on the plane, I'd just as soon no one else knows what you're doing."

As they continued the drive into Omaha, Derek and Kennedy discussed what they were at liberty to tell Matti and what they shouldn't. But much of the time they drove without speaking. Derek kept his eyes on the highway, so Kennedy couldn't see his eyes, but his facial expression was somber and concerned. After they drove in silence for several miles, his tight expression relaxed into a smile, and he asked her, "Do your feet hurt?"

"Not as bad as they did before your mother put medication on them. I'm sure it will be painful to walk."

"If it won't hurt your feet to move, I'd like for you to sit closer to me," Derek said.

Kennedy scooted across the seat without putting much pressure on her feet, but no amount of pain would have kept her from accepting that invitation. There didn't seem to be much to say, but as long as they were on rural roads, Derek held her hand. When they drove into the crowded streets of Omaha and he put both hands on the steering wheel, she slipped her arm around his waist.

Derek followed Matti's directions easily. They soon spotted the restaurant she'd mentioned and met her without any delay. Perhaps noticing how painful it was for her to walk into the restaurant, Derek insisted on filling her plate from the buffet. They'd eaten together so often during the summer that he had a good idea of what foods she liked. As they ate, Kennedy and Derek filled Matti in on the basics of Kennedy's abduction without mentioning anything that would impair the sheriff's investigation.

All too soon for Kennedy they finished dinner, and it was time for Derek to leave. He took her carry-on bag out of his truck and put it on the backseat of Matti's car, while Matti held Kennedy's arm as she hobbled to the parking lot. Perhaps feeling that Derek and Kennedy needed some privacy, Matti got into the car and closed the door.

Kennedy moved close to Derek, hoping he'd make the first move in saying good-bye. If he didn't, she intended to.

"Have a safe trip," he said and turned away. But Kennedy had seen tears in his eyes, and she caught his arm. When he moved toward her, she put her arms around his waist.

"Thanks for everything this summer, Derek. Please call me as often as you can to let me know what's going on. I miss you already."

His defenses must have collapsed for he pulled her close, and when she leaned her head on his chest, the rapid beating of his heart sounded like a drum in her ear. He released a long, audible breath. "Don't think this is easy for me, Kennedy, or that I won't miss you," he said in a husky whisper. "But once you're back in California with your other friends, you'll have a chance to look at our relationship more closely. You'll see that this is for the best."

He released her gently, kissed her lightly on the lips, and stepped quickly into the truck as though he couldn't trust himself to stay any longer. She watched until he left the parking lot and disappeared in the heavy traffic.

Kennedy opened the door and slid into the seat beside Matti, but she couldn't hold her tears any longer. She lowered her head into her hands and sobbed.

"Cry all you want to," Matti said, starting the car and exiting the parking lot into the stream of traffic. "It's hard falling in love with the wrong man. I know from firsthand experience, although our situations are reversed. In my case, I was the one inferior to a Morgan, and I suffered because of it. But if this is any consolation to you, even in my blackest moments I've never been sorry that I loved Tony with a love that wouldn't die."

Still sniffing, Kennedy pulled a tissue from her purse and blew her nose. "But it's all worked out for the best now. You and Tony can finally be together."

"And I have faith that you and Derek will work out your differences, too. But Tony and I aren't over the hurdle yet. I don't know how his grandfather will react when I show up in Valentine. Since Tony and I won't get married until Valentine's Day, I'll have to get a job, and Gabriel Morgan still has enough clout to keep me from finding one in Cherry County.

* * * * *

Matti lived in a large residential complex, and although the rooms were small, it was a cozy apartment. "I'll brew some chamomile tea and we can have some 'girl talk.' "

"I want to soak my feet in hot water while we talk. They aren't as sore as they were this morning, but I have to be able to walk better tomorrow."

"Don't worry about it. You can always ask for a wheelchair," Matti said. "While you change in the bedroom, I'll make your bed. I'll fill a big pan with water and you can soak your feet while we drink tea."

The tea was relaxing and the hot water soothed Kennedy's feet while they talked about Matti's work and her projected move to Valentine. For the time being Kennedy was able to forget the horror of her kidnapping and the fears she had about her uncertain future with Derek.

"Tell me when you want to go to bed," Matti said as Kennedy stifled a yawn. "You'll have a long day tomorrow."

"Normally I'd need to be at the airport two hours before departure, but since I don't have any luggage to check, I think that if we leave here at half past seven, we'll be all right."

"I'll fix some coffee and toast before we leave."

"Don't bother with breakfast for me. I'll have time on my hands before the plane takes off, and I'll eat at the airport." Kennedy paused thoughtfully. "I've been thinking about a solution to your job problem in Valentine."

She briefly explained her tentative plans to turn the West Eighty into a conference center. "I won't know whether this is feasible or not until I talk with my attorney, but do you have enough experience to spearhead a preliminary survey in Nebraska and neighboring states to see if there's a need or interest in a Christian conference center?"

"I don't know," Matti said, "but I might be able to do it. I'll pray about it."

"I've been praying about establishing the center, too. Derek thinks it's all right, but my attorney may throw cold water on the idea. Preparation of a survey would take several weeks, and I'll be paying someone to do it, so it might be a good opportunity for you. I've mentioned my idea to Tony, because I'd want him on the Board of Directors if we decide to organize a corporation. I don't know how long it will take to get this project up and running, but it would be nice if we could have a partial program in place by next summer."

Matti's eyes brightened at the prospect of finding employment so easily, and when her own love affair was in such turmoil, Kennedy was pleased to think that she might have this opportunity to help Tony and Matti.

* * * * *

Intense misery and desolation swept over Kennedy as the big jet hovered over the Los Angeles airport, hit the runway, and taxied to the terminal. Unwilling to talk to anyone, she had arranged to travel first-class, and most of the way she had reclined in her seat with her eyes closed to avoid conversation with her seatmate. Her heart ached with pain, and she yearned for Derek until she felt physically ill.

This was the first time she'd been away since her father's death, and upon her return she felt his death more keenly than she had before she went to Valentine. Kennedy had called Rosita before she left Omaha and told her that she was returning to Los Angeles. She knew the housekeeper would be waiting for her, but she still had an empty feeling. Her feet were better, but she arranged for transport to a cab stand.

She couldn't wait any longer to find out what was going on in Valentine. She especially feared that Lazaro would harm Derek because he'd rescued her. She dreaded to call, but the suspense was unbearable.

While the taxi whizzed in and out of traffic, she dialed the home phone at the Circle Cross. June answered.

"Hi," Kennedy said. "I've arrived safely in California, and I'm in a taxi on my way home. What's going on?"

"No news about Lazaro, as far as we know. The sheriff has ordered Derek to stay out of the manhunt, and he's angry about it. But he and the men are on constant guard to be sure Lazaro doesn't cause any damage to the ranch. Al's staying at Riverside, and Derek, Sam, and Joel are patrolling here."

"You can tell Derek I got home all right. He can call when he has time."

"We miss you, Kennedy," June said.

"I miss you back, but it seemed to be the right thing for me to do."

June agreed, closing the conversation with, "I'll tell Derek you called."

When the taxi stopped in front of her home, the front door swung open and Rosita waved to her from the step. Kennedy paid the taxi driver, thanked him, and limped up the sidewalk.

"Welcome home, Miss Kennedy," Rosita said as she took the suitcase and helped Kennedy into the house. She hugged her again and again and cried over her before Kennedy could sit down.

Wringing her hands, Rosita wailed, "What have you done to yourself? You can't walk, your hair is too long, your skin is as brown as mine, and you look old. You're not my little girl anymore. What has happened?"

Laughing, Kennedy said, "I've been living on a ranch for all summer. It's aged me."

"Oh, mercy me! Let me fix you something to eat."

"I'm not hungry. I need a soaking bath and some rest more than anything else. We can have dinner at the usual time."

"You seem different," Rosita said. "Oh, by the way, Steve Martin is back from Europe, and he's called two or three times to see when you would be home."

Just the news I need to hear, Kennedy thought. She had hoped that Steve would have taken her e-mail message as final, but she should have known he wouldn't. He was persistent—a good trait for a lawyer—but she didn't have any answers for the questions she knew he'd be asking. She wished he would leave her alone.

The next morning, Kennedy called her attorney and made an appointment, telling his secretary, "And I need at least an hour. I have several things to discuss."

"Then it will have to be next week. I'll tell him you called, and he may find an earlier time for you."

She called a few of her close friends and made luncheon dates for the following week. And since Rosita had been so shocked at her appearance, she made an appointment at a beauty salon for a haircut and a facial. Not that she was displeased with her appearance, but she didn't want her friends asking questions she couldn't answer.

* * * * *

It was late the following day before Derek called. "Sorry I didn't call sooner, but I didn't have any news. The sheriff and state troopers combed Cherry County and couldn't find Lazaro. He was finally caught in southern Colorado and is on his way back to prison. Hopefully this is the last we'll hear about him."

"Then I wasn't in danger after all."

"No, and I'm sorry I insisted that you leave. I've made a lot of poor decisions, Kennedy."

She could tell that he was in low spirits, so she said as cheerfully as she could, "All of us have. Don't beat yourself up about it. I had a good visit with Matti and talked to her about helping out with the conference center if we decide to go with it. She's interested."

"How are your feet?"

"Still tender, but they're getting better. What's Wilson doing?"

"Moping around like he's lost his best friend. He misses you."

Kennedy's throat tightened, and she couldn't answer. They chatted for several minutes, but she felt as if she were talking to a stranger, for they didn't say any of the things that really mattered.

She lay on her bed for a long time, dry-eyed, staring at the ceiling. She had disregarded her Morgan pride all summer, but there were limits as to how much she'd humble herself. Although she might change her mind, at this point she was determined she wouldn't return to Valentine until Derek asked her to.

The next morning she got out of bed with new resolve. She would take up her life as if the interlude in Nebraska hadn't occurred. She would finish preparations to take the bar exam in October. She'd worked too many years to become an attorney not to follow it through to the end. Whatever her future with Derek, she intended to become qualified to practice law in California.

Mr. Talbot's secretary called and told her that he could see her at two o'clock the next day. She was glad she had made the appointment at the beauty salon, for she didn't want the lawyer to be as shocked at the change in her as Rosita had been. And after spending two hours in the beauty shop, she thought Mr. Talbot wouldn't be. But when she glanced in the mirror after her hairdresser had styled her hair to look as it had when she left California, Kennedy knew instinctively that it was the expression in her eyes that had changed, not her outward appearance.

Resigned to a quizzing by Mr. Talbot, she drove to his office in time for her appointment. When she walked into his spacious office, he stood and gave her a tight hug as he'd done since she was a child and had come to the office with her parents. If she seemed different to him, he didn't comment.

"Thanks for seeing me so soon," Kennedy said, as she sat across the desk from him. "Besides receiving a report on Dad's affairs, there are several new matters I need to discuss with you. But let's take care of the estate first."

"All is in order, and we'll have the final papers ready for you to sign soon. From our previous conversations, I understand that you want to retain me as your father did."

"Oh, yes. I'd be lost without you."

"Very well. I'll represent you to the best of my ability, just as I did for Kenneth." He handed her a large file of documents. "These are copies of the papers you will have to sign. Take them home and study them closely. I will answer any questions or make any changes you want before we close."

"What have you concluded about Smith Blaine's embezzlement?"

"I've reported him to the IRS and suggested that they make an audit of all of his clients' accounts. By the way, your new manager must be on top of things—that accounting system of his is excellent."

Kennedy felt her face flushing, but she said, "He's very competent. His father managed the Circle Cross for several years, and Derek spent his teenage years on the ranch. I told Smith I didn't need him any longer."

"Good. We can have another meeting whenever you've finished looking over those papers, but what can I do for you today?"

"You received the handwritten copy of my will, I'm assuming, but I want you to draft a new document so we can have it witnessed and notarized. The one I sent was just an emergency measure."

"As your attorney and friend who had advised you to make a will as soon as your father died, should I know why you felt pressured to make that will and send it to me in the manner you did? Even without knowing what the contents were, I don't mind telling you that receiving it disturbed me considerably."

"It would take hours to tell you all that's happened this summer, but I suddenly realized that my closest living relative is my maternal grandfather, Gabriel Morgan. You've heard of him?"

With a slight grimace, Talbot nodded. "Your father was my close friend. I've known for years about the way he rejected your mother."

"When I realized that, if I should die, he would inherit the Blaine property, I had to make sure that didn't happen. I'll tell you more later, but there were times this summer when it seemed likely I might be killed. That problem is solved now. Will you take time to read the will I sent to you? If it is valid enough to prevent Gabriel Morgan from getting Dad's money and the Circle Cross, we won't make any changes now. However, as soon as you have time, I want your advice on how I should handle what I've inherited, and then you can write a new will."

Talbot called his secretary on the intercom and asked her to bring Kennedy's file from the safe. Kennedy watched his face carefully as he read the document.

His eyebrows arched inquiringly when he finished. "In the event of your untimely death, you can be assured that your grandfather won't get anything from you, but there *are* better ways of handling your bequests. I'll gladly advise you on how that can be done. I'll give it some thought, and we'll set up a date in a few weeks to discuss your options. You bequeathed the Circle Cross to Derek Sterling. Do you want that to remain in the new will?"

Kennedy shook her head. "No. I want you to take any necessary steps to *give* the ranch to him now."

It took a lot to surprise Elliott Talbot, and Kennedy smiled at the stunned look on his face. When he was able to speak, he said, "Give? Not sell?"

"*Give* it to him. He doesn't have any money and would never make enough to buy the Circle Cross, but he loves the land, and I want him to have the ranch now while he's young enough to enjoy it. I will keep the Blaine home, Riverside, and a parcel of land known as the West Eighty."

"Does Derek know you're doing this?"

"No, and I don't want him to know until all the paperwork is done. That's legal, isn't it?"

"Yes, but highly unorthodox."

"I know, but I won't keep the ranch unless he operates it, and I won't reward his hard work with nothing but wages. And since you're too much of a gentleman to ask, I'll tell you that I fell head over heels in love with him, and he could have *me* and everything I have if he'd ask. He loves me, too, but he's poor, an adopted kid who knows nothing about his background, and full of pride. He thinks he isn't good enough for me and I don't know how to change his mind, but I haven't given him up yet."

Obviously concerned, Talbot said, "I hope you know what you're doing,"

"I do. Dad always said that the Circle Cross was the least of his investments, and you know I'll have enough to live on for the rest of my life without the ranch. If I can't have Derek I don't want anyone else, and I won't marry someone I don't love just to have children to inherit my estate. I'll be more content if I know that Derek has the Circle Cross, regardless of what happens to me. It will be his decision whether he wants to continue with my plans to register the ranch with the NRHP. I think he'll want to because he encouraged me to investigate the possibility. I haven't filed any papers yet."

"What if he takes the ranch and marries someone else?" Talbot questioned. "Has that occurred to you?"

Kennedy took a deep breath. "It would break my heart. Not for losing the ranch, but for losing him."

Talbot threw up his hands in defeat and looked at his watch. "Is there anything else?"

Perhaps this isn't a good time to tell him what I want to do with the West Eighty, Kennedy thought humorously, *or he might take measures to have me committed.*

"Yes, there is, but I've already used my appointment time, so I'll wait until you've taken care of all we've discussed today. I'll go over the papers you've given me and call you about them soon. You can take your time in preparing everything else. I'm intending to take my bar exams in October, but in the meantime I may get a job to keep me occupied. I have too much time on my hands."

"I can help you with the bar exam," Talbot said, "so write down any questions you have. I'll drop by the house some Saturday and give you pointers on what you should review. And you know you wouldn't have to look far to find a job," he said with a smile. "I'd take you in as a partner anytime."

"That's good to know, and I may take you up on the offer. I'm too emotionally unsettled to make decisions like that now."

* * * * *

Now that Lazaro had been apprehended and everything seemed to be going well at the Circle Cross, Kennedy didn't have any probable reason to contact Derek. How many days should pass before she should call him? To keep her mind off Valentine and all the summer memories, she spent the next three days at the university in the law library reviewing some of the courses she had taken in her early college years. One minute she was elated over the many things she remembered only to groan inwardly about facts that she'd completely forgotten. It would have been difficult enough to prepare if she didn't have the added complication of Derek and the ranch intruding into her thoughts.

On the third day, she closed her briefcase and left the library determined that she would call Derek as soon as she got home. Maybe if she could just hear his voice it would be enough. In the parking lot near her car, she heard someone call.

"Kennedy!"

Oh, great! Just what I need, she thought. She turned to greet Steve Martin, who was hurrying toward her. Steve was slender rather than tall, and Kennedy couldn't help but compare him to Derek's powerful figure. However, Steve was a handsome man with fair features and blond hair, and Kennedy had always liked him.

"Hey, Kennedy. When did you come home?"

"About a week ago."

"I told Rosita to have you call me."

"She gave me the message, but I've been busy. And, really, I didn't think we had much to say to one another."

"Why not? Even if you don't want to marry me, we can still be friends. Besides, I didn't take that as a final answer."

"Read my lips, Steve. It was a final answer."

He shrugged his shoulders, and Kennedy wasn't sure if he took her words seriously. "Are you going up for the bar exam in October?" he asked.

"I intend to. I studied some while I was in Nebraska, and this is my third day here in the library. I didn't realize how much I'd forgotten."

"My mind was completely off my profession while I toured Europe this summer, too, so I also have a lot of work to do. Why don't we study together?"

She shook her head, at first thinking it was a bad idea, but then reconsidered. Why not? Steve didn't seem to be demanding anything of her. "I'm always running into things I don't remember, so we might help each other," she admitted. "We've studied together for the past two years. If we do this, it will be strictly on a colleague basis—nothing more. But let me think about it. I'll call you." She opened the car door and stepped inside. "Are you leaving now, too?"

"No. I have a job, so I have to study on weekends and at night."

"I'll be in touch soon."

* * * * *

Pride has its disadvantages, she thought, as she held the phone in her hands for fifteen or twenty minutes, trying to decide whether she should call. But Derek had his pride, too. She did have some important news to tell him, so using that as an excuse, in the end she dialed his cell number.

"Hello," she said, when he answered his phone on the first ring.

"Is this a bad time to call?"

"Nope! I'm sitting on the porch resting before supper. How are you?"

"Busy. I've been at the university library for the past three days, and my mind is overworked."

"What you need is a moonlight ride along the Niobrara River."

If that was his way of telling her he wanted her to return to Nebraska, he would have to do better than that. "It's too far away for me to do that tonight, so I'll have to pass up the offer. How are you, Derek?"

"All right. But I've been out in a hot wind all day, and I'm tired. Mom and I saw Tony at church on Sunday, and he asked about you."

"I'll call him one of these days." She paused briefly. "Tell me everything you've been doing on the ranch."

"One of us checks on Riverside every day, and it's all right. Mom has been canning tomatoes she bought at the market in Valentine. She made an apple pie today."

"Eat a piece for me, will you? Rosita makes delicious desserts, but she can't match June's pies. And, by the way, the mystery of who wants the Circle Cross has been solved. Mr. Talbot received a letter yesterday from a real estate agency in Denver—they wanted to buy the ranch for a development of an upscale vacation area, expensive homes, and a golf club."

"And?" he asked, with a hint of concern in his voice.

"Mr. Talbot told them that the ranch wasn't for sale."

"Then I guess all of our summer mysteries are solved," Derek said.

"Smith has admitted that he was responsible for the warning notices you received. It seems that he would have made a sizable percentage of money from the sale of the ranch, and his greed made him desperate for you to sell it. He denies killing the cattle, but that crime is still being investigated. The sheriff is almost certain it was Lazaro."

"But what about the NRHP sign they found by the cows?" Kennedy asked.

"They think Lazaro must have found one of Smith's signs and put it there to deflect attention from himself."

Although they talked for a half hour, when Kennedy hung up, she felt empty and unhappy. If she was wise, she wouldn't call him again and instead build a life that didn't include him. But her wisdom had flown out the window the day she met Derek Sterling.

* * * * *

What a difference a month can make, Derek thought, as he cantered along the trail paralleling the Niobrara River on his way to Riverside. It was the last week of September. The leaves of the elm and cottonwood trees were quickly taking on their fall colors, helped along by two nights of frost. Some of the songbirds had already migrated.

It was a month today since he'd taken Kennedy to the airport. He'd wished more than once in the past three weeks that he'd had more faith that she would be safe in Nebraska and hadn't insisted that she leave the state. But he'd been needling her to return to California almost from the day she came to the Circle Cross. He had no one to blame except himself that she wasn't here beside him.

Their few phone conversations hadn't been very satisfactory, for she hadn't once mentioned returning to Nebraska. He rounded the bend and Riverside was before him, looking as it had the day she'd left.

With autumn upon them, he knew he should store the porch furniture, but he didn't want to admit that Kennedy wouldn't show up some day as unexpectedly as she had the first time. Derek had hoped, with the apprehension of Lazaro and Smith Blaine's financial problems keeping *him* occupied, that Kennedy would return to Nebraska. He tied his horse to the hitching post that had probably been in front of the house when it was built. He looked at the front door almost expecting Kennedy to come to greet him as she had so often. A feeling of desolation swept over him when he knew that wouldn't happen today.

His feet seemed as heavy as lead as he climbed the steps to the gazebo and stretched out on the lounge. He closed his eyes and felt as if he could smell the roselike fragrance that always surrounded Kennedy. If only he could hear her voice. But it had been a week since they'd talked, and he'd called her then. He thought she should call him this time.

As he daydreamed, his cell phone rang, and he quickly took it from his pocket expecting to hear Kennedy's voice.

He heard his mother's voice instead. "I'm just checking to see what time you'll be in for supper," June said. "I'm grilling T-bones, and I don't want to start them until I know where you are."

"I'm at Riverside, Mom. Give me a half hour and I'll be home."

Why had he been so sure the call was from Kennedy? Was it wishful thinking?

With the phone still in his hand, he sat up. If he wanted to talk to Kennedy, why didn't he stop acting like a teenager and call her? He walked through the house, found that everything was all right, and locked the house behind him. He activated the alarm system that Kennedy had asked him to install and sat down on the top step of the porch.

It would be mid-afternoon in Los Angeles. He dialed her number.

"Blaine residence," a man's deep voice said.

Derek was stunned into silence for a few minutes. He would have

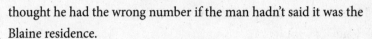

thought he had the wrong number if the man hadn't said it was the Blaine residence.

"Hello?" the deep voice prompted.

"Is Kennedy there?"

"Wait a sec. She's out on the patio with Rosita. I'll call her."

Derek considered hanging up, but he knew he shouldn't jump to the wrong conclusions. There could be numerous reasons why a man would be in the house.

Kennedy's voice soon answered. "Hello."

"This is Derek. If this is a bad time, you can call back."

"Oh, no," she said with a lilt in her voice that convinced him she was glad he'd called. "I can talk now. What's new?"

"I've just checked out Riverside, and I thought I'd report that everything is all right. The new security system you ordered is working well. We've tested it, and we get a warning at the ranch if anybody is messing around."

"What have you been doing today?" she asked, and he told her, all the while wondering who had answered the phone.

"Right now I'm sitting on the steps at Riverside looking toward the river, where I see plenty of fall colors. What have you been doing?"

"Oh, Derek, you make me homesick. I wanted to see the autumn leaves. But to answer your question, I had an appointment with Mr. Talbot this morning, and we're finally getting Dad's affairs settled. This afternoon I've been reviewing court cases. Steve, a friend from law school, and I are working together. Mr. Talbot is coming to the house shortly to counsel both of us."

"Is this the Steve who wanted to marry you?" he asked hesitantly.

"Yes, but he's okay with my refusal. I think he realizes, too, that we're only friends and will probably always be. It takes more than friendship to have a happy marriage."

"I guess so. I try to picture you in your home, but I just can't get a clear picture of what it's like."

"Then why don't you come to see me? I'd love to show you around this area. You can't imagine how beautiful the Pacific Ocean is."

"Thanks, but I can't manage the Circle Cross in California."

"I'm sure that the guys can handle everything for a little while," she insisted.

It distressed Derek that she didn't give any indication of when she planned to come back to Nebraska. "Maybe, but I can't get away right now. I won't bother you anymore. Go ahead and study."

Ending the conversation and wishing he hadn't called her, Derek vaulted into the saddle and headed for home.

Chapter Eighteen

....

Kennedy turned off the phone and left the bedroom where she'd gone to talk to Derek. Steve didn't know about her interest in Derek, and she didn't want him to know. If he did, he'd ask too many questions.

"Sorry to keep you waiting. That was the manager of the Circle Cross reporting in."

By a sheer force of willpower Kennedy focused on the advice and instruction Mr. Talbot gave them over a three-hour period while she made notes on her laptop. Once she closed the door behind the lawyer and Steve, her thoughts returned to Derek, remembering how often through the spring and summer they'd sat on the porch together. Wasn't it time for her to swallow her pride and admit that she'd never be happy at any other place but the Circle Cross?

During the meeting with Mr. Talbot this morning, she had signed the necessary papers to transfer the Circle Cross to Derek. By now, the documents were probably on their way eastward by special delivery. It was possible that Derek would receive them tomorrow or at least the day after that. What would he do? She had a feeling he would call, refusing to accept the ranch. She was convinced he would be angry. June might be able to reason with him, but she wouldn't say anything to his mother until she heard Derek's reaction.

A week passed and Kennedy didn't hear from Derek. When he didn't call, she haunted the Internet, expecting an e-mail from him. Her sleep was troubled with dreams about the Circle Cross. Rosita scolded her for not eating.

Wasting time when she should have been working, she sat in her father's office and stared at the painting of Riverside, imagining Derek sitting on the porch steps. It was the first week of October, and surely by now he'd received the deed to the Circle Cross. She had expected him to call as soon as he received it, if for no other reason than to bawl her out for what she'd done. Although she had believed his appearance and personality had been etched into her heart with an indelible pen, there were times when his features blurred in her thoughts. If only she had a picture of him it would be more bearable, but she hadn't taken a camera with her to Valentine.

Rosita served Sunday luncheon on the covered patio area, which had been designed and maintained by Grace Blaine until her death. Although she didn't love flowers as much as her mother did, Kennedy had tried to preserve the area. A half-canopy of native California evergreen trees shaded most of the garden, with just enough sunlight to nurture the plants her mother had planted.

After they'd eaten, Kennedy said, "Rosita, I'll take care of cleaning up. You can have the rest of the day off. Go visit your sister. I'll fix a salad for supper."

"Thanks," the housekeeper said. "I'll go visiting, but not before I load the dishwasher and tidy up the kitchen. You look like something the cat dragged in. You need to rest. And don't let me come home and find you with your nose in a law book. I don't know what happened to you out there in Nebraska, but I'm worried about you."

Taking Rosita's advice, Kennedy strolled around the garden. She lifted a heart-shaped petal of wild ginger and sniffed the faint, spicy smell. Carefully lifting the leaves of a patch of wild strawberries, she picked a handful of the rich, sweet fruit and nibbled on them, listening to the singing of the orioles, mockingbirds, and finches in the trees above her head. The birdsongs only increased her melancholy and caused her to remember the robins and cardinals she'd heard in Nebraska. Were the meadowlarks still singing along the Niobrara, or did they stop singing in the fall? She had picked a rose and was holding it to her nose when she heard a step on the patio's tile floor.

"Rosita, the new rose you planted this spring smells as sweet as perfume. Have you noticed?"

Suddenly the air seemed to be charged with electricity, and Kennedy knew before she even turned around. Derek stood behind her, the top of his hat grazing the patio's awning. Kennedy was stunned at first, and she couldn't speak or move. Her eyes moved from the scowl on his face to the brown envelope he held. It was undoubtedly the deed to the Circle Cross.

He slammed the envelope down on the table. "Just what are you thinking? Have you lost your mind?"

She wasn't intimidated by his attitude—she'd half expected it—and it was enough that she was with him again. Uttering a glad cry, Kennedy quickly closed the short distance between them, wrapped her arms around his waist, and leaned against him.

"Oh, Derek, I love you so much, and I've missed you more than you can ever imagine."

For a few moments his body remained rigid, unyielding, but suddenly he drew her into an embrace that almost took her breath. Her heart pounded an uneven rhythm as his hands caressed her back and he whispered her name over and over into her hair. She leaned back and raised herself to meet his kiss, which caused her pulse to swirl with excitement.

When he released her lips, he kissed her forehead, whispering, "This is crazy—just what I never intended to do."

"It is *not* crazy," she said, and happiness filled her heart. "This is what we should have done weeks ago. Oh, Derek, I've been miserable not being with you. I've dreamed about you, and when I turned around and saw you here with me, I felt like I'd died and gone to heaven. When did you get to Los Angeles?"

"I came straight here from the airport to straighten you out about that deed, and I end up kissing you."

Kennedy stretched upward and brushed a gentle kiss across his lips. "Let's go inside—it's getting hot out here. You can meet Rosita, and then we'll talk."

"I met Rosita as she was leaving the house. She wasn't too keen on letting me inside until I convinced her of who I am. She looked me up and down and said, 'So I suppose you're the one who's breaking her heart. I knew she was lovesick. She's been moping around ever since she came home, but I couldn't get a word out of her.' She told me how to get to the patio and left."

"Have you had your lunch? I can fix you a sandwich."

"I am hungry," he said, "but I was so mad at you that I couldn't eat until I found you and told you off."

"You sure have," Kennedy said with a laugh, leaning against him, and his right arm came around to circle her waist. "You can tell me off like this anytime." She was deliriously happy, and she couldn't erase the smile from her face as she took his hand and led him into the kitchen.

"Tell me about your flight," she said, as she opened the refrigerator and found ham, cheese, and condiments for sandwiches. He perched on a barstool while she made two sandwiches and poured tea over a glass of ice.

"This was my first plane trip, but it won't be the last. I liked every minute of it. I had a window seat, and I got a whole new conception of the beauty of God's world and how He'd created it. The Rockies are awesome."

"How're June and Wilson?"

"Both of them miss you, but they're all right." He added with a mischievous smile, "Life has been downright dull since you left Valentine. The crime wave has disappeared, and everything is peaceful. You gave us an exciting summer."

She sat across from him while he ate. Every time their gazes met, her heart pounded. The two sandwiches disappeared quickly, and she gave him a large portion of the frozen ice-cream cake dessert that Rosita had served at noon.

After he finished his dessert she poured two cups of coffee, and he filled her in on all of the news of Valentine and the people she knew. "I'm not sure what Smith Blaine is doing now. I hear he's spending a lot of time with his lawyer," Derek said.

"I don't intend to press charges against him, if he pays back the money he stole from the ranch." Standing, Kennedy said, "Do you want anything else to eat?"

After he assured her that he didn't, she put the few dishes in the dishwasher. "You want to look at the rest of the house?" she queried.

"Sure do," Derek said. "I want to learn everything about your California life."

She held his hand when she took him on a tour of her home. "Houses here aren't like midwestern dwellings at all," she said.

"It's a super house, though. What surprises me is that it's so quiet. I learned how noisy the city is on the way from the airport. And I'll tell you that I feel safer on a bucking bronco than I did when that taxi driver was weaving in and out of traffic like a madman. Honking horns, squealing brakes, and the roar of hundreds of engines was deafening, but here in the house, I don't hear anything from the outside."

"We live in a gated area with restricted traffic. There's plenty of noise in downtown L.A." Still holding his hand, she said, "Let's sit on the couch."

Taking a deep breath, he sat down and stuck out his long legs in front of him. "There wasn't much room to stretch my legs on the plane."

"Do you want to take a nap? I'll be quiet."

He stretched his left arm and pulled her close. "I'm not going to waste our time sleeping. I can't stay long." Turning her so he looked straight into her eyes, he said, "I will *not* take the ranch. I don't know why you thought I would. Your lawyer will know how to cancel that deed—I brought back all the papers with me."

"Derek, theoretically the Circle Cross has been yours for weeks. When I started receiving all those threatening notes and realized that my grandfather would inherit my estate if I died, I wrote a will by hand giving you the Circle Cross in the event of my death. I sent the will to Mr. Talbot while I was still in Nebraska. And if you weren't too mad to read the deed, you probably noticed that I've kept the West Eighty and Riverside. So you aren't going to get rid of me entirely if you own the ranch."

She felt he was weakening when he said, "I feel cheap to even think about taking it."

She knew he was struggling with his pride, and she said, "No one need ever know you didn't buy it. Please don't disappoint me—I *want* you to have the Circle Cross."

"Nobody will ever believe I had enough credit to buy a spread like that."

"It's nobody's business except ours. But please don't argue about it now. Tell me how long you can stay so I can decide what to do while you're here. I want to show you a good time."

"I didn't aim to interfere with your work."

"I don't have much to do right now."

"Aren't you studying for that bar exam?"

"Yes, but I'm not sure I can get ready for the one in October, and there isn't another exam scheduled by the California Bar Association until February. Please don't leave right away."

"We're rounding up cattle and herding them closer to ranch headquarters for the winter," Derek said, a speculative gleam in his eye. "All of us are needed for that job, but I'll stay a couple of days."

She clapped her hands. "Great. We'll have a good time. You need a vacation."

"Okay, City Girl, you've talked me into it. I'll call the airport and lock in my reservation for Thursday. Tell me how to find a motel."

"You can stay right here in Dad's room."

Kennedy knew of his determination not to tarnish her reputation, and when he shook his head, she said, "Rosita stays here at night, so there isn't any reason for you to go to a hotel. I don't want to miss a minute of your visit. Did you bring any luggage?"

"A small bag. Rosita put it in the hall closet."

While he changed his plane schedule, Kennedy put linens on the bed in her father's room and fresh towels in the adjoining bathroom. Derek brought his bag from the closet and set it in the room. "I'll call Mom and let her know I got here all right. She'll want to know when I'll be home."

"Tell her I said hi," Kennedy said. "After you talk to her, let's walk around the neighborhood and then take a drive outside the city and into the mountains. Tomorrow we'll tour the city of Los Angeles."

* * * * *

When he went to bed the next night, Derek's mind was so conflicted with all he had seen since his arrival in California that he couldn't rest. Kennedy had kept him on the go from the time he arrived at her home, but he knew they'd only seen a very small area of Los Angeles and its vicinity.

Derek hadn't thought his admiration for Kennedy could become any greater, but as he'd watched her weave in and out of multilane traffic through and around the city, he could only look at her in wonder. And he'd had the nerve to josh her about not knowing how to ride a horse! She'd made arrangements for them to take a six-hour tour of the city, but at his insistence she let him pay for the tickets.

Sitting on the upper deck of the tour bus, they'd traveled to the city center of Los Angeles, the Farmer's Market, Sunset Strip, Beverly Hills, and Bel Air. They saw a dazzling array of stars' homes, well-groomed parks, manicured gardens, and hillside estates.

They had spent an hour at Grauman's Chinese Theatre and the Walk of Fame, looking at the autographed cement blocks bearing the signatures of many of Hollywood's famous stars. Perhaps the most startling revelation of the day was when they stopped by the tribute to James Arness, star of the long-running *Gunsmoke* television series. Derek remarked that as a kid he spent a lot of time watching Marshal Matt Dillon's shows.

"So did I," Kennedy said. Then, slicing a saucy grin in his direction, she said, "In fact, the first day I saw you walking toward me at the Circle Cross, you reminded me of Matt Dillon. I'd had a teenage crush on him, so apparently he had the qualities I wanted in a man. I fell in love with you that first day."

Derek had been stunned, and he stared at her without answering. He realized now that he should have said something, but when he didn't, Kennedy walked on, pointing out other autographed blocks featuring celebrities she thought he would remember. Momentarily, he wondered if he should ask her to marry him. Was it pride or stupidity that kept him from asking for what he wanted more than anything else the world had to offer? He would marry Kennedy if she was as poor as a church mouse, however poor that was supposed to be, but would other people believe he wasn't after her money?

He was even more aware of her wealth now than he'd been before, for when they were on the bus tour, he'd noticed a large edifice in the downtown business district that had BLAINE BUILDING carved in the stone lintel over the wide entrance. He'd asked about it, and she reluctantly admitted that her father had built it but that the building was hers now. Having seen the university she'd attended, the large church where she worshipped, and the widespread evidence of the extent of her wealth, he couldn't humble himself to propose to her.

* * * * *

"I want to spend most of the day at the beach." Kennedy was outlining her plans while they ate breakfast in the dining room with Rosita bustling around serving the ham and cheese omelet, mixed fresh fruit, and coffee she'd prepared. "We don't have to swim. I just want you to enjoy the ocean. It's awesome. But cowboy boots aren't too good in the sand. I don't suppose you could wear a pair of Dad's sneakers. I haven't done a thing with his clothes yet, as you probably noticed from his room. It's not something I want to do."

"I'm not used to wearing sneakers. I'll be better off in boots."

She looked at the shiny leather of his black boots. "Sand won't be good for them, but you can have them cleaned at the airport before you go home."

Kennedy was enjoying Derek's company and he seemed to be having a good time, but except for their passionate kiss on the day he arrived, he'd acted more like her brother than a man in love. The deed to the ranch hadn't been mentioned, although Kennedy had brought it in from the patio and laid it on the dresser in Derek's room. She'd told him she loved him, but he hadn't said that he returned her love. She knew that he did love her—it was obvious in his eyes when he smiled at her and the way he couldn't keep from touching her. They held hands when they walked, and when they watched television, he pulled her close and kept his arm around her.

Kennedy concluded that he was never going to propose to her, and the two days she'd anticipated so much were disappointing to her. He was obviously enjoying the sightseeing, but she sensed that he was eager to start for home. Delaying his departure for two days had been done to humor her rather than because he wanted to stay. She woke up early on his last day, put a robe over her pajamas, and quietly went to the kitchen. Making a pot of coffee, she took her Bible and went out to the patio. Apparently neither Derek nor Rosita was awake.

She opened the Bible at random, and the words from the fifth Psalm were before her: " *'Listen to my cry for help, my King and my God,*" she read softly, "*for to you I pray. In the morning, O Lord, you hear my voice; in the morning I lay my requests before you and wait in expectation.'* "

Kennedy closed her eyes and prayed inwardly, *God, I don't know what to ask from You. Is it just stubbornness that I want Derek? Is it Morgan pride that makes me determined to marry him when it isn't what he wants? I love him enough that I want him to be happy regardless of my own feelings. Does he think I'm trying to buy a husband by giving him the Circle Cross? Or is it his past that stands between us? How much does his past really matter? I have one day left. Please, I beg of You, give me the right words to say or the wisdom to keep my mouth shut.*

Tears seeped from her closed eyes, and she remembered the good times she'd had in this home with her parents. When she questioned if she was always destined to be alone, she supposed she was feeling sorry for herself and she swiped at her tears. She had Derek for one more day, and she didn't want him to see her tears.

She forced a smile when she heard his step behind her, and she motioned to a chair. "Well! You're dressed and ready for the day, and I'm still in pajamas."

"Remember I'm still operating on Central Time, so my inner alarm clock got me up early."

"Yes, I remember that a rooster wakened me too early on my first night at the Circle Cross."

"Rosita is up, too, preparing breakfast. She sent word that the food will be ready in thirty minutes, and," he added with a wide grin, "if you want any breakfast, you'd better get dressed."

"She's been bossing me around since I was a kid, so I don't pay much attention to her orders, but I do need to hurry. It's a long drive to the beach, and I want to have several hours there. Would you like to eat breakfast here on the patio?"

"Yeah, that would be super."

* * * * *

Derek watched Kennedy as she hurried into the house. He had noticed the tears she'd tried to hide behind her smile, and he had a hunch he was the cause of her unhappiness. He'd been awake most of the night trying to figure out what he should do. As usual, he had questions but no answers. Should he accept the Circle Cross? Should he try to trace his ancestry before he asked Kennedy to marry him? Should he forget about the past and marry her anyway? Should he just explain that he wanted to be her friend but nothing more? The last would be a lie, and Derek wasn't in the habit of lying. He *wasn't* content to be just a friend; his love for Kennedy caused his heart to ache constantly. Did he want to own the Circle Cross if she couldn't share it with him? He'd been introduced to what her life was now; would she be happy to live in rural Nebraska?

Although he'd enjoyed seeing the city yesterday, he'd felt smothered. Remembering their first meeting with a smile, he knew that she *was* a city girl and he was a cowhand. If he asked her, he was pretty sure she would marry him, but if she grew tired of the Circle Cross, what then? He sure couldn't live in Los Angeles.

* * * * *

They were on their way to Malibu Beach by nine o'clock. Derek had seen this beach featured in numerous movies, so the area seemed somewhat familiar. Houses perched on the hillsides overlooking the sandy beach below. Although the Santa Monica Mountains flanking Malibu's beaches couldn't compare to the Rockies in size, they formed a spectacular backdrop to the oceanfront.

When they reached Kennedy's favorite beach, climbed the sand dune, and looked out over the Pacific, at first Derek was speechless. A large steamer loomed on the horizon. The tide was coming in and, as he watched the breakers rolling toward the shore and the surfers taking advantage of the opportunity to ride the swelling waves, he whispered a portion of the Bible from Psalm 104 that he didn't realize he knew:

" *'There is the sea, vast and spacious, teeming with creatures beyond number—living things both large and small. There the ships go to and fro, and the leviathan, which you formed to frolic there.'* "

"It is awe-inspiring, isn't it?" Kennedy said quietly. "I've been here hundreds of times, and the scene never fails to charm me. Let's walk first and then we can rent an umbrella and eat the lunch that Rosita fixed for us."

Derek soon found out that his boots weren't made for walking in the sand, so he took them off and walked barefoot.

"I'll take off my shoes, too, and we can walk in the water," Kennedy said.

They rolled their pants to their knees, and the cool water surged around their ankles. Carrying their boots and shoes in their left hands, they joined right hands and kicked their feet like children. This beach had always been part of her life, but Kennedy seemed to enjoy it as much as he did. The tide was depositing shells on the wet sand, and she said, "Let's find some pretty shells for June."

As they chose whole, colorful shells, Derek said, "I want to buy a gift for her and the guys, too. I feel guilty about leaving them with all the work during this busy time, but I'm not sorry I came."

"Neither am I. You've probably never had a vacation."

"There's always something to be done on the ranch. And there hasn't been anyplace I wanted to go."

After they filled their pockets with shells, they turned around and Kennedy said, "We can walk through the shops as we go back to the car. You might find something you'd like to buy."

They washed their feet and dried them on Derek's handkerchief before they put on their shoes and climbed to the top of the sandbank. In one of the shops, he bought a shell necklace and earrings for his mother and bolo ties for each of the ranch workers. He also bought a box of chocolates for Kennedy and one for Rosita.

"This will please Rosita. She's a chocoholic."

As they put his purchases in the car, Kennedy asked, "Are you hungry now?"

"I could eat," Derek admitted.

"Then we'll eat our picnic lunch on the beach. Do we need to rent an umbrella?"

"Not for me. I'm used to sun and wind."

"It's hazy today and we won't get burned, so let's not bother with an umbrella," Kennedy decided. "If you'll carry the picnic basket, I'll bring a blanket and the thermos."

* * * * *

They found a secluded place in the shadow of a sand dune, spread the blanket, and ate the sandwiches and cookies Rosita had prepared for them. Tired from their long walk, they lay on the blanket side by side, holding hands, and Kennedy closed her eyes. She didn't know when she'd ever been more content. She gloried in the sound of the splashing water, the calm breeze, and a quiet place with Derek beside her. What else could she want for complete happiness?

Knowing the answer to that question, Kennedy withdrew her hand from Derek's, leaned on her right elbow, and scanned his handsome, rugged facial features. He opened his eyes and smiled sleepily at her.

"Derek, I want to ask you something."

"Go ahead."

Still she hesitated, but taking a deep breath, she asked, "Will you marry me?"

Although it was a serious moment, she almost laughed at the amazement mirrored in his dark eyes. He sat up quickly and stared at her for what seemed like hours to Kennedy. He seemed speechless, but eventually he cleared his throat.

His gaze was filled with wonder, but his voice was calm and steady when he answered, "Yes. Yes, I will."

Kennedy was temporarily dazed, for she hadn't expected him to surrender so easily. But when she finally realized that she'd achieved her heart's desire, she threw herself into his arms, laughing and crying at the same time, calling his name over and over. Her heart overflowed with gratitude that he'd said the words she thought she would never hear.

Holding her close, Derek admitted softly, "I'm not sure it's the right thing for you, but I love you so much that nothing else matters if I can't have you. Not even the Circle Cross. I don't want it without you beside me. I know I'm not good enough for you, but I'll spend my life trying to make you happy so you won't ever regret marrying me."

Her eyes brimming with happiness, she leaned back and looked up at him. "Do you know how miserable you've made me because you wouldn't tell me that?"

"I was only doing what I thought was best for you," he said humbly.

"I know." His lips captured hers, and she surrendered to the sweet tenderness of his kiss. He released her lips and rested his chin on her head. As they sat in silence, his rapid heartbeats told Kennedy even more than his words had conveyed.

"The 'yes' was easy, but now comes the hard part," Derek said. "How are we going to make a marriage between us work? Our worlds are far apart. What I've suspected before I've learned for sure in the past two days. You know I can't live in your world, but can you live in mine?"

Reluctantly, she moved out of his arms. She would have preferred to stay in them forever, but there were decisions to be made. "I *will* live in your world; I know you wouldn't be happy in a city. I haven't given it much thought, for I really didn't believe you'd ever marry me, but I'm sure I can adjust. I liked Valentine and the Circle Cross, and in spite of the trouble, I was content being there this summer. Besides you and June, I have family in Cherry County, but only friends in California."

"You'll be giving up a lot."

She shook her head. "But I'm gaining more than I'll lose. It will be a new life for me, but I can practice law in Nebraska as well as in California. The bar exam is given in October, and it will probably be that long before I can be ready to leave here. And since I'll be living in Nebraska, I will qualify to practice law there. I'll talk it over with Mr. Talbot." Making decisions as she talked, she added, "I'll have to put my home up for sale and decide what to do with all the furnishings. We won't need them at Riverside. I have some difficult decisions to make."

"I know, but I want to be together as soon as we can make it. These past weeks when you've been in California have been the worst time in my life. I've been grouchy with everyone, even Mom. I wish we could get married right away."

"Let's get married before you leave California," Kennedy said eagerly. "I won't feel sure of you until we are married."

His hands slipped up her arms and drew her closer for a moment. "Whoa! Don't tempt me, my love. We need to use our heads on this decision—not our hearts. But don't worry, I won't back out now. Not that I still don't have doubts, but I've got faith enough to believe that we can deal with our problems. Just last night I prayed for a sign to know what to do, and I thought that if you asked *me,* it would be God's will. He answered that prayer when you proposed."

"And while you were in Dad's room praying, I was praying in my room across the hall. The only possible way seemed for me to take the initiative, so our decision is in the will of God. And since He's placed a blessing on our union, it will work out for the best."

"I believe that, or I would never marry you."

"Since this has happened, it's changed my plans for our day. I expected to stay here for several more hours, but I'd like to leave now and take you to meet Mr. Talbot. He's my friend and mentor and has sort of taken Dad's place. He questioned my wisdom in deeding the Circle Cross to you, and I think he should meet you. He's a good judge of character, and he'll soon realize that I've made the right choice."

"I'll go, but I want you to promise that you won't put my name on any of your other investments. And I don't want to know your financial worth, or I'd probably take off running all the way back to Valentine."

Laughing at him, Kennedy said, "But when we're married, you're going to be my heir, regardless."

"No matter," he said stubbornly. "I'll take the Circle Cross, but I don't want anything else. Maybe we'll have kids someday who can inherit what your parents left you."

She pulled his head down and kissed him soundly. "All right, I promise, and I'll tell Mr. Talbot that you don't want your name on anything except the Circle Cross, for he would need to know."

* * * * *

Derek had an early morning flight and they had to leave the house at four o'clock, so after their meeting with Mr. Talbot, who assured Kennedy that she'd made a good choice, they returned to the house and had dinner with Rosita. They helped her clear the table and put the dishes in the dishwasher. After she went to her room, Derek and Kennedy cuddled on the couch, making plans.

"Are we going to keep this secret?" Derek asked.

"Not as far as I'm concerned. I'd like to shout it from the highest mountains."

Derek tightened his embrace, and when she looked up, his lips slowly descended to meet hers, and for a moment she surrendered to the mastery of his kiss. "I'm still afraid that people will think I'm marrying you for your money rather than because I love you so much that I can't live without you."

"It isn't my fault that I have money or yours that you don't have much. We can't ruin our future happiness by worrying what people will think. You tell June as soon as you get home, and as soon as she knows, I'll send a notice to the *Valentine Midland News*; that is, if June doesn't reject me as a daughter-in-law," she added with a laugh.

"That won't happen. Mom is a wise woman, and she'll welcome you into the family. She knows I love you."

Unconsciously running her fingers through his thick hair, Kennedy said, "I'll send a notice to the newspaper; I suppose it will be best to mention in the notice that the date of the wedding hasn't been determined yet."

"Why don't you also put the announcement in the *Omaha World Herald*? It has a wide circulation in Cherry County. When *do* you think we can get married?"

She flung her hands out in indecision. "It may take a few months before I can settle my affairs and move to Nebraska. I'll have to contact a Realtor about the house, but I won't stay here until we get a buyer. I will definitely plan to spend Christmas with you."

"Maybe we can get married on Christmas Eve," Derek said eagerly—and although Kennedy was still somewhat embarrassed at her boldness in proposing to him, she knew he hadn't felt obligated to accept her proposal.

Chapter Nineteen

....

The next morning before he entered security at the Los Angeles International Airport, Derek put his arm around Kennedy's shoulders and pulled her to one side. "With your beauty, your brains, and your money, you could have your choice of hundreds of worthy men. I still can't understand why you chose me."

"Because to me you're the most worthy man in the world, and I love you."

"I pray that I'll never let you down," he whispered.

"You won't. Let's talk every night," she said. She lifted her face for his kiss, wondering how she could bear to be separated from him for several more weeks.

* * * * *

While he waited in the airport for the plane's departure and all during the nonstop flight to Nebraska, Derek compared the difference in his attitude and hope for the future on his flight to California to how he felt now. Approaching Los Angeles, he had been miserable, unhappy, angry, and dreading a future without Kennedy. If he refused to take the Circle Cross when Kennedy obviously wanted him to have it, would he feel obligated to leave the ranch? Was it right for him to uproot his mother from the place she loved? Where could he go to find a better opportunity than he had now? Would he be forced to leave ranching altogether and find a job in a factory or an office?

Now three days later, his future was assured at the Circle Cross

LOVE FINDS YOU IN VALENTINE, NEBRASKA

and Kennedy would become his wife. Throughout his life Derek had
struggled with a feeling of inferiority, but never as much as he felt it
now. He still couldn't understand why she had fallen in love with him
and was willing to give up the life she'd always lived just to marry him.

Derek knew that they hadn't discussed the greatest reason that
their marriage wasn't a good idea. He hadn't even thought about his
ancestry when he'd told her he would marry her. He had no idea what
psychological, physical, and emotional traits he would bring into their
marriage. And he didn't mention it later as they planned their future.
Perhaps the only solution was to ensure that they didn't have any
children. But he liked kids and had always wished he could have some
of his own. And though they hadn't talked about it, because Kennedy
was an only child and was concerned because she didn't have a close
family, he figured she'd want children, too.

Since the day Kennedy had asked him if he would let her
research his biological parents, the thought had entered his mind
occasionally. At that time, he was totally against it, but now he wasn't
so sure it wouldn't be a good idea. But why find out now when they
were already making plans to marry? If his past did come back to
haunt him sometime, they would have to deal with it then. He wasn't
sure he would ever mention it to Kennedy again. She knew all the
skeletons in his life. If she was content to take him as he was, why
should it bother him?

Once his plane landed in Omaha, he telephoned Kennedy while he
waited in the parking garage for his truck to be brought to him.

"I'm back in Nebraska," he said. "The plane arrived on time, and I'm
ready to leave the airport."

"Be careful on the drive home and call me when you get there,
please," Kennedy said warmly.

"I will. Love you," he said, and his heart swelled when he said it. Who would have thought that such a change could have taken place in his life in less than a week?

"Love you, too," she said. "Bye."

The drive to the Circle Cross passed quickly—or so it seemed to Derek as he contemplated his dreams for the ranch. Having his name on the deed was a small matter. He would never make any changes without discussing them with Kennedy, although he figured she would give him free rein as she always had. He would like to provide better quarters for the men who worked on the ranch. He knew that Sam wanted to get married, and Derek thought he would build a comfortable home for him and his bride.

When he drove into the ranch yard, Wilson barked, jumped off the porch, and ran circles around the truck once Derek turned off the engine. When he stepped out of the cab, the dog put his front paws on Derek's waist and barked a welcome into his face. Derek rubbed the dog's head.

"No, I didn't bring her with me," he said. "But cheer up, old buddy; she'll be here in a few months."

"Welcome home, son," June called from the porch. Although there was love shining from her snappy eyes, Derek also noted anxiety. He hadn't told his mother about the deed he'd received from Kennedy or why he'd decided on a quick trip to Los Angeles. Doubtless she'd worried about him all the time he was gone.

Derek ran up the steps, picked up his diminutive mother, and whirled her around and around. "Derek!" June shouted. "You're making me dizzy. What's come over you?"

"I'm in love," he said.

"So? I've known that for weeks. How's Kennedy?"

"She's lost her mind," he joked. "She's going to marry me."

"Praise the Lord!" June said. "God made you for one another, but I was beginning to think you'd never see it."

Suddenly serious, Derek settled his mother on her feet. "I'm not good enough for her, Mom. I shouldn't have agreed to it, but I love her. And for some strange reason, she loves me back."

"Tell me all about it," she said. "Who else knows?"

"You're the first to know. Kennedy will e-mail announcements about our engagement to the *Midland News* and the *World Herald*, but she wanted to be sure you knew about it first."

"When will you be married?"

"We haven't decided. She has to settle her affairs in California before she can move to Nebraska. She intends to be here no later than Christmas."

"Let's have a prayer together, son. God has been gracious to both of us."

Derek didn't hesitate to kneel beside his mother. He knew it was only by the grace of God that he had come to this moment.

* * * * *

Only occasionally did sadness creep in as Kennedy laid her plans to leave California. Rosita wept constantly for the first two days after Derek left and she learned of their plans. Understanding how Rosita felt, Kennedy was patient with her at first, but finally she said, "Rosita, stop it! I know this is a big change in your life as well as mine, but don't you want me to be happy?"

Sniffing, the housekeeper said, "Yes, but why can't you marry Steve and be happy here in California? He's a good man."

"I agree, but I don't love him."

"Then your man ought to move here."

Knowing it was impossible for Rosita to realize how miserable Derek would be in a city, Kennedy didn't try to explain. "It isn't going to happen that way, so you'll have to accept it. I've arranged with Mr. Talbot to buy a home for you near your daughter, and you'll have a trust fund to provide for your needs as long as you live. And I'll pay your way to visit us in Nebraska once every year. Please don't carry on like this and make me feel guilty."

Rosita took the scolding in good grace and settled down to help Kennedy make arrangements to move and close the house.

June's happiness over their proposed marriage had balanced out Rosita's sorrow.

She called Kennedy immediately after Derek had returned to the ranch and said, "There's no one else on earth I'd rather have for a daughter than you."

Tears misted Kennedy's eyes, and her voice trembled when she said jokingly, "And how do you know I'm not marrying Derek to have you for my mother?"

"Derek says you're moving to Nebraska, so I suppose you'll be living at Riverside."

"Yes. It seems the logical place to live," Kennedy said.

"I'll enjoy having my grandchildren close by," June said.

Happily, Kennedy said, "We haven't talked about children yet, but I hope to oblige you. I still can't believe it's true. Be sure to let me know when the notice is printed in the paper, and get some extra copies for me. It will take a lot of people by surprise, I suspect."

June chuckled. "Frankly, it may cause more talk than when your mother and father got married. Your grandfather may disinherit you, too."

"Oh, he did that long ago. But I'm not so sure he will object. The one time I've talked with him, he made complimentary remarks about Derek. But it doesn't matter what he thinks."

"I know, Kennedy, but I wish you could make up with him. He's your closest relative. Besides, he's an old man—and a lonely one, I suspect."

"I may be ready for that. I'm so much in love now that I can even love my enemies. I won't make the first move, though," Kennedy said belligerently. With a soft chuckle, June said good-bye.

* * * * *

Tony was the first person to contact her after the notice of their engagement was printed in the local paper. Kennedy was pleased to hear from him.

After expressing his best wishes and his approval, he said, "I'll admit I wasn't completely surprised, as I observed you together when we hosted the kids from Omaha—but I didn't realize it had gone so far. He's a good man, Kennedy, and he deserves to have somebody like you. I told Matti, and she'll be calling you. The newspaper notice indicated that you'll be making your home at Riverside after the wedding."

"Yes, I'm selling the house in California. I intend to move to Valentine before winter. I liked Cherry County in the summer, but I'm not sure I can deal with your blizzards."

"Oh, it's not bad to be snowed in for a few days. People around here know how to prepare for the bad weather."

"I've already made arrangements with a Realtor to list my home. In the meantime, I've got to sort out the things I want to bring with me. Pray for me, Tony. It's going to be a break with the past."

"You and Derek are both in my prayers."

* * * * *

When Matti called to rejoice with Kennedy that she had found with Derek the kind of love Matti shared with Tony, she asked Kennedy when they were getting married.

"We haven't settled on a date yet. I'm getting my affairs in order so I

can leave, and it's not going as fast as I'd hoped. Now that Derek and I have decided to get married, I can hardly bear being away from him."

"I know what you mean. I'm working in Omaha longer than I expected to, but my resignation is for the first of December. Tony has found a small, furnished apartment for me in Valentine until we get married. Now I don't know if I should mention this, and don't hesitate to say no if you want to, but you know that Tony and I are getting married on Valentine's Day. Why don't you and Derek get married when we do?"

For a moment Kennedy was speechless. "But we're expecting Tony to perform our wedding," she said hesitantly. "Who would we get if we had a double wedding?"

"Tony has asked his good friend Daniel Trent, who pastors a church in St. Louis, to marry us." Giggling slightly, she continued, "You probably wonder why I'd wait almost six months to marry Tony, but it's a childhood dream of mine. My parents were married on February 14, and I always thought I'd like to be, too. It will be really romantic."

"Well, this is all so sudden. I'll have to think about it and see what Derek thinks. We've planned to get married as soon as I move to Valentine, but it *would* be cool to have a double wedding. Let me talk to Derek and see what he thinks."

* * * * *

The first day of February Kennedy wakened slowly, stretching in the luxury of her bed at Riverside, hardly believing that she'd returned to Nebraska more than two months ago in time to spend Christmas with Derek and June. She widened her eyes in the darkened room and looked around. It was only six o'clock, but she didn't think she could go back to sleep. The date on the clock face reminded her that it was the first of February.

She couldn't believe she had been back in Nebraska for two months and that within two weeks, she and Derek would be married. Although he had wanted to get married as soon as she moved to Cherry County, Derek, too, thought a double wedding would be a cool idea. After waiting all summer, they decided that two more months wouldn't matter, especially when they could see each other every day. Lying in bed with her eyes closed once again, the activities of the past three months passed through Kennedy's mind like a programmed DVD.

The sale of her home in California had happened more quickly than Kennedy had anticipated, though at first it seemed to take an interminable amount of time. Within two weeks after the house had been listed, she had a buyer—a newly married couple who had asked to buy the house furnished. But Kennedy had reserved special items to bring to Riverside—her father's desk, her mother's cedar chest, and the dining room suite that her parents had bought when they moved to California. After she gathered all of her personal keepsakes, including her toys and baby bed, she contacted a moving company and arranged for the items to be taken to the Circle Cross.

Her car was only a year old, so Kennedy decided to bring it with her to Nebraska. She'd been uncertain about driving from Los Angeles to Nebraska alone, and when she talked to Derek about it, he said, "I'll fly out and drive home with you. We're ready for winter at the ranch, and the men can handle everything until we get here."

"Oh, I'd love to have you do that. Why don't you bring June with you, and if you have time, we can sightsee on the way to Valentine?"

"That's a neat idea, my love. She hasn't been on a plane or seen much of the country, and she would like that."

"I intended to load the car with my computer and other items I won't trust to a moving van, but since you're coming, we can rent a small U-Haul trailer for those things. My car isn't very big, as you know, but there's enough room for the three of us.

Kennedy remembered keenly her sorrow at leaving her home and Derek's tenderness and concern for her. Holding his hand had made it easier to walk out the door for the last time.

Her furniture hadn't been delivered for a week after she returned to Valentine, and during that time, she and June had removed some of the furniture in Riverside, which she replaced with items from her California home. They had replaced the double bed she'd slept in all summer with a new king-sized bed.

While she had been in California, Miranda had taken another job. With Smith Blaine in trouble up to his neck because of his embezzlement and Lazaro returned to federal prison, Derek wouldn't have objected to her living alone. But Kennedy persuaded Matti to give up her furnished apartment and live with her at Riverside until they were married.

Before she left California, Kennedy had arranged for Mr. Talbot to study the legal pros and cons of turning the West Eighty into a conference center. Meanwhile, Matti was spearheading a feasibility study to assess the future of such a facility in rural Nebraska. The results of Mr. Talbot's and Matti's efforts would determine if she continued her plans to remodel the building on the West Eighty into a conference center.

Kennedy stretched again when she heard Matti walking around upstairs and, rather than getting up, turned her thoughts to their wedding plans. Because neither Matti nor Kennedy had parents or siblings to give them away as traditionally happened, the couples had decided on a private ceremony. Their only guests would be Tony's parents, his siblings and their families, June, and Rebecca, the mother of Daniel Trent, Tony's friend who would marry them.

Kennedy had insisted on an open reception at the nearby Holiday Inn, and considering the large population of Blaines and Morgans in Cherry County, the caterers were preparing for more than two hundred people. The guests would be received in the lobby of the hotel, and a sit-down dinner would be provided for everyone in the large dining area of the hotel.

"Are you awake yet?" Matti asked, as she entered the room with a cup of coffee in each hand.

Kennedy sat up in bed and put a pillow behind her back. "Not *wide* awake," she answered, "but the coffee will help."

She took one of the cups, and Matti sat cross-legged on the foot of the bed.

"Only two more weeks," Matti said, "and we'll both be married. It's hard for me to believe even now that, after all those long miserable years, Tony will be my husband."

"Has the wait been worth it?"

"I wouldn't want to live through those years again, but I'm sure that Tony and I will cherish being together even more because of the years we were separated. I thank God that I didn't marry someone else."

"Did you have many offers?"

"No, and there was only one guy whom I even considered, but when he asked to marry me, I couldn't. I'd dated him for over a year. I felt guilty about leading him on, for he really loved me, but I knew I'd never love anyone except Tony."

"I didn't have any serious relationships," Kennedy confided, "but one man I'd known for several years proposed to me a few weeks before I came to the Circle Cross. One look at Derek took care of that."

Kennedy took the last sip of coffee and threw back the covers. "Enough of this. We've got two showers coming up this week *and* a final trip to Lincoln for the last fittings on our wedding dresses. Besides, Derek keeps talking about the annual Bull Bash. I have a feeling I'm going to attend whether or not I want to go," Kennedy said. "Isn't that a few days before our wedding?"

"Yes, on Saturday," Matti answered. "*Everyone* turns out for that event—there's something for everyone."

"Derek wants to buy some more registered stock, and he says the Bull Bash is the place to see what's available. As the wife of a rancher, I'll be expected to go along."

"Then you'd better stop by Young's Western Wear and buy some long johns and a heavy coat," Matti said, smiling widely. "If Derek is like most ranchers, he'll look at every animal along the street, and I've heard that there are a lot of them."

* * * * *

Kennedy kept her phone beside her bed, for since her return to Riverside, Derek had always called her as soon as he'd eaten his breakfast. His call on Bull Bash day awakened her, and as she rolled over to pick up the phone, she noticed that it wasn't good daylight yet.

"Good morning, sweetheart," he said. The tenderness in his voice stirred her senses. "Sorry if I woke you up, but I have problems."

Kennedy wakened quickly. "Oh, no! What's wrong?"

"Several of our horses broke out of the corral last night, and we have to round them up."

"Can't you wait until tomorrow to do that?" she wailed. "You don't want to miss the Bull Bash."

"I know, but I don't want to lose the horses, either. Although the weather is supposed to be good, blizzards can pop up quickly in Cherry County, and I won't take any chances."

"Derek, if some emergency happens at the Circle Cross on Valentine's Day, are you going to miss our wedding?"

Laughing, he said, "No, I promise you, I'll be standing at the altar right on time that day. If there's an emergency, the men can take care of it."

"Promisc?"

"Yes, I promise. Sam and I are going after the horses, but Al and Joel will be in Valentine. You can ride into town with Mom."

"But she's going to be busy helping in the church's food booth, and so is Matti. I'll drive."

"Maybe we'll find the horses in a hurry and I can come to town for part of the fun."

Chapter Twenty

Disappointed, Kennedy drove into Valentine alone, completely surprised at the crowded town. Was there anyone in Cherry County besides Derek and Sam who hadn't shown up for the Bull Bash? Her first stop was at Young's Western Wear, where she bought a heavy hoodie and a pair of woolen gloves. Then, mingling with the crowd, she went to the art show at the library, where she listened to a cowboy poet reading his original poetry. The Sandhills Piece Maker's Quilt Guild had a wide variety of small quilts, wall hangings, and table runners in one of the stores, and she bought several of them.

When Derek hadn't come by midafternoon, Kennedy encountered Al walking among the livestock pens.

"Al, do you know what kind of bull Derek would like to buy for the Circle Cross?"

"Why, yes, ma'am, I do. He's always talking about buying a Red Angus bull from the Arrowsmith Ranch near Bassett, Nebraska."

"Will you show me the kind he would like?"

Favoring her with a perplexed glance, Al nodded and headed toward one of the pens. He pointed out a huge animal chained inside the temporary stock fence. "That's the kind of bull he wants, but he'd rather have a bull calf and raise it to suit him."

"How much would a calf cost?"

Looking frightened, Al said, "Five or six thousand dollars, maybe. Miss Kennedy, I don't know what you have in mind, but I won't be a part of it. If you're going to do what I think you are, Derek will kill me."

Kennedy patted the cowboy on the shoulder. "What Derek doesn't know won't hurt him. You go ahead and forget you talked with me today," she said, with a fond smile in his direction.

Al backed away from her, looking as frightened as if she had a contagious disease. After a short talk with the owner of the Arrowsmith Ranch, Kennedy went to the First National Bank and asked to see the president. She told him the price the ranch owner had asked for a bull calf. When he assured her that the price was reasonable, she said, "I want to buy it and take it to the Circle Cross today for a wedding gift. The owner has assured me that if Derek doesn't like this one, he'll exchange it for an animal Derek does want. Will you guarantee the check I'm giving him?"

The president smiled broadly. "Miss Blaine, you're already a good customer of this bank, and I'll be happy to do anything for you."

Two hours later, with some trepidation, Kennedy followed the cattle trailer that contained the Red Angus bull calf as the truck left Valentine and drove toward the Circle Cross. She knew how touchy Derek was, and perhaps she shouldn't have bought the animal, but she also knew that Derek would be hesitant to spend the money necessary to upgrade the ranch's stock.

Looking extremely cold and weary, Derek came out of the barn when the rancher drove into the ranch yard. Kennedy parked her car quickly and ran toward Derek, who had the oddest expression on his face.

Putting her arm around his waist, she said quickly, "I've been trying to decide what to buy you for a wedding gift." She gestured toward the truck, where the calf bellowed loudly. "Will that do?"

Derek looked down at her, and she couldn't tell if he was angry or stunned by what had happened.

"Darling, please don't be angry. The man says that if you don't like this bull, you can come to the ranch and pick another one."

Kennedy held her breath. She'd never seen Derek look like this. Was he embarrassed? Would he even marry her now?

Suddenly, he swept her into his arms. She could feel his uneven breathing on her face as his arms tightened around her waist. "I don't deserve you, my love," he whispered. "God really smiled down on the Circle Cross the day you came here."

Disregarding the rancher and the Circle Cross's men, he tipped her head backward and kissed her soundly.

With his arm around Kennedy, Derek walked to the truck and shook hands with the Arrowsmith owner. He peered through the bars at the bull. "From the looks of him, I couldn't have chosen a better one." Squeezing Kennedy tightly he said to her, "I knew you'd turn into a good rancher. Let's unload our new bull."

"Then you really do like him?" Kennedy asked anxiously.

"I like him, but I wonder how you knew this was the kind of stock I wanted."

Laughing because she was so happy and because she wanted to protect Al, she said, "Maybe a little bird told me."

* * * * *

Only one more day until I'm Mrs. Derek Sterling was Kennedy's first thought when she woke up. Putting on her robe, she went to the kitchen, where Matti already had French toast prepared for their breakfast.

"What time are we meeting for rehearsal?" she asked.

"Seven o'clock. Daniel and his mother won't arrive in Omaha until around noon. Tony wanted to allow time for plane delays. His parents and his sister's family are driving in from Lincoln. They have reservations at the Holiday Inn where the reception will be held and where the rehearsal dinner is. You know all of this, I guess, but if you're as excited as I am, you've probably forgotten most of the details."

"You're right." Kennedy held out her left hand and caressed the engagement ring Derek had given her—a French-cut pave setting with sixty-six brilliant cut round diamonds. Kennedy hadn't wanted him to spend so much money, but he begged her to pick out a ring she really wanted, and she had. "Once Derek slips a gold band on my finger to match this one and Daniel pronounces us husband and wife, my sanity will return, but until then my brain isn't functioning very well."

Tony came after Matti in midafternoon so they could spend time with his parents at his home. Wanting the wedding to be as family-oriented as possible, Kennedy later drove her grandfather's Buick to the ranch house to pick up Derek and June. He drove them into Valentine in the Buick, and they were the last to arrive at Tony's church, where they would be married in a small chapel rather than the main sanctuary. All of the other wedding party was there, including Daniel Trent and his mother.

Daniel was a broad-shouldered man with dark eyes and hair who looked like an athlete. Tony had mentioned that Daniel was an "exercise freak," and Kennedy could tell that he did work to keep his body in shape. His mother, Rebecca, on the other hand was overweight, which didn't seem to bother her in the least. Her dark blue eyes gleamed from a face that seemed prematurely wrinkled, so perhaps her early widowhood was still painful for her. But she was an outgoing woman about June's age, and the two of them bonded right away.

"I feel as if I know both of you already," Rebecca said to Derek and Kennedy. "Tony was so happy to be reunited with his long-lost cousin that he told us a lot about Kennedy in his frequent e-mails." Turning to Derek she said, "I believe he said you were in school together."

"Yes, we met when our family moved here. We were friends during high school, but we didn't see much of each other after he went away to college."

"Where did you live before you came to Valentine?" she asked.

"In Chicago," Derek said shortly, and Kennedy knew he was annoyed that Rebecca's questioning reminded him of things he preferred to forget during this time of happiness. She hadn't wanted anything to remind Derek of his unknown past during their wedding festivities. Rebecca apparently sensed his restraint, and although she continued to visit with them for a few minutes, she didn't ask any other personal questions.

Kennedy had been a bridesmaid at two of her friends' weddings, so she was aware of what to expect, but Matti laughed nervously a few times while Daniel led them through the steps of the ceremony he would perform the next day.

When Kennedy opened the door and stepped into the hallway at Riverside after they came home from the rehearsal dinner, she said to Matti, "When I walk through that door tomorrow night, I'll be Mrs. Derek Sterling."

"But you shouldn't walk through the door. Derek is supposed to carry you over the threshold."

"He'll never think of it," Kennedy answered.

Giggling, Matti said, "Well, stand outside until he does."

"I'm so excited from all the visiting and eating that I won't be able to sleep. Do you want to watch something on television?"

"I don't think so. I still have to pack my clothes for our honeymoon." She grabbed Kennedy's arms and swung her around the hallway. "Imagine, little ol' poor girl, Matti Gray, honeymooning in Hawaii."

"You deserve it, my friend. It's a honeymooner's paradise."

Matti stopped twirling and leaned against the wall. "I wish Derek and you were coming with us."

Kennedy took off her coat and hung it in the hall closet. With a mischievous glance toward Matti, she retorted, "Now, girlfriend, as much as I like you, I don't want you *or* Tony on my honeymoon. I'm looking forward to hibernating here at Riverside for a few days with nobody except Derek, even if I have to handcuff him to me."

"Sure, I understand. We'll see lots of each other from now on." Heading toward the stair steps, Matti said, "Try to sleep."

* * * * *

Kennedy heard the clock in the living room strike midnight, but she must have gone to sleep soon afterward, because she didn't wake up until Derek called her at seven the next morning.

"I know the groom isn't supposed to see the bride on their wedding day," he said, "but that doesn't mean I can't call you, does it?"

"No, and I'm glad you did. It's seems like a long time until two thirty."

"This day is made to order for us. It's rare to not have snow on the ground in February and with temperatures in the low fifties."

"So Tony and Matti won't have any trouble driving to Omaha and taking their flight to Hawaii."

"It doesn't seem likely." With remorse in his voice, he stated, "I still feel guilty that we didn't plan a trip."

"Don't! Darling, I'm perfectly content to spend our honeymoon at Riverside. Really, I am. But I'm holding you to your promise to take a vacation next summer."

"I'll go anyplace you want to," he said.

"I know you will, but it's a honeymoon just to be with you and know that you're my husband. I mean it, Derek." He started to speak, and Kennedy said sternly, "And don't let me *ever* hear you say again that you don't deserve me."

Laughing, he said, "I don't, but that wasn't what I started to say. Daniel and Rebecca have decided to stay an extra day or two, and Tony asked if we could take them out to dinner before they leave."

"Do we have to?" Kennedy groaned. "I wanted a few days for just the two of us, but I don't suppose we can turn Tony down. We might just invite them to Riverside. I'll think about it."

"I know how you feel, sweetheart, but we'll have the rest of our lives together. I like Daniel and Rebecca," Derek said. "And it was good of him to come all this way to marry us. Besides, I'm glad that Rebecca will be at the wedding, so Mom won't have to sit alone."

"Only a few more hours," Kennedy said.

"They'll drag for me, though," Derek said. "I'll never really believe you're mine until Daniel pronounces that we're man and wife."

* * * * *

Kennedy's fingers felt as if they were all thumbs while she and Matti helped each other put on their wedding dresses in a classroom close to the chapel where the marriages would be celebrated. As she settled a white cotton eyelet scooped neckline gown over Matti's head and shoulders, she considered their wise decision not to wear identical wedding garments. Though they would be married in a joint ceremony in the same chapel on Valentine's Day, their weddings were otherwise individualistic.

Kennedy smoothed the full skirt over the slight hoop and tied a blue satin ribbon around Matti's waist while Matti put on the pearl earrings and matching necklace Tony had given her as a wedding gift. Kennedy placed a short veil over Matti's red hair, which was styled in an informal upsweep with her face framed by wavy tendrils. She turned Matti around to see the final results. "Oh, you're beautiful! I only hope I look half as pretty as you do."

"You know you'll outshine me," Matti said generously. "Your hairstyle is stunning," she said of the glamour-girl coif the local hairdresser had created. From the deep part on the left side, her hair cascaded in waves several inches below her shoulders.

To complement her blond hair, Kennedy's had chosen a gold Chantilly lace over ivory satin gown with flared cap sleeves and a matching cathedral-length veil. She wore the diamond pendant her mother had worn on her wedding day and her own diamond earrings, a gift from her parents when she'd graduated from high school. When the dress was in place, Matti fitted Kennedy's feet into ivory peep-toe pumps.

Kennedy opened the door into the hallway so they could hear the music being played on the piano by Tony's sister, who was a music teacher in Lincoln. Kennedy recognized "From This Moment," the selection to be played before the "Wedding March."

"Let's go," she said to Matti. "We should be at the chapel door by the time she finishes this arrangement."

"Are you nervous?" Matti whispered in a trembling voice as they walked down the hallway.

Gripping Matti's arm, Kennedy grinned and joked, "No, I'm shaking like this because I'm cold. Seriously, though, I'm not nervous about *being* married. I've been waiting for this moment since I arrived at the Circle Cross and saw Derek for the first time."

The music stopped and, after a slight pause, strains of the "Bridal Chorus" from Wagner's opera *Lohengrin* reached their ears. Clasping hands, the girls moved into the open doorway. A short distance away, Derek and Tony waited for them. Derek's heartrending, tender gaze met hers, and Kennedy's spirits soared.

It would have been difficult to find two more handsome men. Derek wore his gray tux with a matching shawl collar easily, as if he dressed in such garments every day. Kennedy was used to Tony being dressed in formal clothes, but she marveled at the happiness shining in his eyes as he waited for Matti in a classic tux, white shirt, and black bow tie.

The processional was probably the shortest one in history, for only a few steps brought them to the pulpit where Daniel Trent stood. They took their places between Derek and Tony.

Before he asked the couples to join hands, Daniel read in a solemn voice, "Dearly beloved, we are gathered together here in the sight of God, and in the presence of these witnesses, to join these men and these women in holy matrimony. This honorable estate, instituted of God, was adorned and beautified by the presence of our Lord Jesus Christ at the marriage in Cana of Galilee. The family is the foundation of human fellowship. Therefore, marriage is not to be entered into by any unadvisedly, but reverently, discreetly, and in the love of God."

Soon Kennedy and Derek stood hand in hand and took their separate vows. Kennedy had been determined that she wouldn't shed any tears today, for it was the happiest day of her life, but when Daniel held up the platinum wedding band with a geometric design that Kennedy had chosen for Derek and said, "The wedding ring is the outward and visible sign of an inward and spiritual bond which unites two loyal hearts in endless love," her eyes misted with tears. She intended to do everything in her power to keep those vows.

When she slipped the ring on Derek's finger, she leaned forward and kissed his hand. And judging from the euphoria she experienced when Daniel at last pronounced them man and wife, Kennedy wondered if she'd ever been completely sure of him until this moment.

Although Derek's kiss was gentle and brief, Kennedy saw the tenderness of his gaze, and happiness filled her heart. To the majestic strains of "Trumpet Voluntary," Tony and Matti preceded them down the aisle, kissing and hugging those in attendance. When Kennedy and Derek reached the seat where June sat with Rebecca Trent, Kennedy stopped abruptly.

With a big white ribbon around his neck, Wilson sat on the pew beside June. Sensing Derek's silent laughter, Kennedy turned on him.

"I thought Wilson deserved an invitation," he said.

Wilson's ears perked straight up, and he gazed at them with solemn eyes.

"I agree. If it wasn't for Wilson, I might not be here today." She knelt and threw her arms around the dog. He barked joyfully, wagged his tail, and licked Kennedy's cheek. Then he jumped to the floor and walked down the aisle before them, as if he considered he had earned that privilege.

* * * * *

Tony's parents had insisted on providing a stretch limousine to transport members of the bridal party and their families from the church to the reception at the Holiday Inn. Matti and Kennedy would have been content to travel in private cars, but because Tony's mother had been disappointed when they didn't have a more elaborate wedding, everyone had agreed to travel in the limousine.

Kennedy had expected several guests, but she was surprised when she saw the huge crowd of people waiting for them in the entrance hall once the limousine parked under the hotel's canopy. She picked out Sam, Joel, and Al, as well as Miranda, from the noisy crowd that greeted their arrival with applause. Miniature bubbles drifted around their heads as their guests cheered. The reception coordinator directed the wedding party to take their position in front of the floral-draped fireplace.

"Kennedy and Derek, you stand first in the line; June comes next," she said. "Then Matti and Tony, with your parents beside you. The guests will greet you first and then move on toward the buffet. They can start eating, and after all the guests have been seated, we'll cut the wedding cakes."

Matti and Kennedy had both chosen four-tiered cakes, but otherwise they were different. Matti and Tony had chosen a vanilla cake with a roasted pineapple and coconut filling. Derek had assured Kennedy that he had no preference, so she decided on layers of chocolate chip cake filled with dark chocolate mousseline and white-chocolate cream. As an extra touch, the bakery had prepared a special peanut butter and jelly cake for children.

The line of guests seemed endless, and the high-heeled sandals Kennedy had chosen for style rather than comfort pinched her feet. She shifted from foot to foot to ease her back muscles, and, perhaps sensing her discomfort, Derek often placed his strong hand on her back.

They had been standing and greeting well-wishers for more than an hour when Kennedy turned to the next guest and stared, tongue-tied, amazed, and very shaken. Gabriel Morgan stood in the line, accompanied by his housekeeper, Esther Holmes. Kennedy's back stiffened, and Derek turned quickly to see this unexpected guest.

"I didn't receive an invitation, but I hope I'm welcome," Gabriel said, a glint of humor and uncertainty in his sharp eyes.

Kennedy sliced a fast look toward Tony, but he was talking with one of his parishioners and wasn't aware of his grandfather's entrance. Derek gently squeezed her right underarm. A fleeting memory of her mother's sorrow caused Kennedy to hesitate momentarily, but she knew that with his gentle touch, Derek was encouraging her to let bygones be bygones.

She slowly held out her hand, and the infamous Gabriel Morgan clasped it tightly.

"We didn't send invitations to anyone," she said, "but it's an open reception, as we indicated in the newspaper. Of course you're welcome,"—but Kennedy hesitated before she added, "Grandfather."

Tony must have heard what she said, for he glanced toward her, and his face turned ghostly pale. By now, all of the guests must have been aware of Gabriel Morgan's presence, because an unearthly quietness settled over the room.

Gabriel Morgan's strong voice sounded loudly in the crowded room. "I came to congratulate all four of you, but also to publicly apologize for many of the things I've done that brought sorrow to you and Tony and your families. I hope you'll find it in your hearts to forgive me."

Kennedy stepped closer, put her arms around him, and kissed his dry, wrinkled cheek. "It won't be easy to forget the past, Grandfather," she murmured, "but I'll try. Thanks for coming."

Tears filled Gabriel's eyes as he turned to Derek. "Congratulations," he said. "I'm glad she chose you, and you have my blessing if you want it."

Derek quickly grabbed his outstretched hand. "Thank you, sir. I do want it. I appreciate having you here today. Kennedy doesn't have much family left now, and I want you to get acquainted with her. You'll find out that she's worth knowing."

As Gabriel moved on, Esther Holmes took Kennedy's hand and whispered in her ear, "God bless you, my dear. He's a sad and lonely man, and he wants to make amends. Please be kind to him."

Kennedy breathed a prayer of thanksgiving when Matti and Tony also accepted Gabriel's presence and his apologies. When she swiped at her tears, Derek leaned close and whispered with a smile, "My love, history is being made tonight. Our wedding day will always be remembered as the day the Blaines and the Morgans finally buried the hatchet."

"It's about time," she said, latently wondering what her father would say to her if he were present.

Chapter Twenty-one
....

Except for a few occasions when she'd stayed overnight with childhood friends, Kennedy had always slept alone. She'd actually wondered if she *could* sleep in the same bed with anyone. After Derek carried her over the threshold, without being reminded, and in love they came together as husband and wife without hesitation or embarrassment, she had gone to sleep easily. The last thing she had remembered was Derek's whisper: "I love you, City Girl."

Waking with Derek's arm around her and her head on his shoulder was about as near to paradise as she would experience. She was happy that Matti and Tony would have their honeymoon in Hawaii, but she had all she wanted—the Circle Cross and Derek as her husband. He was still asleep, and she lay quietly, not wanting to disturb him.

She closed her eyes again and thought of their wedding day and night and how right it all seemed to be. She and Derek had traveled a rocky road before they got to this point, but how good it was to have him beside her at last. Moving slowly, she slipped out of bed, put on her robe, and went to the kitchen.

To prove to him that she *could* cook, she fried several slices of ham, scrambled eggs, and had bread in the toaster when Derek ambled into the kitchen. His hair was ruffled, and he looked sleepy. He rounded the table, took her in his arms, and kissed her.

"I was scared when I woke up in bed by myself. I thought maybe it was all a dream and that we hadn't gotten married after all." He looked at the clock. "I can't believe I slept until ten o'clock."

"Just remember you're on your honeymoon," Kennedy reminded

him. "You've promised that you won't work for a few days."

"Unless there's an emergency," he amended.

"So what are we going to do today?"

"Now that the weather's so good, this will be a fine time for you to see a lot of Nebraska you haven't seen. We'll head out soon and go wherever you want to."

"I'd like to go right now, but we'll need to take Daniel and Rebecca out this evening. Let's plan to leave tomorrow morning and stay overnight someplace."

"Sounds good to me."

They ate leisurely, and Kennedy was happy to see that the stress she often sensed on Derek's face was gone. He seemed more relaxed than she'd ever known him to be. They were sipping slowly on fresh cups of coffee and discussing her grandfather's presence at the wedding reception when his phone rang.

"If that's somebody wanting you to work, I'm going to handcuff you to the porch post," she warned.

Derek listened for a while before he said, "Yes, that will be all right. We're going away for a couple of days, but we won't be leaving until tomorrow. So come on out."

Answering Kennedy's uplifted eyebrows, he said, "That was Daniel Trent. He apologized for barging in on us but asked if he and his mother could visit us for a short time this morning."

"I'll be glad to see them, but I'm surprised they would bother us *today*, of all times!"

"I'm sure they have a good reason, but we'd better get dressed."

"You go ahead. I'll rinse the dishes and put them in the dishwasher."

Although they rushed, Derek was just pulling on his boots and Kennedy was brushing her hair when they heard a car pull into the driveway. Derek opened the door, and Kennedy was surprised to see not only Daniel and Rebecca but June on the porch also. All three of their visitors had strained expressions on their faces.

Derek and Kennedy exchanged astonished glances, and she stood to one side, allowing Derek to be the host. She intended to do everything in her power to keep him from feeling inferior to her because of her wealth and family background. He must realize that Riverside was *their* home now, not hers.

"Daniel and Rebecca, it's good to see you again. Hi, Mom," he said. "Come on in to the living room."

"I have coffee made," Kennedy offered, but the three visitors shook their heads as they sat where Derek indicated. She and Derek sat on the couch. A strange silence filled the room, and Kennedy didn't know what to say. Finally Rebecca Trent cleared her throat.

"I apologize for bothering you today, but I didn't want to leave without talking to you. When we met you, Derek, both Daniel and I were amazed at how much you look like my brother. I called him at once and asked him to send me one of his photos when he would have been about your age."

With a sharp intake of breath, Derek shot a sidelong glance of disbelief toward Kennedy. She moved closer to him, and he grabbed her hand.

"Daniel received the picture on his phone last night," Rebecca continued. She nodded to Daniel, and he lifted the lid of his cell phone and turned it to face Derek and Kennedy. They stared at a full-screen photo of a face so nearly like Derek's that it seemed impossible to believe that it wasn't his picture. Speechless, they both looked to Rebecca for an explanation.

"Daniel didn't know until I told him last night, so this is a surprise to him, too." Swallowing with difficulty, she continued, "I got pregnant when I was sixteen, and I gave my child up for adoption. Derek, having watched you closely for the past two days, I'm convinced that you must be my son. Not only do you have physical traits like my family, but your mannerisms remind me of the young man who fathered my child."

Derek's fingers tightened around Kennedy's hand, numbing it, and she wiggled her fingers until he relaxed his grip. Daniel's face was ashen, his eyes downcast. June sat with her head bowed.

"We'd like to hear what else you have to tell us," Kennedy said quietly, for she knew Derek was beyond words. "As you can imagine, this has come as quite a shock—but a pleasant surprise, too. Derek has been troubled all his life because he didn't know about his biological parents."

"We stopped at June's house before we came here, and I learned about Derek's childhood from her," Rebecca said, and her lips trembled. "I opposed giving up my baby, and my parents took charge of the adoption. They went through an adoption agency with a nationwide adoption program. I never knew what happened to him. It nearly broke my heart when June told me he'd been abandoned on the streets of Chicago, so I have no idea how that happened. I eventually married his father, but I didn't try to search for my child because I felt sure that he would be in a good home and I shouldn't interfere."

"And I didn't try to find out," Derek said, finally able to talk, "because I was afraid of what I'd learn. I struggled against marrying Kennedy because I didn't know what kind of background I'd bring into the marriage."

"You have no need to be ashamed of your heritage," Rebecca said. "Our families are God-fearing people, even if we have no great riches among us. My parents were very reputable people, youth leaders in our church, and they thought my disgrace would hurt their influence among the other young people. They later regretted their decision, but it was too late. No one else knew. Even after we married, I didn't tell your father I was pregnant. We lived together happily until his death ten years ago, and he died without knowing that he had *two* sons. I've paid all my life emotionally for deceiving him and for abandoning you. Will you forgive me?"

"I'm sure I will eventually," Derek said slowly, "but I just can't take it all in now."

"I've always wanted a brother, Derek," Daniel said, standing and reaching out his hand to Derek. "I didn't like being an only child."

Quickly taking Daniel's hand, Derek said, as his lips spread in a boyish smile, "It hadn't dawned on me that you're my *brother*." The gentle look of childlike wonder on his face was the most precious sight Kennedy had ever witnessed.

"I'm convinced that you are my firstborn," Rebecca said, "but I would like to verify it if you don't object to DNA testing."

"Not at all," Derek readily agreed. "I'd like nothing better than to have the mystery of my past cleared up." But turning to June, Derek said, "Mom, how do you feel about all of this?"

"Happier than I ever thought I would be. I knew you were a special child and have never considered that you didn't come from good parents, but for your sake, I'm glad to learn the truth."

"Then you don't mind sharing me with Daniel and Rebecca?"

With a wan smile, June said, "You know me better than that, son."

* * * * *

Promising that they would come to visit Rebecca in the summer and meet his extended family, Derek and Kennedy stood on the porch and silently watched Daniel drive away.

Kennedy looked at Derek, wondering what his reaction would be when they were alone.

To escape the cold wind, they hurried inside. Derek still had a dazed look in his eyes, as if he wondered when fantasy would be gone and reality would set in. He started laughing and flung himself down on the couch in the living room.

"So, City Girl, what do you think of your husband now?" he asked. "Not only is he the owner of one of the best ranches in Cherry County and married to a millionaire, but he suddenly finds out that he was born into a reputable middle-class American family. Can you believe it?"

She sat in his lap, put her arms around his neck, and planted a kiss on his lips. He responded as she expected him to do, but before their kiss deepened, Kennedy said, "I'm deliriously happy for you to finally know that your biological background is nothing to be ashamed of. But to answer your question, if you were still just a *cowhand*, I wouldn't love you any less. I've loved you since the first day I saw you, even before I knew that you were an adopted kid. Your past never mattered to me. For your sake, not mine, I'm delighted to have you learn about your heritage. But I'm glad we didn't find out until *after* we were already married."

He looked at her questioningly, and she added, "If you had learned beforehand, you might always have wondered if I would have married you as long as your past was unknown. Now you'll never doubt that I love you for what you are today, not what you were in the past. And I want you to stop thinking you're inferior to me," she said sternly.

Derek grinned, and Kennedy read his thoughts.

"And I *am not* like my grandfather!" she said. "Except in his opinion of you. The way he accepted you and acknowledged you publicly as a good husband for me will go a long way in my forgiveness of him."

"I appreciated what he said. So actually both of us have gained a family in the past few days. What better wedding present could we have?"

"You know, Derek, I'm going to like being married to you."

"I guarantee it! We had to go through a lot of heartaches before we got to this point, but it's worth it, my love."

Kennedy agreed with a kiss. "Only God could have brought us together, so let's thank Him and ask His guidance for the future."

Kennedy nestled her head in the curve of his shoulder and listened in gratitude as Derek poured out his heart in thanksgiving to God. This was the first time she'd heard Derek pray, but his fervent words of humility, praise, and thanksgiving brought added happiness to her heart. She was doubly blessed to have a husband who not only loved her more than himself but also loved God.

"Oh, Derek," she whispered brokenly, as she molded to the contours of his strong body, "thanks for marrying me."

POST CARD
Love Finds You

Want a peek into local American life—past and present?
The *Love Finds You*™ series published by Summerside Press
features real towns and combines travel, romance,
and faith in one irresistible package!

The novels in the series—uniquely titled after American towns with unusual but
intriguing names—inspire romance and fun. Each fictional story draws on the
compelling history or the unique character of a real place. Stories center on romances
kindled in small towns, old loves lost and found again on the high plains, and new
loves discovered at exciting vacation getaways. Summerside Press plans to publish at
least one novel set in each of the 50 states. Be sure to catch them all!

NOW AVAILABLE IN STORES

Love Finds You in Miracle, Kentucky by Andrea Boeshaar
ISBN: 978-1-934770-37-5

Love Finds You in Snowball, Arkansas by Sandra D. Bricker
ISBN: 978-1-934770-45-0

Love Finds You in Romeo, Colorado by Gwen Ford Faulkenberry
ISBN: 978-1-934770-46-7

COMING IN FEBRUARY, 2009

Love Finds You in Humble, Texas by Anita Higman
ISBN: 978-1-934770-61-0

Love Finds You in Last Chance, California by Miralee Ferrell
ISBN: 978-1-934770-39-9

COMING IN APRIL, 2009

Love Finds You in Maiden, North Carolina by Tamela Hancock Murray
ISBN: 978-1-934770-65-8

Love Finds You in Paradise, Pennsylvania by Loree Lough
ISBN: 978-1-934770-66-5

summerside
PRESS